The Peeper

John Bukowski

Published by Rogue Phoenix Press, LLP
Copyright © 2025

ISBN: 978-1-62420-862-1

Editor: Amanda Armstrong
Cover: Designs by Ms G

Dedication

To my good friend Elizabeth Haines, one of the best beta readers there is.
Thanks a lot Z!

Chapter One

I was turning to the sports page when the newspaper jumped in my hands.

"He's struck again." Cheryl said, flicking the paper a second time for emphasis.

"Pardon dear," I said, folding the paper and putting it on the table.

"You never listen to me," scolded my wife of nineteen years, seven months and six days. "I said he's done it again. Another murder. He's run his score to three with this Freemantle person." Her finger stabbed the salacious headline:

Police investigate another bizarre slaying of a suburban housewife.

"How do we know they're even connected?" I replied, nodding toward the *Tribune*, Midlothian, Ohio's one and only daily paper. "The news people say that, but the police haven't."

"Oh, please," Cheryl said. "Don't be an idiot. I grew up here. We have the occasional killing, drugs and such. But three in a month? All women? And so bizarre? Please. He must be a real sicko."

I could feel her behind me, shaking her long, silky hair, its streaks of brown and grey replaced by bleach-bottle blond after her latest trip to the spa. I smiled at my buttered toast. "How do we know it's a *he*?"

"Don't be an idiot. You better hurry; you'll be late for work."

"I can afford to be late. I have a doctorate in veterinary medicine," I said, nibbling a crust of bread. "And I work for the county." I sipped more coffee. "And I'm a unionized supervisor."

"Any idea when the doctorate unionized supervisor is going to get a promotion? Or maybe a raise? Or maybe a bonus?"

"I better get to work." I picked up my lunch bag and kissed Cheryl on the cheek. "Why don't you take some steaks out of the big freezer downstairs? I'll grill. We can open a bottle of wine, have date night." I gave her a hug. She didn't hug me back.

"Oh yeah, I almost forgot. I have a thing tonight, um, a *ladies* thing. Dinner and a meeting."

"Didn't you just have one of those?" I asked.

"That was the *monthly* meeting. I'm on the board, you know. We meet *every* week. Might not get back till late. There's cold chicken in the fridge."

~ * ~

Morning traffic wasn't bad – only used my horn once. The working portion of Midlothian's citizenry putzed their way to Hokkaido Plastics, Deer Park Medical Center, or The Sunshine Café. I putzed toward the county municipal buildings.

Twenty minutes of breaking, accelerating, and grumbling put me in the county lot. I angled toward a parking space two over from a sheriff's cruiser, when a darting orange streak forced me to hit the brakes. Heart hammering, I got out and looked around. There, huddled by the police cruiser's right front wheel, was an orange tabby cat. Almost a kitten really, a scraggly, under-fed teenager. It looked as scared as I felt.

"Hey little guy. You've got to be more careful. I almost hit you." I scanned the parking lot. "Where's your mom?" The cat shrunk against the tire as I approached. "Don't worry, little one. I won't hurt you. You look hungry." The cat eyed me suspiciously but didn't move. "Stay right there." I walked back to the car and got my lunch bag. It contained a ham sandwich, an apple, and a snack-sized bag of Fritos. I lifted a slice of ham slicked with butter off the sandwich and walked back to the cat. Now it was behind the tire, only its head peering out at me.

"Here you go," I said, tossing the meat to within a foot of the hiding feline. At first it didn't move, eyeing the ham as if it were poisoned bait. Then it pounced, carrying the treat back under the holding it like it was a trophy mouse. I smiled, watching the cat dash with its prize to the large maple. Then I ambled left to the municipal offices.

The county office building was constructed during the cold war and always reminded me of a bomb shelter; the concrete walkway descending into concrete walls bermed into a mound of industrial fill with grass on it. A few shrubs and trees had been added to break the grey monotony.

I entered through the double glass doors as receptionist Peggy Roberts was having the first in her daily series of heated 'chats' with her mother.

I waved and said, "Morning."

Peggy waved perfunctorily back, her focus still on the maternal curse occupying the other end of the line. Turning right, I walked past licensing toward environmental services, heading for room 138.

My heels clicked thirty-seven paces down linoleum that might once have been brown. The smell of hot macadam gave way to eau de old building, with its bouquet of dust mites, floor wax, and wood seasoned by more than half a century. At my destination, light shone behind the black letters reading 'Pesticide Control Program.' Below the frosted glass was a white placard informing one and all that Randall Corlane, DVM was supervisor of this illustrious program consisting of exactly four persons: myself, one administrative assistant, and two inspectors.

What's a veterinarian doing in pesticide control, you ask? Well, vets and pests go together like, well ... dogs and fleas. We're the docs who know all about mites and ticks, fleas and lice, mosquitoes and biting flies. We're also the guys who know about the mange, malaria, and other diseases these creepy critters carry, as well as what kills them but not their hosts (in theory, anyway).

I turned the brass knob that hadn't been replaced since Nixon occupied the White House and entered to the smell of ground roast rising from the Mr. Coffee in the corner.

"Morning Jan."

"Morning Randy," said Janyce Sterling, the aforementioned administrative assistant. Just a couple years out of community college, Jan was every bit the modern young woman, with piercings and multicolored hair proclaiming her individuality as it did for thousands of girls just like her. For Jan, professional attire meant the jeans only had small holes in them and the thong was only visible when she bent over.

"How was your evening?" I asked, pouring coffee into my OSU mug and adding one sugar.

"I spent most of it in bed."

"Weren't you feeling well?" I looked around for the cream.

Jan leered a grin. "Oh, I *felt* fine."

I shook my head. "Which guy this time?"

"Kyle."

"The one with all the muscles and tattoos?" There was powdered creamer but not actual cream.

"Uh huh. I spent a few hours exploring both."

I raised my hand in surrender. "Too much data."

"You'll never guess where his snake tattoo is?"

I chuckled. "Have pity on an old married man and spare me the erotic details."

"I thought you'd enjoy living vicariously?" She raised her pierced eyebrows. "Or if you want, I can introduce you to one of my girlfriends and you could live cariously?"

"You know you're half my age, don't you? And that I've been married almost as long as you've been alive."

"I notice you didn't say *happily*. Her name's Rochelle Kolodny. She likes older guys. Even semi-happily married ones."

"This sexual harassment thing works both ways."

"I know. I just like to see you blush, *Randy*."

I obliged.

Those of you who think the above erotica could not happen in a modern-day professional setting have never worked in county government. The limits are pretty much set by the employees, unless they have a strong hand at the tiller. My hand has always been a tad wimpy, eschewing confrontation. Plus, I didn't see the harm.

"We have any cream?" I asked.

"You don't take cream."

"I know. Is there some in the breakroom?"

She shrugged. "Probably some half and half. Why?"

"Um, I have a friend who could use a square meal." I dumped the chip crumbs from a Styrofoam bowl. "Do me a favor and put a note on my desk – 'Get Meow Mix'." Then I left for the breakroom.

~ * ~

When I returned from my errand of mercy, Jan was deep into People

4

Magazine, so I grabbed my now lukewarm coffee and slipped around the cloth partition that separated boss from employee.

There are few personal offices in unionized county government. Like home fries, we're cubed. Mine was a semi-private cube (three walls) with a window. I had a beautiful tunnel-like view of a tree and a parking lot. Not bad for government work.

I put down my mug and turned on my computer. Then I heard the office door open.

"Hey, darlin." The cheerful voice of Nolan Webster, the senior inspector, carried easily over and around my partition. I didn't need to see him to know he was dressed in threadbare jeans and that he hadn't shaved. He always sported the same ratty, almost-beard, as if his hair grew out partially then stopped. I wondered if he trimmed it that way.

"Hey Nols," Jan said.

"Miss me last night?"

Jan sighed heavily. "Yes, but I managed."

"I'll bet," Nolan said. "You've got the well-ridden glow. How about me? Does mine show?" I didn't need to look around the partition to see his leer in my mind's eye.

"Was it human?" Jan asked.

"And lively. Um, Skipper in?"

Jan must have waved him around.

"Hey Chief."

"Hey yourself, Nols. Where's Tweedle Dum this fine morning?"

"Cash may be AWOL today. I left him at the bar around seven. He was already stinko."

Carter (Cash) McCall was the junior member of my team. Imagine a skinny, male version of Jan, in coveralls with 'County Inspector' on the breast pocket.

"You are a bad influence on that young man, sir."

"Don't blame me, chief. Said young man was dead set on diving in the tank. Upset about something but wouldn't tell me what. Just that he saw something that freaked him out. Sounded scared. Hey, did you see the paper?"

"What?" I mumbled, entering my password to unlock the screen.

"The paper. The Peeper's added to his score."

"The *Peeper*?"

"That's what the press is calling him. From the way he, you know." Nolan tugged his eyelid and scissored fingers across it.

"That's disgusting," I said.

"They say he has some skill with a knife. Single stroke to the heart." He stabbed fist to sternum. "Knows his way around the anatomy. Like that guy on Ripper Street."

"They never caught bloody Jack, did they?" I asked.

"Not the season I'm binging. Probably won't catch the Peeper either."

I checked my email. "Are you *rooting* for him?"

"Nah. But it does add spice to Midlothian's humdrum summer."

"I prefer humdrum."

"Any complaints last night?"

One of the chief responsibilities of the PCP was chasing down misapplication complaints. These could range from concerns about routine yard treatments to accusations that someone poisoned the family pet. They all had to be checked out, even the backyard feuds and alleged dog-icides. So, I ran down the messages.

"Two. One out on Parkersburg Road, the other in town—Drury Lane."

"Let me guess," Nolan plopped his butt on my grey-metal desk. "Some yuppy accuses Farmer McPeet of spraying insecticide on little junior while he played video games on his Parkersburg-road computer. And a domestic feud – neighbor A killed neighbor B's prize rosebush because B's TV plays too loud."

"You're ruining the suspense," I said.

"Which one do you want me to hit first?"

"Are your time sheets finished? They're due today."

"I'll finish them later."

"That's what you said last month. And the month before."

"How about I hit Drury Lane now, then Parkersburg. I can grab lunch afterward at that new place near the freeway."

"You mean the strip club?"

"Bozo's is *not* a strip club. The waitresses just wear casual summertime attire."

"Like hot pants and halter tops?"

"No one calls them hot pants anymore, pops. They're booty shorts now."

"Tell you what, *son*. Get your booty out to Drury Lane and I'll hit Parkersburg."

"You? Inspecting?"

"Hey, I started out doing inspections. Back when this place was just me."

"Was that the Jurassic or the Mesozoic era?"

"The bronze age. And I want those three months-worth of time sheets as soon as you finish at Drury."

"Yes, Mein Fuhrer."

I waved off his sieg heil. "And be careful leaving the lot. There's a stray cat hanging around." I sighed. "Poor thing."

Chapter Two

Majestic Knolls was a new development; one of those hummer-house clusters that spring up among the farmland along with the strip malls and fitness clubs. I pulled my county Buick onto the concrete drive at 421 Hummingbird Way. Another McMansion was fifty feet to my right. Parkersburg Road was visible over my left shoulder. Beyond Parkersburg was McPeet's Orchard, fruit trees lined up neatly past the split-rail fencing.

I'd no more than stepped into the summer heat when I knew that McPeet had recently sprayed for cherry maggot. There was the telltale scent often described to me as 'that smell in the pest-control aisle at Walmart.' I'd explained a thousand times that said smell was mainly the solvent carrier-vehicle used to dissolve the active ingredient. The insecticide itself stayed where sprayed, but the solvent odor wafted here and there, so that people thought they were being poisoned by the equivalent of new-car-smell.

As I retrieved my sport jacket and clipboard from the passenger seat, a woman of about forty came out the front door. She was tall, a mile of tanned legs under her shorts, full figure tenting her polo shirt, blond hair tied into a ponytail. I waved to her and prepared for explanation one thousand and one.

"Good morning. Are you Ms. White?"

"Weider-White," she replied. "With a hyphen."

"Of course. I'm Randall Corlane from the county Pesticide Control Program."

"Pleased to meet you." She held forth a tanned arm. "Call me Suzanne."

We shook hands. "I'm Randy." I smiled my 'I'm here to help' smile. "What seems to be the problem?"

She wrinkled her nose. "Can't you smell it."

I took a moment pretending I couldn't. "That mildly sweet, chemical odor?"

"The *insecticide* smell. That, that ... farmer." Speaking as if McPeet were a disease, she pointed accusingly. "He sprayed his poison yesterday. During *my* barbeque." She looked back at me and lowered her voice. "There were children present."

"I see." I nodded in understanding. "Was anyone at the barbeque exposed?"

"What do you mean? We all were."

"No, I mean *physically* sprayed. Did you or anyone else see the mist cross Parkersburg Road, droplets landing on your property and or person." It was patter I'd worked out over the years – civil and officious. Sounded a bit like Jack Webb. I added a 'just the facts' expression.

"Well ... no. But ..." She wrinkled her nose again and swept her arms wildly. "That smell. It's everywhere."

"Well." I smiled. "What you are smelling is not insecticide."

"Fine, fungicide or herbicide or what have you. It's *all* poison."

"No, what I mean to say is that the odor by itself does not constitute pesticide exposure. What you're smelling is ..."

"What do you mean, no exposure? If I can smell it, I'm *exposed*. My guests could smell it too. And my son, my child. Jason has asthma, you know."

I didn't know, but I tried not to raise my voice to match hers. "No, I understand why you'd feel that way. But what you are smelling is not pesticide. It's like, well, when you're in the pest-control aisle at Walmart."

"I wouldn't be caught dead at Walmart."

If 'farmer' was a disease, then 'Walmart' was all seven plagues rolled into one. "Of course not. But what I mean to say is ..."

"It's even worse in the backyard. Come, I'll show you."

I admired her long legs strutting around the side of the house, then hurried after.

A flagstone path led to the gate in an honest-to-goodness white picket fence, albeit a plastic one. The fence surrounded a postage-stamp yard complete with patio, stainless-steel barbeque (no doubt for tofu burgers), and assorted patio furniture. No child's toys dotted the area, confirming that little Jason spent his leisure hours at the computer. Standing in the center of the crabby lawn, I could spit a loogie into the neighbor's yard, which was identical sans the fencing.

"Do you smell *that*?" Ms. Weider-White said.

I did indeed. The smell was most definitely stronger. And the smell was most definitely different, but familiar. It reminded me of the freezer where we placed the euthanasias back in vet practice; a smell I'd grown to know intimately until playing God drove me from clinics into public health. But this backyard odor was stronger, heightened by temperatures in the eighties.

Nodding, I walked toward the rear of the yard. What the novelists call 'the stink of death' was more pungent to my left. Looking over the fence in that direction revealed a drainage ditch, the bottom of which I could not see. I looked for a rear gate in the fence – there was none.

"Do you think your neighbors would mind my walking on their property?" I pointed to the fenceless yard on the right and smiled. "I'm a little old for hopping pickets."

Weider-White shrugged as if she didn't know what her neighbors would mind, or who they were.

I headed back through the front gate and down the outside of the fence until I'd reached the ditch.

"What are you looking for?" she asked.

"The source of your smell." I followed the odor like a fly homing on a dog pile. I didn't have to follow long. Twenty paces put me near the corrugated pipe where the ditch ran under Parkersburg Road. The stench increased with every step, until my breath caught in my throat, and I involuntarily turned away, thanking the lord that I hadn't just eaten.

On my approach, several crows took flight, leaving their lunch unfinished at the bottom of the ditch. The main course appeared to be a nude body shoved partially into the pipe. A turgid pool dammed up against the rotting head and shoulders, long blond hair floating in the stagnant water. It looked to be a woman, but it was no longer easy to tell. One nipple had been cut off, replaced by a jagged hole from which maggots squirmed. A second hole sat just below the sternum, more maggots dining therein. That's what I saw in the second before I turned away. But that wasn't all I saw. The vision imprinted in my mind was of the eyes that were barely visible under the lip of the pipe. One was gone, no doubt curtesy of the crows. The other was open, staring at the sun. The lids had been removed.

~ * ~

"You okay now?"

I thumbs-upped the paramedic, then sipped more water.

"Need another dose of salts?"

I shook my head. Smelling salts had twice snapped me back from the memory of the sightless eye. My mind could deal with the rest of the ghastly horror show, but that bare, lidless eye kept it reeling. I knew I'd been up close and personal with a grisly headline. And I knew I'd be seeing it again in my nightmares.

A chubby man in a checked jacket left an unmarked (if you don't count dents) brown sedan and walked toward me. I'd seen this middle-aged gent around the municipal building from time to time. I'd even exchanged pleasantries with this balding, county detective owning the unfortunate name of Milton Garlicki.

"You okay there, Doc?"

I nodded.

"When did you find it?"

Another involuntary shudder hit me as he pointed to the gurney being hauled from the ditch, a blanket blessedly covering the strapped-down form.

I took a sip to wet the burnt cotton in my mouth. "About forty-five minutes ago."

"How'd you happen to be down by the ditch?"

I tapped my nose. "Followed this."

His head bobbed in understanding. Taking out a pen and pad, he asked, "What were you doing out here?"

Two burly guys in coveralls trundled the gurney toward a black station wagon with 'County Morgue' stenciled in white. The bundled form had once been a person – a woman. The Peeper's latest victim. No doubt as pretty as the others. Now, so much worm food.

"Doc?"

"Oh, sorry. What did you say, Milt?"

"What were you doing out here?"

"Application complaint. Ms. White, um, Weider-White contacted the office. McPeet sprayed his trees and she wanted to complain."

The detective smirked and shook his high forehead. "Someone should tell these city folks that *they* moved next to a farm, not vice-versa. Huh?"

"Well, I don't know about that. But that's why I was here."

Milt seemed satisfied. "Mind coming to my office to make an official statement?"

I stood, my knees wobbling. "No, not at all." I managed a wan smile. "I'm headed that way anyway."

He stomped toward his car; I tottered toward mine.

"Just one thing," I added.

Milt turned, giving me a blank expression that was as close as he got to inquisitive.

"Mind keeping my name out of the paper?"

He smiled; a piece of breakfast sausage was stuck between front teeth. "I'll do what I can."

~ * ~

"Are you just getting home? I thought you were already in bed."

Cheryl put down her tea. She was still in her dinner clothes, a tight-fitting pants suit with moderate cleavage. I often wondered why straight women dressed up for each other. Cheryl must have wondered as well as she buttoned up as if in embarrassment.

"Mmm, had some work to finish up."

"Must have been important. It's after ten."

"How was dinner? LeeAnn drink too much again?"

Dinner out with lady friends was at least twice per week. Her best friend, LeeAnn Miller, was usually there, along with others from the BFF League, which is kind of a lady's club with no definable purpose except eating, drinking, and gossiping. They had meetings as well, no doubt to plan eating, drinking, and gossiping. Between my work and her dinners, meetings, lunch dates, health-club sessions (she'd added the latter a few months ago, as if there wasn't enough on her plate), we saw each other maybe ten hours a week. And still, we didn't have much to say. C'est la vie.

"Why must you always pick on LeeAnn? What was the big work emergency?"

I took off my jacket and tie. "Catching up. Got delayed down at…" I waved. "I'll tell you later."

"Well, I'm going to bed."

"Me too," I said. "After I check messages."

"Don't forget to turn off the hall light *again*." She headed down the hall to her bedroom while I headed up to mine.

You're probably wondering why I didn't tell my partner of almost twenty years that I had found a body today. A murder victim. One of the Peeper's victims no less. The same Peeper we'd discussed over morning coffee. You're probably thinking that I should be bubbling over with the big news; 'Guess what happened to *me*?' frothing from my lips. But I wasn't.

I'm not sure why I kept my mouth shut. Something in me just said 'wait'. Maybe I didn't want to relive the shock. Or maybe I wanted to hold onto it for a while, hold onto something that I knew but she didn't. This experience, this memory, was mine, mine alone, not community property. After years of sharing everything, knowing everything, one feels the need to keep a few secrets. At least I did. I couldn't remember feeling this way when I was thirty, but the longer my wife and I endured, the more I wanted to keep my own council, to expand my private space. Or maybe we'd drifted far enough apart that private space was all I had left. Anyway, I wanted to keep a few secrets. I'm not sure a psychologist would find that healthy, but it was true.

A few of those secrets were on my bedroom computer. Oh, I'm not talking about the occasional porn-site tonic that middle-aged men use to cope with existential fear and the boredom of long-term fidelity in a world of casual sexploration (eg. Jan's acrobatics). I'm talking about family secrets— my other family. The family that was separate from nineteen years of marriage. The family of which my neighbors and workmates were largely ignorant. My cyber family.

I admit to being none too bright about computers; the word Luddite comes to mind. I can hardly even figure out my cellphone. These machines weren't around when I was born, and even when they became available, we didn't waste money on such diabolically newfangled gadgets in the Corlane household. But since my parole from Corlane correctional, I've become a bit of a social media addict, with close to five thousand cyber friends. Not real friends in the traditional sense, but, like a drowning man, a lonely man will reach out to any hand, even a virtual one.

Cyber friends are like their photos—two-dimensional. All you really know about them is what they share on their feed: grin-and-shake shots (maybe a sexy one or two), syrupy slogans, political rants, cartoon hearts, happy faces, and restaurant reviews. You flirt a little. You get and give a birthday greeting, maybe a Happy Holidays. You have a stronger emotional connection with your accountant. But the anonymity of it felt comforting (at least to me), and the electronic flirting raised my middle-aged temperature a bit.

As an old married man, casual flirting was as far as I ever took it, lest innocent double entendre descend into something more. You married women may be thinking that the slope twixt the two is a tad slippery. You may also be thinking it's a bit pathetic. And maybe it is. But it was something I could live with. Because even when the status quo is less than ideal (or even less than less), inertia is strong and the devil you know is at least the devil you know. Change is change for the worse, as my late mother used to say.

I scanned my feed and found myself staring at one of the sexy variety photos, a selfie of someone with the unlikely sobriquet of 'Krazy Kat'; many cyber people hide behind a double layer of anonymity, cloaking even their true names from online friends they don't really know. Selfie was perhaps the wrong word for this photo. Selfies was more like it, as cleavage was the star of this particular production. Thing one and thing two were focused in the foreground, with blond hair and powdered face hazed into a background blur.

There were already several dozen salacious replies from male admirers, most of the 'Beautiful!' and "You are hot!' variety. My cyber policy was not to compete with such comments, tooting my version of 'Hey Baby' as one more wolf whistle from a crowded construction site. I'd read somewhere that the way to appeal to women, besides buying them stuff, was to make them laugh. So, I relied on a line from Manchurian Candidate, the original with old Blue Eyes. "Always with a little humor, Comrade".

'Make sure you have a leash when you take those puppies out,' I typed. 'They look like they could hurt somebody.' I smiled at just the right combination of risqué and funny. I pressed send, watched my comment flash up among the multitude, then moved on.

There was a new post by Nancy Collingwood, one of my online crushes (as with Krazy Kat, what harm could it do?) This twenty-something cop who looked like Charlize Theron had posted 'Heading to work out – wish me luck' with a selfie of shorts and police tee shirt stretched over her trim figure. I thought for a moment, looking for that witticism that would set my reply apart from the catcalls and crude remarks. My fingers hovered over the keys for several seconds, then I wrote 'Don't overdo. I'd hate to see that lovely property of the police athletic league damaged.' I pressed send.

At this point, you might be asking why I bothered? Why was a man in a long-term relationship flirting with an online fantasy he was never going to meet? A psychiatrist might say it was a need to sate the middle-aged male ego, to reaffirm, at least in his own mind, that he wasn't over the hill, could still attract. Or Sigmund might opine on the voyeuristic comfort of dalliance without risk, long-distance infidelity, the vicarious thrill of exchanging a few compliments and risqué remarks with a stranger one will never actually meet. Cheryl's most risqué remark was "not tonight, I have a headache." A sociologist might discuss the societal trend toward a sterile, virtual-reality existence, where human contact is limited to text messages, tweets, and FB posts. Maybe that's all true, maybe it's all bullshit. But again, I didn't see the harm; except maybe deep down in the soul, below the layers of inertia and humdrum routine that become our lives.

Moving on, Karl Wolff asked me to like Walker-Wolff insurance. I had never done business with Walker-Wolff insurance, but in my experience one agent was pretty much like the next. What harm could it do? I liked them.

The name Walker-Wolff needled at my brain like a half-remembered song title. Their offices were in Florida, so it was doubtful I'd heard an ad or seen a billboard. But the name was familiar and brought up a vision of long, tanned legs walking in the sunshine. Probably saw that on a Florida Tourist Bureau ad and made an odd, mental connection. I was about to scroll on when a series of associations flashed through my brain.

Walker-Wolff.

Weider-White.

Long legs strutting in shorts and polo.

Hair swirling around a lidless eye.

I shook off a shudder and poised my curser over the next notification in the string. Before clicking down, I paused in indecision. Why not, I thought. What harm could it do? Might even build some healthy PR for the PCP, maybe county government in general.

I moved my cursor to the search field, typing in Weider-White. There were two: one in North Dakota, the other Midlothian County. I paused again, then shrugged and sent a friend request. In the spirit of friendly public relations, I also wrote a casual remark on her timeline.

The next notification was a comment on a reply of some earlier comment to some photo or other. I exed it into cyber nothingness.

Then to my surprise, a new notification binged into my box. Nancy Collingsworth had poked me – seven times in a row. My witty repost had struck pay dirt. I smiled and poked her back. A couple more clicks and I was posting on her page.

'Hi there. Hope you had a great day!'

Not exactly Dickens, but I'd already used my witty remark quota for the evening. What was left? You look hot? What's your sign? How about those Reds?

I started to log off when a message notification binged onto the screen. "Speak of the devil," I muttered. Nancy Collingwood again, fifteen seconds ago. For a moment, I hesitated, feeling a little guilty (and a bit naughty). Then I thought again, what can it hurt? I opened Messenger.

'Hi yourself. I had a great day, thank you for asking. How about you?'

I started to write, 'Fine,' then paused. I wasn't fine. I hadn't had a good day. In fact, as days went, it was on the crappy side. Maybe one of the crappiest ever. Goose pimples rose at the memory. I wrote instead, 'Not so hot, but thanks for asking.' I sent the message.

Normally, I would have left it there and gone to bed. Cheryl might still be reading. Maybe I'd walk down and tell her about The Peeper. Maybe I'd just wash up and try to sleep, visions of lidless eyes making that impossible. But instead, I stared at the screen, waiting, anticipating. I watched twenty seconds tick off my computer clock, then thirty-five. A new message flashed into view.

'That's too bad. Want to talk about it?'

I thought about this. Did I? I hadn't wanted to talk with the guys at the PCP. I hadn't wanted to talk with Cheryl. I didn't want neighbors asking what it was like, or reporters sticking microphones in my face. Did I want to talk with this attractive stranger? I wasn't sure, so I played it neutral.

'That's okay. Don't want to hold you up.'

The reply was quick and to the point.

'Nonsense. I'm all ears (and other sensitive parts). Shoot."

So, I shot. I shot the shit with this mysterious stranger for half an hour. I told her about finding The Peeper's calling card. I told her about work frustrations. In thirty minutes, I shared more than I had with my wife in the past thirty days.

Chapter Three

"Randy? You okay?"

"I'm sorry, Irv. What did you say?"

Irving Zimbauer was head of County Environmental Services. As such, he oversaw Water and Waste-Water Management, Solid-Waste and Recycling Services, and me. Mine was the smallest group under his command, more an afterthought really. Ohio's smallest county had added a Pesticide Control Program as a nod to local protestors alarmed by a *Tribune* story on the link between cancer clusters and insecticide applications. Alarmed protestors tend to alarm county commissioners, especially when such protestors are vocal around election time. Like oysters, commissions sometimes produce a pearl when irritated long enough. In this case, said pearl took the shape of a four-person office headed by yours truly.

"I said, have you been getting enough sleep?"

"Sleep?" I replied. "Yes. I slept fine." And I had. My online conversation with Nancy (probably not her real name) had lanced the boil of my bad day. I left the computer feeling better, then took a drive during which cool jazz and summer breezes blew the cobwebs from my brain. Then I slept like the dead (make that a baby). I woke feeling good, refreshed, ready to start again.

"Then why don't you report on PCP's numbers for June."

"Ahem. Sure. Last month, we chased down fifty-two application complaints, issued ten violations, and sent eighteen samples to the state labs for analysis." I droned on for another two or three minutes, until I was starting to put even myself to sleep. Irv said thanks, apparently relieved that he had dotted my particular I. He then dismissed us, satisfied that another monthly meeting moved him thirty days closer to his retirement condo in Boca Raton.

I migrated back to my cube, where my great morning headed south.

~ * ~

When I came in the office, Nolan's skinny butt was now balanced on Jan's desk. Today, my admin was wearing a tee shirt that said, 'If you can read this, stop staring at my tits'. The letters got progressively smaller, like on an eye chart.

'Come on, darlin," Nolan said. "I could show you a thing or three."

"I'm pretty sure there's nothing of *yours* I want to see," Jan replied.

"You do *work* here, right?" I asked my head inspector.

"You bet, chief. Nothing going on right now."

"Well go and find some paperwork to do."

"Okee dokee. See The Peeper struck again? That makes four."

"Yeah. I heard about it."

"Out on Parkersburg Road. Speak of the devil, huh?"

I pointed to the door and got a Boy Scout salute in return.

"And after lunch," I added, "you and Cash make a perimeter application in the conference room. Then take some swab samples for the lab."

"Cash is out today," Jan said.

"Again?" I asked.

"What for?" Nolan asked.

"Huh? What for what?"

"The perimeter application in the conference room."

"Oh. I don't trust the results the lab's been giving us and want to see how they do with a known application as a control."

"I mean, what chemical do you want me to *apply*?"

The phone rang. I heard Jan say, "Hello, Midlothian County Pesticide Control Program."

I thought for a moment, then shrugged. "Permethrin. Standard strength. Same as for that positive control sample you sent them last month."

"That *you* sent them," Nolan said. "Against union rules, by the way."

"Well, let's stick *with* the rules and have *you* do this application. Okay?"

"You got it." Another BSA salute.

"Only this time, don't tell the boys in the white coats what we sprayed.

I want to see if they can identify it on their own."

Nolan left as Jan was saying, "Okay. I'll tell him. Bye."

Before I could round the corner to my three-walled fortress of solitude, my admin said, "Irving wants to see you."

"I just saw him at the monthly meeting."

"I'm assuming he knows that but wants to see you again.

I shrugged and left.

~ * ~

"Hi Irv. What's up?"

My boss was plopped behind his institutional desk, which was identical to mine, including the coffee-stained blotter. His forty excess pounds hung over the belt of his polyester slacks. The bottom button of his white, short-sleeve shirt was undone, revealing a tuft of belly hair that his too-short tie failed to cover. He leaned his balding head back in his sprung desk chair as he spoke around a bite of raspberry Danish.

"You investigate a complaint at Majestic Knolls this week?"

My stomach flipped. "Yeah."

He put down the pastry, wiped fingers on his slacks, then looked at a note. "A Mrs. White?"

"Weider-White," I corrected. "Ms. What about it?"

Irv retrieved his Danish and looked back at me. "She's pretty upset."

Now was the time to mention the body. Now was the time to say, 'I don't doubt it. Me too.' But instead, I said, "Oh?"

"Said you hit on her?"

I was expecting maybe a reference to The Peeper, maybe a reference to McPeet, maybe both. Maybe a reference to the incompetence of county government and its inability to protect taxpayers from harmful chemicals. But this? You could have knocked me over with a sampling swab, and I guess my face showed it.

"Did you?" Irv asked.

"What? No. What?"

"Something about having a bad day, "trying day" is how she put it. And then you tracked her down online and hit on her."

"Listen, Irv. I don't know …"

Irv smiled like the cat that lunched with the canary. "Is she a looker?"

I stammered and I guess I blushed because his grin lechered up a notch.

"Ahem. Listen, Irv. I did not *hit* on her."

"Let me guess. Tall, blond, big jugs?"

My face felt hot. "I sent her a friend request, that's all. You know, social media, the internet."

"That's *all*?" He was obviously enjoying this.

"Ah, practically. I reached out. Thought maybe I could improve department PR."

He took a bite of Danish and a sip of coffee. I watched chipped porcelain tip up and down. Then the back of his hand wiped the smirk off his face.

"Listen, Randy. I know you've hit the married, middle-aged doldrums." He spread his palms wide. "Haven't we all. And I know you're cursed with a twenty-something nymphomaniac for an admin." I muttered something, but he waved me off. "Just not on business. Okay? Improve your PR with blondes who haven't made application complaints. Capiche?"

I started to mutter something else, then thought better of it. I nodded.

Irv waved again and went back to his last few bites. I went back to room 138, waiting outside until the heat left my cheeks.

~ * ~

In my office, Nolan was once more perched on my admin's desk.

"I like your eye chart, darlin," he said.

"You've been gawking at it long enough," Jan said.

"I'm trying to decide if I'm nearsighted or far sighted."

"Far sighted," Jan said, still looking at her *People* magazine. "So why don't you stare at it from the conference room."

Suddenly, I couldn't take it anymore. "Nolan!"

They looked up, bemused expressions on both faces.

"Chief?" Nolan said.

A scathing rebuke brewed in my head, a combination 'get out, get back to work, do what I told you, you're fired.' A tirade that would burn three inches off his scrawny tail. But I didn't say it. Such spleen ventings are useless in unionized government, even counterproductive. The venter may have a stroke, but the ventee complains and is given time off with pay, which would leave me an inspector short. So, I stood there, blood pounding in my ears, face taking on the colors above the fruited plain.

"You okay, boss?" Nolan asked.

I finally managed to breathe. "Yeah. Just a bad couple of days." Although the last couple of years hadn't been that great either.

"I heard," my admin said. "Blondie shot you down. Huh?"

"What? Where did you hear *that*?"

"Peggy told me. Bummer. I keep telling you—let me fix you up with Rochelle."

I stammered something, but I doubt it was intelligible. My brain wasn't at that level yet.

Nolan smirked. "News travels. Small office." His smirk became a shit-eating, fatherly grin. "Feeling the seven-year itch, skipper? Got that yen to feed the monkey some new peanuts."

"You have such a way with words," Jan said. "You should write for Hallmark."

Nolan's shit-eater changed to a worldly smile. He patted my shoulder. "I know just what you need. I'm taking you out to lunch."

"It's only 10:30."

He shrugged. "An *early* lunch. I'll drive."

"No," I said, looking up at a giant sexy clown cutout with two strategically placed pompoms, a come-hither smile on her two-dimensional face. "Not here."

"Why not? You gotta eat somewhere. Am I wrong?"

"Not at Bozo's."

"Burgers are supposed to be top notch."

"We'll get in trouble."

"How?"

"Somebody will see the car and call the office. Employees jerking off on county time."

"That's why we took *my* car instead of your county cruiser." Nolan pointed to the crowded lot. "Just another civilian plate among the multitude."

"What are all these people doing here at eleven fifteen?"

"Early bird happy hour. Half-price burgers before noon."

"What if somebody from the office sees us?"

"And what are *they* doing here?" Nolan winked. "Come on." He was out of the car before I could protest further.

Inside was a brightly lit tavern with all the charm of a Denny's. High-set globe lights danced off the stainless-steel bar and Formica tables. Shiny, red vinyl coated every chair and stool. A kaleidoscope of reflections gleamed off fifties-style napkin holders. The air teemed with a not unappealing mix of frying meat, cheap perfume, and off-gassing glues from the new construction. I found myself smiling.

"Told ya," Nolan said.

"Welcome to Bozos. Two today, gentlemen?"

My eyes traveled from the checkerboard linoleum to the sound of the young, female voice. On the way, they found a set of shapely legs (not as long as Suzanne Weider-White's, but they'd do) below red shorts that might have been painted on. Traveling further north revealed a flat, pierced belly and a white halter top, cleavage popping from the scooped neckline like dough from a tube of refrigerator biscuits. Brunette hair framed two enormous, darkly painted eyes.

The curvy lips below the eyes said, "Sir? Two today?" I nodded dumbly.

Her dimples widened, and she said, "Just follow me."

Nolan gave me an elbow nudge and I jerked forward; eyes glued to her rear set of dimples.

The hostess handed us each a menu and said, "Shyreen will be serving you today."

"Close your mouth, Skip," Nolan said. "You're catching flies."

"We shouldn't be here," I whispered, sitting down.

"Look around," Nolan whispered back. "Nobody cares."

I looked. They didn't. The all-male crowd was drinking, eating, and staring, not necessarily in that order.

"Relax," he said. "Live a little."

"Hi, I'm Shyreen. Something from the bar, gentlemen?"

Our server was a carbon copy of the hostess, except she was blond and didn't need the services of a push-up bra.

"Yes, Shyreen. That's a lovely name." Nolan's smile was of the Cheshire variety. "We'll have a pitcher of LaBatts, darlin."

"What are you doing?" I whisper-shouted.

Nolan matter-of-facted me right in the eye. "Is there any union rule against a beer or two at lunch?"

"Well, ah, … Well, no. But …"

"And is there any rule about *how* or *where* one spends one's lunchtime?"

"Well, ah, well, no, um, as long as it's legal."

"Then what are you worried about? I'm driving. Relax. Lighten up. You worry too much, Skip."

I was about to protest when I thought, 'maybe I do.' There were rules against intoxication, but two beers would hardly accomplish that. And even if they did, I never heard of anyone getting canned for one too many—not in a union shop. I was fifteen years a straight arrow, minding the rules while others flaunted them, yet none of those flaunters ever got canned, or even demoted. So, I figured I was entitled to one afternoon (late morning) unwinding. And I could use a beer right now; getting chewed out by the boss does that to me. And it was practically the weekend. Thus rationalized, I unclenched my bowels and tried to relax into the red vinyl.

Shyreen brought the pitcher and two frosted mugs. The first glass was for thirst, as they say. By the second, I was biting into the best, greasiest burger I ever had. I didn't even object when Nolan ordered a second pitcher. Shyreen was happy to oblige. I gave her a sly, oh-so-charming grin. She gave me a daughterly smile.

My ancestry is Scotts-Irish, supposedly dating back to Castle Corlaigne in the old sod. As such, Corlanes have been known to hold their liquor, nipping a wee dram from time to time. But after finishing most of a pitcher of Canadian beer, this particular Corlane was feeling a wee bit happy. I had no idea of the ancestry of my tablemate, but I did know he was matching me mug for mug, with no noticeable effect.

"Where does your family hail from, Nols old boy?" I made an effort not to slur, and mostly succeeded.

Nolan shrugged. "Around. Now let me ask *you* something, Doc?"

"Shoot." It's hard to make the shoo sound without a little slur, at least when you're half toasted.

"This broad on Parkersburg. What's her name, Wider-Wide?"

"Weider-White." This time I may have slurred. "I did not hit on her!"

"Shh. Yeah, sure."

"I *friended* her. There's a difference."

"Right. Keep it down, okay boss."

"Okay, maybe I commented on a photo of her in a bikini. But it was casual. 'Beautiful picture'. Or something like that. That's all. And *she* posted the picture, not me."

"Okay, okay. I get it. You didn't hit on her."

My hand snatched air as Nolan grabbed the pitcher before I reached it.

He poured the last of the beer into his mug. "But you wanted to, didn't you?" He took a gulp and winked. "Didn't you?"

Our eyes met. I grinned sheepishly. For some reason, I did not mention The Peeper, even though it was a perfect subject changer. Instead, I grew philosophical in a beery kind of way. "Let's just say it is an occupational hazard of almost two decades of wedded bliss. A time when the better half no longer...wants your peanuts. Or vice versa."

"I know," Nolan said. "I mean, I've heard that happens. What did she look like, this Wide-White?"

"Weider-White," I said, giving a strong H sound after the last W. "W-E-I-D-E-R *hyphen.*" I dotted the air. "W-H-I-T-E."

He held a finger to his lips, speaking softer than me. "Got it. What did she look like?"

I thought for a minute, calling her image to mind. I started to blurt something, but Nolan's finger again covered his mouth with the sound of air escaping a flat tire. So, my hands sculpted the universal figure of an attractive woman, keeping it wider at the top of the hourglass.

He nodded and smiled. "Long legs?"

I spread my hands to their limits.

"Blond?"

I smiled and slurped dregs from my glass.

Nolan didn't respond for a moment, just gazed into the ozone with a grin. "Married?"

I shrugged. "Probably divorced."

"No ring, huh?" He sipped beer and gave me an odd look, even for Nolan. "Ring doesn't always matter though, does it?"

I think I blushed. Or maybe my face flushed from the alcohol.

"Want some pointers?" he asked.

"Scuse me?"

"Pointers. For next time. The next Weider-White or Fenster-Fine or Jones or Smith."

I waved him off and leaned back. What I really wanted was a nap. Maybe on the conference-room table at work. I'd told Nolan to do something in the conference room after lunch. What was that? I couldn't recall.

"Doc?"

"Hmm?"

"Let me give you some advice." Dad Hardy was back. "I'm a bit of a computer geek and know all about social media. I'm also a bit of a player if I don't mind saying so. And both those things have taught me that you don't go on their page and send suggestive comments. That looks too much like harassment."

"I didn't..."

He shushed me again. "I know." He finished his glass and resumed a hushed, fatherly tone. "It's okay to meet online, break the ice. But then what you want to do is talk to them. In person. Get a feel for how the land lays." He wiped his mouth. "Do your homework. Learn some things about her. Is she lonely? Is she bored? Where does she hang out, favorite restaurants, watering holes? Casually bump into her. Drop a well-placed compliment. Maybe buy her coffee or a drink. Ease into it, a little at a time."

"Ease into what?" My 'ease' rhymed with leash. "I'm a married man." I smiled.

I got that odd look again. "I notice you didn't say happily." He winked and waved for Shyreen. "Come on. I'll grab the check and get you back to the office." He winked again. "Just something to think about. For next time."

Chapter Four

The rest of the afternoon was a bit hazy. I remember seeing the cat and coaxing it over with the packet of kitten chow in my pocket. I also remember napping in my office instead of the conference room, which now smelled like the pesticide aisle at Walmart. I think Jan left early with a snide remark, "See you Monday, glassy eyes."

Cheryl was out when I got home, saving me one of her patented "you're an idiot" rebukes, so I skipped dinner and went to bed. I woke at three in the morning with a three-alarm headache and the feeling that a camel had used my mouth for a footbath before kicking me in the stomach. I took a pee, took two Tylenol, and turned on my computer.

It's surprising how many people are online at three in the morning. There are insomniacs like me, as well as friends from parts of the world where day and night change sides. I had nine notifications waiting.

Five people had commented on South Bay Movies, but I didn't feel like trivia just then. Barb Snyder from Beaumont Texas liked my 'Happy Birthday!' (what can I say, I'm a poet). Several friends commented on a video of a black lab hauling a snow-disc up a hill then mounting the plastic and sliding down, tongue wagging from its blocky head. The highlight of my online visit was another poke from Nancy Collingsworth, fifteen consecutive pokes in fact. A naughty thrill struck me as I looked behind me then poked her back.

I flicked back to watch the snow-boarding pooch, smiling each time he tugged the disc to the top then climbed aboard. With the skill of the big Kahuna, the dog shifted weight expertly, first leaning forward to send the sled skidding down the snow, then leaning back to slow the descent at the bottom. Then he'd hop out, clench jaws on the rim and start back up for another run. I think I watched this eight or ten times, smiling a little less with each viewing. That dog's life was a lot like mine, doing the same thing over and over. Except my canine friend was having a good time.

Finger poised, I was about to X the screen dark and myself back to bed, when the numeral one popped inside the message symbol. I held the arrow over the X, then watched it float like a Ouija planchette to the wavy message icon.

A small snapshot that looked like Ms. Theron in her prime sat next to an oblong box containing block printing. This particular Charlize had a police cap perched jauntily over pony-tailed golden hair, shade from the cap's brim adding mystery to her dark eyes.

'Hey there. What you doing up? Another bad day?'

That was an understatement, I thought. But was it? Was today so bad? At least something happened. Something besides waking up and moving from A to B to C to bed. There'd at least been some emotion—anger, embarrassment, flirtation. Something approximating life. I lifted my fingers and typed.

'Just restless and contemplating.'

'Contemplating? What? Life? Love? The Kamasutra? Spill it, I won't tell.'

I thought for a moment, then typed, 'Dust.'

'That's gonna need some explanation.'

'Did you ever think about dust?'

'Can't say I have, except maybe during allergy season.'

'I have. Just lately. I've thought a lot about it. How it just sits there, unmoving, uninvolved. It watches. It waits. It accumulates, slowly, gradually. But it doesn't experience. It marks time. No one notices it, pays much attention. Then before you know it, it's half an inch thick and another year has passed. Dust and life. Ying and Yang.'

I pressed send, then waited. The screen remained blank. I waited some more. Still blank. After a time that seemed like hours but was probably sixty seconds, I congratulated myself on chasing off yet another female in a long line going back to tongue-tied, high-school phone calls and awkward college dates. After a longer time, at least when judged by the molasses tick of 4 AM, I reached to click off messenger. To my surprise, a reply flashed on the screen.

'Wow, that's deep. Enigmatic. But kind of gloomy. Surely, things aren't that bad for a handsome guy like you.'

This caught my full attention, especially after my funereal comments on the nature of dust and life. Handsome? This was new. This was direct. No double entendre there. An actual, straight from the shoulder compliment. What was the catch? What did this mysterious woman want?

My mind raced through possible options. Was Nancy Collingsworth the nom de guerre for a pock-marked Central American gold digger masquerading as a cute Dayton cop? Was it a scam to send money for her mother's operation in Chile? Join her bible group? Jehovah's witness protection program? What? Why was this hottie calling me handsome at four o'clock in the morning?

I must have considered twenty possible motives, except for one—that she actually thought me handsome. I guess that's what two decades of "don't be an idiot" can do to the male ego. I was reminded of the old saying about not wanting to belong to a club that would have yourself as a member. Hadn't Woody Allen said that? But he'd had Mia Farrow and her sexy daughter. And I looked better than Woody. My profile photo may have been fifteen years old, without the current snow dusted on a thinning roof, but I was the same weight as when the picture was taken (almost anyway). So why not?

My ego and social-media bravado returned, tuning up for a sexy come back. But what? I thought a bit, then typed.

"I was a naughty boy today. Now I'm paying the piper.' I added a bagpipe sticker and a frowning emoji. Again, not Dickens, but with a touch of humor.

'Ooh! Naughty can be nice. What did you do? I won't tell.'

How to answer? 'I got drunk at lunch' was too plebian, something mechanics and truck drivers did. And as a cop, she probably had her fill of drunks. So, I thought of my afternoon at Bozo's and typed.

'Was surrounded by beautiful women but had to disappoint them.' Before I hit send, I changed 'them' to 'some.'.

'Ooh, you bad boy! Didn't know you were a playa.'

'I have my moments. How about you?'

I don't know if it was the feminine attention, the hangover, the hour, or the fact that I was in Micky and Minnie PJs, but I was running out of sexy repartee. The lame 'how about you?' was meant to volley back to her court, just another version of 'how was your day?' She served back more than I bargained for.

'Getting ready to hit the gym early. Still trying to lose my winter weight. You've peeped me in workout togs, so you know I like to get sweaty.'

This was getting good.

"Don't do too much. I'd hate for you to lose the good parts."

We parried back and forth for a few minutes, me trying to keep up as the dialogue shifted from double to single entendre and back again. But like the lady from Niger, I didn't know how to leap from the tiger's back without ending up inside. And part of me didn't want to. I felt nervous, sure, but alive. More alive than I had since, well a long time. My senses sharpened so that I heard the faint hum of the computer, smelled lint drying on the screen, tingled in places I hadn't tingled in a while. My headache and queasy gut disappeared. My muse returned, so that risqué repartee flew from my fingers.

I opined that 'It sure looks hot in those sweats.'

Ms. C replied that 'sometimes it sizzles.'

'Does that lead to a cold shower? Or do you have other ways to turn down the heat?'

'Lol! My showers are always steamy. My cool downs too.'

And so it went. Lob and backhand. Rush to the net, then back to the service line. It lasted for only a few minutes, but they were tantalizing minutes. I actually found myself sweating and breathing hard. And that wasn't the only thing getting hard.

Bear in mind, I was doing no more than typing, and with a woman I had never met or even seen. A woman who wasn't even technically there, although she was, somewhere. Yes, she was there. And that fact made this old married man more than a little uncomfortable. Discomfort vied with titillation, dancing back and forth like Fred and Ginger. I found myself glancing over my shoulder more frequently, although I knew Cheryl was asleep in her downstairs bed. A noise startled me, sending my mouse to the X in the upper right corner. The drop-down menu asked if I wanted to 'close the current tab' or 'close all tabs' before I realized the sound was the AC kicking on. I sighed in relief and made a decision.

This might not technically be cheating, but that was debatable. Time to end things. Time for an 'it's getting pretty late (or is it early)' comment. I started to type, but Ms. Collingsworth beat me to it. Then she took the strength from my fingers and the wind from my sails.

'Well, I'd love to keep chatting (or is it flirting?) but got to get my buns moving. Time to get pumped for another day of protect and serve. Maybe we could pick this up later. Maybe more than mutual peeping. How about we meet for coffee? Or would drinks be better? '

I gaped at the screen, fingers poised above the keys, cold air from the vent drying my clammy brow. More time ticked by; fingers poised but immobile. I couldn't move. I couldn't breathe. I felt light and airy, like I was floating above the screen watching the raised fingers of some piano-playing statue. My heart raced. My gut flipped. Lights dotted before my eyes; my vision barely able to note another message popping on my screen.

'Cat got your tongue? Or can I suggest another use for it? '

This final barely intended jab freed the steel bands around my chest. I managed a ragged breath. The stiffness left my body and I sunk back into my chair, with just enough strength to fold the screen of my laptop shut. I closed my eyes until the lights stopped flashing.

Sitting there, eyes closed, waiting for the fireworks to subside, I was reminded of Halloween about three years ago. An unexpected, out-of-season snowstorm had struck Midlothian, leaving behind two inches of the white stuff. I'd procrastinated on buying new tires, as I was wont to do in any situation that combined money with decision making. Coming home from a late afternoon, my worn rubber hit a freeway that Midlothian's road crews had yet to plow. The first turn at forty per resulted in my one and only experience twirling three-sixty while screaming at the top of my lungs and praying that no one would drive into my predicament. After sliding off the shoulder with a thud, I felt the same post-adrenalin fatigue I was feeling now.

Oddly, the memory made me want to drive. I was sure as hell too keyed up to sleep. A drive would make me feel better—It always did. And I had a lot to think about before crossing any Rubicon.

Chapter Five

When I got back from my drive, the hangover was gone, and my fatigue was reduced to an occasional yawn. Cheryl wasn't up yet, so I made myself an early breakfast of eggs, toast, and coffee. I was surprisingly hungry. A quick rinse of the dishes and I was the first one in the office, even with a drive-through stop for a large Dunkin coffee; a real treat given that our program's ten-buck Mr. Coffee made java that tasted like it came from a ten-buck Mr. Coffee.

Kirby wasn't in the lot (that was the name I'd given my orange-tabby friend). I prayed that he (she?) hadn't gotten hit by a car; I always cried a bit when I saw someone's best friend flattened on the highway. Then I headed inside, recapturing my good mood as I punched alarm codes and walked past the still empty reception desk.

I was looking over budget projections when I heard the office door open—Jan arriving, eight thirty, on the dot. After a few minutes of rustling in the outer office, I smelled the Mr. Coffee starting up. Too bad it never tasted as good as it smelled. Then the phone rang, and Jan picked up. No doubt one of her boyfriends was calling to say she'd left her diaphragm or panties or dignity at his place.

I felt funny, a little naughty listening in. Like I was eavesdropping or a Peeping Tom or something. Peeping? That's the term Nancy Collingsworth had used. I hadn't thought much about it at the time, but now it seemed like an odd choice of words. Especially with all the news about the Peeper, and given that she was a cop, and given that Dayton is only twenty miles from Midlothian. Young Ms. Sterling's voice broke my train of thought.

"Hello. Midlothian County Pesticide Control Program. How can I help you?"

I smiled again. The kid gave good phone, I had to hand her that.

"No, I'm sorry but Dr. Corlane isn't in yet. Who may I say called?

Who? …Does he know what this is about?... Alright. I'll be sure to give him the message."

The phone clicked.

"Who was that?" I called.

"Shit! Randy is that you?"

"Who else were you expecting?"

Her young body popped around the partition. Today's tee shirt had a large cartoon rooster with a leering grin. Below read "I ♥ big cocks". Not much double entendre there, I thought.

"A boss who didn't hide and scare the shit out of me. You almost gave me a heart attack."

"You're too young for a heart attack. Who was on the phone?"

She handed me a message. "Some guy named Milton Garlicki, if you can believe it. Said he's a homicide detective."

"Wonder what *he* wants?"

"For you to call him back. You kill somebody?"

I stared at the message. "Not that I recall."

Jan's eyes raised into question marks.

I shrugged. "Might have a *pet* question. I always get those questions. In fact, every vet since Cheiron has been asked about every pet since Dino the dinosaur—occupational hazard."

Now it was her turn to shrug. "I know Dino from reruns, but I'll take your word on this Sharon person." Then she returned to her desk.

I put the paper on my blotter and made a mental note to call around ten, when Jan took her coffee break, or in her case, diet Pepsi break. I didn't want her around when I talked to Milt. Visions of a lidless eye goose pimpled my forearms.

I shook my head. "Yeah, probably a pet question." But that lidless eye said there was more to it than that.

~ * ~

I never called Milt. Instead, I headed over at lunch. Sheriff's headquarters was just on the other side of the parking lot, and if I was lucky, he'd be out grabbing a bite when I stopped by. Playing message tag appealed to me more than discussions of dead women—approach avoidance being my middle name. It was not to be.

"Knock, knock."

Milt looked up from a Big Mac oozing secret sauce as I ducked my head into his office.

"The desk sergeant said to just come on back."

He motioned to me. "Come on in doc. No need to stop by during your lunch hour. A call would have done." He burped. "Have a seat."

The detective offices made pesticide control look like the Taj Mahal. Milt's grey-steel desk was similar to mine, but piled high with files in one corner, food wrappers and assorted trash in another. The rest was a series of scuff marks, cigarette burns, and felt-tip graffiti. The air smelled heavily of BO and rotting things, not the least of which were the teeth in Detective Garlicki's mouth. I pulled up a metal chair, checked the stained seat for wet spots, then sat down.

"What'd you want to see me about, Milt?"

Garlicki wiped his mouth on a sheet of typing paper. "Wanted to run something by you, since you're the pesticide guru in these parts."

I looked about the room. "Let me guess. Roach problem?"

He laughed. "Yeah, but we got a county service for that." Milt rummaged through some papers, knocking a couple of French fries on the floor. He found what he was looking for and handed it to me. "That's a report from the coroner. They ran a tox screen on that body you found yesterday."

"Tox screen? Seems to me the cause of death was pretty straight forward." I shuddered at the thought. "Why are they running tox screens?"

He shrugged and grabbed his burger. "Some cooperative program with a nearby college, Wright State I think." He bit into the big Mac but didn't let that stop his talking. "The egg heads at their lab got some federal money to develop this new technique, some atomic absorption whatsits; need test samples to standardize the thingy." He shrugged. "Every stiff gets sampled and sent in, regardless of circumstances."

I looked at the report. "Permethrin?"

He nodded. "Traces of that were found on the dead girl. Would that be something McPeet sprayed on his fruit? Maybe drifted over?"

I studied the paper. "I think Charlie uses preharvest malathion.

Besides, he's got good technique, sprays only when the wind is right. Can't see him drifting all the way over to that ditch. Especially given Weider-White's panty-bunch concerns."

"You want to check with him for me? Just to be sure."

I nodded. Something about permethrin needled my brain, but I couldn't place it.

"You got any leads on this guy?"

Another burp. Another breeze of rotten cabbage. "You know I can't tell you that doc."

"No comment, huh?"

"Yeah, I got a comment. This puppy is one sick SOB and I'm gonna catch him."

Chapter Six

I didn't feel much like eating after my talk with Garlicki, so I just grabbed a yogurt from the vending machine. Lidless eyes do as much for the digestion as they do for sleep patterns, or maybe my early morning had more to do with sixty ounces of Canadian beer and a rather uncomfortable online chat with a sexy lady cop. My mind slid effortlessly to lunch at Bozos, Shyreen's lush, sensual curves as she brought our pitchers and food; her laughing eyes—beautiful dimples front and back. I smiled as the image drove out more macabre musings. My smile widened at thoughts of Nancy Collingwood in sweats. But as minds do, mine meandered to Suzanne Weider-White's long legs strutting in the sunshine, my eyes following, my nose noting the telltale stink of death. My stomach lurched and I threw the half-eaten yogurt into the trash.

I was going through time sheets when I heard Jan reenter the outer office. She was crooning some rap thing in a sing-songy, white-girl way.

"Jan?" I called over the partition.

"You bellowed, master."

"Where's Cash? I need his time sheet."

"He's not in today, Randy."

"Called in sick *again*?"

"Didn't call. Didn't show."

This was unusual. The International Brotherhood of Communication Workers allowed us nine sick days and five personal days per annum, and Carter McCall made sure to use them all. But he always called or set it up in advance—always.

"Personal day?"

"Not that I know of."

"Would Nolan know?"

"Nolan knows so little that it's hard to know what Nolan knows."

"Did Cash say what was wrong when he called in yesterday?"

"He didn't call yesterday either."

I didn't like it. "Call his house and find out what's up."

"Is that an order, Doctor Lecter?"

"*Please.*"

"That's better."

I heard "cock-a-doodle-doo," bellow from the outer office and knew that Nolan had arrived. "Read your tee shirt. So, here I am, ready, willing, and more than able."

"As amusing as that prospect seems," yawned Jan, "I think your boss wants to talk to you."

Nolan popped around my partition. "You wanted to see me, Mein Fuhrer?"

"What's up with Cash?"

Nolan plopped his jeans on my desk. "I was wondering that too."

"*You* were wondering? *You* told me he was out sick."

"Yep. I told you that a few days ago." He dotted the air. "Correction— I *assumed* that a few days ago. But I haven't seen him or even heard from him since. Doesn't Jan know?"

Jan's voice carried over the partition. "You told me yesterday he was *still* sick."

"No," yelled Nolan over his shoulder, "I said I *assumed* he was still sick. Big difference, Miss I heart big cocks."

My headache was coming back. "Nolan!"

"You okay, Skip?"

I rubbed my temples. "Can someone give Cash a call to see how he is or where he is or whatever? Please?"

"I just did," Jan yelled. "No answer."

"Did you leave a message?" I yelled back.

"Nope. No machine or service to leave one on."

I looked at Nolan still perched upon my desk with a smirk on his face. "Mr. Webster?"

"Sir!" He saluted.

"Do you have any inspections scheduled this afternoon?"

"Two."

I rummaged through my drawer for Tylenol. "While you are out and about, please stop by at young Mr. McCall's residence and check if he is okay." I found the pill bottle and washed two caplets down with lukewarm coffee.

"I'd love to, but my inspections are both in Norbert, which as you know is eighteen miles east of here, while Cash lives downtown. That's a lot by four o'clock. Which do you want me to do first?"

I was about to tell him to first stop quickly at Cash's but knew the 'quick' stop would turn into an hour shooting the shit followed by a late lunch at Bozo' followed by a beer siesta followed by going home. I was suddenly very tired.

"Do your inspections. *I'll* stop by to see Cash." I slid a pad to Nolan. "Write his address down for me. *Please.*"

~ * ~

From my impression of Carter McCall, I figured he lived either in his parents' basement or over the garage of some seedy urban house. As I knocked on the door of a downtown basement efficiency, I could see that I was partially right on both counts. The neighborhood was one favored by one-star Midlothian's; there were two condemned houses and a toilet on the corner lawn. A three-year-old rugrat dressed only in a diaper played in the dirt lot across the street, periodically hollering "Good Lawd!" as he beat on what looked like a Ken doll without an arm. The only other sound was the hum of a 1990s air conditioner trying to cool the basement flat.

No one answered my knock, so I called "Hey, Cash? Are you home?" The rugrat paused, arm raised, to give me a suspicious stare before resuming Ken's punishment. When no answer to my call was forthcoming, I tried the knob. To my surprise, the door opened.

I'd been assaulted by foul odors of late, first the stink of day-old death on Parkersburg Road, then Garlicki's office stink and delightful halitosis. The smell inside the dark and funky apartment was somewhere between the two. A flick of the wall switch brought forth a sixty-watt bulb that didn't do much to dispel the gloom but did send a few roaches scurrying into the baseboards.

"Cash? Are you here? It's Randy Corlane."

Still no answer. My mild concern from the office ramped up a notch.

"Cash?" I walked gingerly across the crumb-dusted carpet, stepped carefully around the unmade fold-a-bed sofa, and headed for the bathroom. I was half expecting the odor to flare as I reached the WC, either from a clogged toilet or a dead body. But the assault on my nostrils remained constant; not quite gag-making but far from pleasant. The bathroom was small, filthy, but without the feared commode clog. A mildewed towel lay across the linoleum, along with a pair of girl's panties. "You dog," I muttered as I gave the latter a kick that revealed a monogram in red lettering.

"Why does KAN sound familiar?" I didn't ponder this question long, because next to the initials was a large brown splotch that looked to be dried blood.

~ * ~

"You okay, doc?"

Garlicki and I were outside Cash's cheap apartment in the hazy city heat. The effects of finding first a body then a possible crime scene had caught up with me. The combined smells of bachelor flat and unkept detective suddenly caused the room to spin, or maybe it was my head spinning. But the air smelt better outside, and things swam back to focus. I nodded.

"Sorry. What were you saying?"

"I said, the reason those initials probably seem familiar is because of the first victim. Karen Ann Nagel."

"KAN?"

The fat cop nodded. "Preliminary blood tests match her type. We'll send out to the state lab for DNA, but I'm betting there'll be a match."

"But what would her panties be doing at Cash's apartment?"

Garlicki smiled. "Exact thing I want to ask when we find him. You've no idea where he is?"

I shook a negative. "He hasn't come in for a few days. We guessed he was sick."

"We?"

"My admin and chief inspector back at the program."

"Names?"

"Um, Jan Sterling and Nolan Webster."

Garlicki wrote in a pad. "I'll talk to them. What was this McCall guy out sick with?"

"I'm not sure. Initially I think it was too much happy hour."

Garlicki chuckled. "Been there, done that. Especially at his age. But that only explains a day or two. Something else happen to him?"

I shrugged. "You'll need to talk to Nols—Mr. Webster. He was closer to Cash than I was, I mean am."

"I'll do that." He closed the notebook and stepped aside to allow a technician carrying a black case to enter. "Dust it all, Hal," Garlicki said.

"No problem," the tech replied. "The place is a postage stamp."

"Listen, Detective. Can I go now? I need to clear my head."

He patted my shoulder. "Sure, Doc. Try not to take it too hard. It's just a pair of bloody drawers. Not like that mess out on Parkersburg."

A lidless eye swam into my brain and things began to tilt again. I walked unsteadily to my car.

"Oh, Doc?"

I turned.

"I may need to talk to you again." He smiled. "Like they say on TV, don't skip town without checking in. Okay?"

"Thanks," I said, not sure why I said it.

~ * ~

By the time I got home, Cheryl was at a BFF League function, a play over in Dayton or something. I read the note and thought about popping a pot pie in the microwave, but I still couldn't get the image of the bloody panties out of my head. They bounced back and forth across my brain, dancing a tango with the implication of finding them in Cash's bathroom. So instead of eating, I cracked a beer and went to my room to check emails.

Halfway through the emails I was halfway through the beer and starting to unwind. But instead of losing stress, I felt like I was bleeding off nervous energy, like a kettle that had gone from a whistling boil to low simmer. Rather than fatigue, I felt excitement. A co-worker/subordinate may be a serial killer; I had discovered the implicating evidence. Was this cause for excitement? Had life become so dull that any break in routine, even brushing shoulders with a serial killer, was exhilarating? I wanted to tell somebody, anybody; I'd even settle for Cheryl. I pondered this as I mindlessly deleted junk emails. I pondered further as I checked social media comments. Then my thoughts were broken by a new shock. Nancy Collingwood had sent me a private message.

A dozen things raced through my mind. Should I delete the message and forget about it? Should I block Nancy? Should I be brutally frank about my marriage? All of those seemed right, yet somehow wrong. More importantly, they didn't seem exciting; I was in the frame of mind for excitement. Besides, what was the harm so long as I steered free of meeting her? After all, it was social media, which was as safe sex as there is. I smiled and opened Messenger. The note was just one line.

'I'm sorry if I scared you off.'

The nervous energy was back—a titillating, tantalizing, naughtiness. I looked over my shoulder, even though I knew Cheryl was in Dayton. I looked at the picture next to Nancy's message, the photo that looked so much like Charlize Theron. My heart beat faster. My fingers stiffened over the keys. A lump stiffened in my throat, another in my pants. How to respond? I thought of several comebacks but settled on punting.

'It's not that. Last night there was a…' What? A power outage? 'Cable problem. Sucker crashed on me. Didn't get your message until today.' A reprieve, but only temporarily.

I waited. Part of me hoped she wouldn't answer, so I could end this now. Part of me dreaded that she wouldn't answer. She answered.

'You're a bad liar, Randy.'

'Well, I guess you threw me for a loop. More than usual.' Now what? Might as well get it out on the table. 'Not sure it's a good idea to meet. My wife might not understand.' That feeling of naughty excitement fled like a summer breeze.

'So, you must be the last of a dying breed. HAPPILY married.'

I was back in that comfort zone, able to talk with her—open up. We'd met the impasse, and she was still chatting with me. I again wondered what was wrong with her. I chastised myself for the latter thought and typed.

'I don't know. What's in between happy and unhappy? Neutrally married?'

'LOL! I think you just call that married these days.'

'Well, whatever you call it, that's me. Although we see each other so seldom, it feels more like housemates.'

'Little woman not at home tonight?'

'You guessed it. Out with her girlfriends. Seems like she spends a lot more nights with them than she does with me.'

'Have you ever thought maybe that's because she's not with girlfriends?'

'??'

'Maybe she's spending time with the opposite of girlfriends?'

'Girl enemies?'

'Funny, but dense. I meant opposite the girl part.'

Boyfriend? This had never even occurred to me. Could Cheryl have a boyfriend? Nancy responded as if my thoughts traveled across the cybersphere.

'Let me guess. Goes out ALOT. At concerts and restaurants where she'd be hard to track. Dresses up. Maybe exercising more than she used to. Little interest in you. Little interest in the bedroom. How right am I?'

At first, I laughed, as if the thought was too absurd to contemplate. Then I found my thoughts racing, traveling back to the last time I'd seen Cheryl getting ready to go out. Was it two weeks ago? Three? Our marriage had been reduced to two roommates that worked opposite shifts and communicated by notes. Long periods where we never saw each other at all. Yet the bookend images from that time were almost identical. Three weeks ago, I'd seen her leaving for the evening wearing a heavily cleavaged top and more than a little perfume. Then I recalled the other night, getting home late, her still dressed in skintight and decolletage.

'Are you there, Randy?'

I didn't answer. I couldn't. The idea was too new. And I wasn't yet sure how I felt about it.

'Looks like I've given you food for thought. So, I'll leave you to it and say goodnight—for now.'

I went to bed and stared at the ceiling, thoughts tossing back and forth. The idea was absurd. The idea explained a lot. After forty minutes, I resolved to wait up for Cheryl. See how she was dressed. Smell for male scent. Grill her about the evening, specific details about the play and who she was with; details that could be fact-checked in the morning. I'd feel guilty for doing it, already felt guilty in fact. But I had to know. I had to know how my marriage stood. Was I still neutrally married? Was I on the path to divorce? What might the latter entail? Sometime between eleven and eleven-thirty I drifted off, visions of Nancy Collingwood in my head.

~ * ~

I woke with a start; it was still dark. Something didn't feel right. Uneasiness hung in the air like smoke misting my vision. At first, I thought there must be a fire, but the air smelled okay. No, that wasn't quite true. There was no acrid odor of burning easy chairs and bookcases, but the air smelled not quite right—kind of musty or funky. Again, I was reminded of the euthanasia freezer in vet practice.

I looked for the bedside clock but couldn't find it. It felt like two or three in the morning, dawn still a few hours off. My mouth was dry as cotton, so I arose to get a drink. That feeling of uneasiness increased with each step toward the hallway. By the time I stopped outside the upstairs bath, I knew something was wrong. It was more than the odor, which although not overpowering, was sickly familiar. My feet stumbled toward the stairway, the smell growing stronger.

"Cheryl," I called into a darkness that seemed much too deep for our house.

I stumbled on, moving down the stairs like a golem in some horror story. I drifted past the sofa, past the end table, past the big screen; the light from upstairs growing fainter with each step, the smell growing stronger, more insistent.

The hallway to the master was cave black; I entered it in drifting, stuttery steps. I couldn't see anything, but somehow knew when I had reached the door to the master bedroom, Cheryl's room. I knew the door was open. I went inside.

"Cheryl?"

No answer. I drifted toward the bed, the sickly, nauseating odor growing.

"Cheryl?"

I flicked on the bedside lamp.

My wife lay upon the coverlet. Her face was brightly rouged, her flesh oddly red, as if in the throes of passion. She smiled a rictal grin. Her eyes stared at me, unseeing. Her eyelids had been cut off.

"Arrgh."

I woke for real, a strangled gasp upon my lips. The images from the dream were fresh in my brain. I doubted they'd ever drift into obscurity as dreams usually do. I knew they'd linger forever.

Chapter Seven

Cheryl was still asleep when I left for work. A note on the kitchen table said she hadn't gotten in till after one. As I drove to the office, I ran the numbers. Play would start around 7:30 or 8:00 o'clock. It would run for two hours maybe two and a half, that's 10:30 at the latest. Forty minutes to drive home from Dayton, light traffic that time of night. Let's make it eleven-thirty. Maybe she stopped for a drink or late supper (surely, they would have eaten before the show; had she mentioned that?) A couple drinks would make one o'clock feasible. Of course, so would another roll in the hay and extra cuddling.

The mental gymnastics continued at the office, making work difficult. But oddly, I was as worried that my wife wasn't having an affair as I was that she was having one. When I thought that Nancy must be wrong, part of my mind was at ease. But part of me was disappointed. Cheryl having an affair solved so many things, created so many opportunities, overcame inertia. Part of me was excited by the prospect.

"You okay, Randy?"

I looked up at Jan leaning against my partition. Today it was hot pants and a Bozo's tee-shirt with its two strategically placed pompon drawings.

"I haven't seen that top before."

She grinned. "You like it? Nols gave it to me."

"You guys getting a thing going?"

"No, I just like teasing him." She frowned. "Get up on the wrong side of the bed this morning?"

I leaned back and sipped coffee. "Can I ask you something?"

"Anything. As long as I don't have to promise a good answer."

"You're a woman."

"What gave me away?"

"Seriously."

"So, we're serious this morning." She sat on my desk, legs crossed, hands raised like she was ready to take dictation. "Shoot."

"How do you know if a woman is having an affair? How can a guy tell?"

She shrugged. "Ask her."

"I'm serious."

"So am I. Ask. If she says yes, you know. If she says no, you look for signs of lying. Nervousness. Turning away. Changing the subject." She frowned. "Trouble at home?"

"No. I mean, I don't know."

She leaned in and whispered, "I'm gonna need details."

"Well, I was chatting with this…this person on social media. You know, messaging back and forth."

She grinned. "Was this a lady person or a man person?"

"That's not important."

"Okay. So, what did this attractive lady you were flirting with say?"

"I never said it was a woman, or that she was attractive, or that we were flirting."

"Nope." Her grin broadened. "What did she say?"

I blushed, which made Jan laugh. "She said that a wife who spends a lot of time away from home, starts working out, doesn't want to have… shuns intimacy." I blushed deeper. "That this woman might be having an affair."

"I see. And how do you feel about this possibility?"

"What do you mean, 'how do I feel?'? I'm worried of course. And, well, I'm also…"

"A little excited?"

I didn't answer.

Jan stood. "Well. There's three ways to approach this. One, ask, like I said. Then there's the coward's way out—hire a private detective."

"Have her followed?"

"Haven't you ever watched Cheaters?"

I shook my head. "What's number three?"

The grin was back. "Assume the worst and test the waters yourself."

She walked to the partition, then turned back.

"By the way, in case you are interested, my friend Rochelle is blonde,

47

five-seven, long legs, and big hooters. I've told her about you, and she's interested." Jan snatched a sticky note off my desk, jotted an address and phone number on it, then stuck it on my copy of Pest Control Quarterly. "Just in case." She grinned and returned to admin country.

I caught flies while staring at the partition. Then I heard the phone ring.

"Midlothian County Pesticide Control Program," Jan said. She listened. "Just one moment."

"Randy, for you. Line one."

"Who is it?" I yelled back.

"Your detective buddy with the unpronounceable name."

"Garlicki?"

"That's the one."

I picked up the phone, feeling guilty. "Hello. Randall Corlane."

"Hey Doc, Milt Garlicki."

"What can I do for you, Milt?"

"You can come over and answer a few questions."

"I've told you all I know about Cash and..." I lowered my voice. "About that person I found on Parkersburg. I don't know what else I can tell you."

"Not about that one, Doc. Although we're still talking Parkersburg Road."

"I don't understand."

"News hasn't hit the streets yet, but we got another one."

"The Peeper?" I whispered.

"Looks that way. And today's victim was your friend from Parkersburg Road."

"Weider-White?"

"Got it on the first try. Found her in a dumpster behind Walmart."

"I guess she would be caught dead there," I mumbled.

"What's that?"

"Nothing. When did it happen?"

"Looks to have been dead at least twenty-four hours, although in this heat, who can say?"

"Well, well, why do you want to talk to *me*?"

Garlicki paused. "Just come over. Okay?"

~ * ~

There was no union rule about how you spent your lunch hour, even if that was at the county sheriff's office. I sat back in Garlicki's guest chair, which fortunately was still free of wet stains. The office still smelled, as did Garlicki.

"So, what did you want to ask me, Milt?"

"I was talking with your employee, Nolan Webster. Seemed like a nice enough guy."

"I suppose."

"You think he's an honest guy?"

I thought about that. Nolan could be a pain in the ass and was often the swollen hemorrhoid in my workday, but I couldn't recall him telling me a lie. I'm sure he lied to Jan about his sexual prowess, all guys do that. He probably lied to Uncle Sam on his taxes. But he never spun tales where I was concerned. More's the pity. Maybe he knew that I was powerless to discipline him, or maybe he just knew that I wouldn't. Either way, he always laid the bare facts on the table and smiled, as if daring me to react.

"I've found that to be the case," I replied.

"Good to hear. Anyway, I was talking to him about our friend Carter McCall, who hasn't shown up by the way."

"Find anything else at his apartment?"

"Besides the panties and old pizza boxes, you mean?" He paused. "Maybe. Anyway, this Nolan tells me that the last time he saw our friend was at Bozo's, you know, the new hoochy bar out by the highway?"

"I've heard of it," I said.

"I'll bet," Milt said. "Webster tells me you've even been there. That right?"

"Listen, Milt. It was lunch. Just lunch. Burgers and beer. Nols was driving and wanted to go there. It was his car, so..." I felt my face warming again.

"Don't worry, Doc. I don't give a shit about that." I relaxed a bit. "What I do give a shit about is that Webster told me you had more than a passing interest in Ms. Weider-White. That she'd complained you'd hit on her."

I stopped relaxing. "Listen, Milt. I don't know how this story got going."

"*Did* she complain?"

"Well, yes. But I did *not* hit on her. I friended her. On social media. You know, the internet. Building a little interpersonal PR for the county. That's all."

"Then why did she complain?"

"I don't know. Not really."

"What did this interpersonal PR entail?" Now I paused. "We're checking her webpage, so best to fess up."

"I...I, well, commented on a photo she'd posted."

"Photo of what?"

"Well, er, photo of her in a bathing suit. A photo that *she* posted—publicly."

"And?"

"And I said, 'beautiful picture', or something like that."

Milt looked at his pad. "How about, 'I'd like to start at the equator and circumnavigate both hemispheres'?"

"What?"

"That was your post on her page."

"No, wait. That's...that's impossible. I mean, that's not what I wrote."

"That's what we *found*." I sat there, mouth agape. "You trying to get a thing going with this lady?"

"What? No. I mean..."

"Must have pissed you off when she complained, huh?"

"I didn't like it, but I wasn't mad enough to do anything."

"Got a reprimand from your boss, I understand." He suddenly changed tacks. "How are things at home, Doc? You and the missus getting along okay?"

"We...we're fine."

"Been married a lot of years?"

"Almost twenty."

He whistled. "That's almost three times the seven-year itch. Must be getting restless to spread some oats not quite tame, as my Polish grandma used to say."

"Listen, Milt."

"I mean, we got you at Bozo's. Then this message to Wide-White." He chuckled and looked at his pad. "Got a witty way with words, Doc. I'll give you that. They say a sense of humor is the surest way to open the gates of heaven." He looked squarely at me and stopped smiling, the amiable Polak gone. "I ask around, what else am I going to find out?"

I shook my head and started to speak, when thoughts of my conversation with Jan stopped me cold. Garlicki caught the hesitation.

"I search your house, what am I gonna find?"

I swallowed hard and returned his stare. "Nothing except a Playboy from 2011. Special Edition: Women at Work. It's in my underwear drawer."

His cop eyes remained steely on mine, then his grin returned. "Don't worry, Doc. We aren't in the search-warrant phase yet. Just circumstantial evidence, probably coincidence. You finding the panties. Your connection to Wide-White." He shrugged. "But don't do any wholesale housecleaning. It won't look good." He flipped his notebook closed. "Give me a call if you come up with anything else you think I ought to know." He smiled, a piece of something grey and fatty stuck between his middle teeth. "Thanks for your cooperation."

~ * ~

I sat staring out my window at the tree in the parking lot. I smiled when I saw Kirby rub against the trunk; not hit by a car and looking a bit friskier from a couple square meals. Then my thoughts clouded. I didn't make that comment on Suzanne Weider-White's page. Oh, I made a comment, but one that went something like 'lovely picture'; hardly insulting. Yet, the comment that Garlicki read me sounded familiar, like a cruder version of something I *would* write—double entendre with a touch of humor. How had it gotten there? Who had posted it? Who knew me well enough to post it? How had they assigned it to me? I needed to find out.

"Hey, Bozo." Nolan's voice rang from the outer office. "Like your pompoms. Want to shove some pie in my face?"

"No, Nols," Jen said. "I'm pretty sure there's nothing I want to shove in your face. Maybe up your ass."

"Now we're talking," Nolan said.

Here was the answer.

"Nolan," I called.

His face popped around the partition. "You rang fearless leader."

"You got plans at four o'clock?"

"Clocking off the grindstone. Why?" He casually looked at the picture of Cheryl sitting on my desk and smiled.

"How about I buy you a beer. I need your advice on something."

He plopped his jeans on my desk. "I'm available right now."

I shook my head. "This isn't work related." His eyebrows raised. "Come on, I'll buy you *two* beers."

He smiled. "Okay, but I get to choose the tavern."

~ * ~

Shyreen brought two frosted mugs of Canadian beer: her dimpled smile turning pretty into gorgeous. I thought how her skin was as smooth as vanilla pudding, the rich, homemade kind my mother used to make before she died.

"Thanks Shy," Nolan said. Then we both watched her walk away.

When the lovely blond turned the corner, I turned to Nolan. "After your talk with Garlicki, do you think it was wise to come *here*?"

Nolan shrugged. "What's the diff? He already knows I come here. And he knows you come here."

"I do not *come* here."

Nolan smiled. "I don't know. The way you looked at Shyreen, you seemed close to it."

"Not funny."

"Hey, you're not mad that I told Garlic man about our little trip here, are you?"

"No, but I am mad you told him about Weider-White's harassment complaint against me."

He waved me off. "Relax. It just came up in conversation. He wanted to know if you came here all the time. I said no; I took you here to relax after getting chewed out. Why would he even care?"

"Because she's dead."

Beer spurted out his nose. "Double Wide is belly up?"

"Have some respect."

He raised his palms. "Fine. Dead. Deceased. Gone to her eternal rest." He dropped into hushed tones and leaned in. "How did she get it? Farmer McPeet's pesticides?"

I thought his response seemed oddly callous. "No, they're blaming the Peeper."

"No shit?"

"No shit. And maybe me."

"I don't follow."

"Remember when I told you about friending Weider-White? About what I wrote on her bikini post?"

"Sure. Something like 'sexy lady' or some such. Not very original."

"It was 'lovely picture'."

He chuckled. "Oh, that's *much* better."

"But that's not what it says on her post now."

"What do you mean?"

"Someone changed it."

"Changed it? To what?"

"That's not important. What is important is that *someone* managed to hijack my comment and change it; made it more, well, sexually suggestive."

He pushed his beer away and grinned. "Now I *got* to know what it said."

I felt my face flushing again. I looked both ways and whispered, "I'd like to start at the equator then circumnavigate both hemispheres."

He laughed. "That is *much* better. Way to go, Doc Randy."

"I never wrote that."

"It sounds like you."

"That's the point." I blushed deeper. "It does, a little. Someone who knows me made the change. I need to find out who. Find out why. Find out how."

"So, that's why you asked me out for a beer? Advice on how to track down a hacker?"

"Well, you said you were a computer geek with a working knowledge of social media."

He gulped beer and pondered. "Well, I guess I might be able to help you out. Sort of in the way of a computer consultation. That's what we're talking about, right? A consultant doing some casual, after-hours detective work?"

He seemed to want an answer, so I nodded.

"Let me see," he continued. "Consultants get paid, don't they? I mean, generally?"

I sighed. Most people would see it as a favor to the boss. A little social capital for performance-review time. But this was county government and neither performance reviews nor bosses held much power.

"How much? Besides the cost of beer and a cheeseburger that is."

"Hundred bucks?" He smiled. "Cash. You know, below Uncle Sam's radar."

I sighed again, this time in relief. I was expecting a hundred per hour. I nodded again.

"I'll need to see your setup. Get into your computer and social media account."

"What? Why? It was Weider-White's account that was changed."

"Yeah, but *she* didn't change *your* comment. She could have hidden it or deleted it from her timeline, but she wouldn't have had the power to change what it said. Not even the social media administrator would have done that. No, the change came from your end."

"Well, I don't know. My computer is, well…"

Nolan put a hand on mine. "Got a little porn stored there, boss?"

Heat rose in my face again. "No."

"Okay, fine. Whatever. But trust me, I don't give a shit. I'm a professional."

"Professional pesticide inspector. Maybe *semi*-professional."

He waved me off. "That's during the day. By night, I am Wonder Webmaster, wizard of the keyboard. And Wonder Webmaster is only concerned with your system vulnerabilities and any cracker exploitation, thereto."

"Cracker?"

"Bad-guy hacker."

"There are good-guy hackers?"

"Sure. Yours truly for example. Now, when can I come over to access your system?"

"Let me go home and check the calendar—see when my wife is...I mean, see when I've got some free time."

Nolan's smile said he knew more than was good for him. "Now," he said. "How about that cheeseburger?"

~ * ~

I managed to hold Nolan to two beers before paying the tab. He was still talking with Shyreen when I left, so he probably had a few more. There was too much on my mind to muddle it with alcohol. I had a bad feeling about today—a really bad feeling.

I drove mechanically, my brain occupied with possibilities. Was I under suspicion for murder? Did they think I was The Peeper? Was my wife having an affair? Who changed my comment, and if they did it once, what else could they do? Had all the information on my computer been compromised? Yes, a really bad feeling.

Without realizing it, I found myself driving down the freeway, the summer sun riding low over my left shoulder. Evidently some deep part of my mind, one below the worry, knew what I needed to unwind. I tuned in cool jazz and ran the window down a bit, letting the warm afternoon breeze blow away the stress. I started to relax, my mind wandering to visions of Nancy Collingwood in workout sweats.

Cheryl wasn't home when I got there, per usual, a concert in Cincinnati being tonight's excuse. I'd worry about the implications of that later. For now, I needed to clean up any embarrassment from my computer before turning it over to Nolan.

I quickly checked mail and notifications, glancing through the junk and near-junk. Only one item caught my eye—Nancy Collingwood had sent me a message. I found myself clicking on it almost without thinking.

'Hi. Hope you had a nice day, with time to think. Let me know if you want to talk.'

I started to exit Messenger when my eyes lit on the Dayton PD cap in her photo. She was a cop. Although not a detective, she still ought to know about police procedures—I mean, a cop is a cop is a cop. Maybe she could tell me if I was worrying for nothing or for something. I started to type.

'Hi yourself. Another bad day. Heard some bad news about a friend. Can I ask you about it? Your professional opinion?'

I waited. This is silly, I thought, as the seconds ticked by. She probably isn't even online. I should just go to bed and check in the morning. A reply popped onto my screen.

'Sorry to hear about your bad news. 🙁 Sure, ask me anything.'

How to proceed? In all my driving and thinking, I hadn't formulated any questions, or even known I'd be asking them to an attractive female cop. I decided to stick as close to the truth as possible, in order to get the most useful answers possible.

'My friend may be in trouble with the law. He found some incriminating...'

I changed He to She.

'At a possible crime scene. Then someone she knew was found dead. The police asked her not to leave town and not to do any wholesale housecleaning that might look like disposing of evidence. Should my friend be worried or is this routine?'

Laying it out in writing like that made it seem bad, but I was hoping Nancy would allay my fears. She didn't.

'It sounds like your friend might be a suspect. So yes, a little worry is warranted. Did the cops Mirandize her?'

I hadn't thought of that. On TV, you weren't really in trouble until they read you your rights.

'No. Just informal questions. That's good, right?'

'Yes and no. What exactly are we talking about here? Does this have anything to do with The Peeper killings?'

She was a cop all right. I paused; fingers poised over the keys. Well, I thought, in for a penny....

'Maybe.'

I had hoped Nancy would ponder my "friend's" predicament; think long and hard before suggesting I wasn't in much trouble. She hadn't. Now she *was* pondering. I waited long seconds for a response, more than sixty of them. I'd just about decided to nudge her with a 'still there?' when she answered.

'Kind of puts your other problem in perspective, doesn't it?'

I thought about this and smiled. I wouldn't be the first guy whose wife cheated, or whose marriage failed. But not everybody was wrongly suspected of being a serial killer. That made divorce seem like a Sunday walk in the park. I thought some more. I needed professional advice, and not from Wonder Webster. I needed a cop on my side. I made a decision. I typed.

'That invitation to meet still open?'

I sent the message then realized more explanation was needed.

'Don't get the wrong idea. I need advice. Professional advice on police procedures. For my friend. She's getting worried.'

Her response was quick and to the point. 'I hear you. Advice it is—for now. How about the bar at O'Toole's? Eight PM tomorrow. That okay?'

I almost panicked. That was not okay. Nothing about it sounded okay. It'd be getting dark around eight; darkness suggested things that broad daylight didn't. Further, O'Toole's was a well-known and well-attended Dayton Bistro; Cheryl and her friends sometimes met there. A bar? Alcohol? I shook my head and typed.

'Can we make it coffee at the Northfield Diner? That's about half-way for both of us. Say noon tomorrow?'

I'd only been to Northfield once, noticed the diner as I drove down the main drag; a friendly little place with chrome napkin holders and smiling strangers. Strangers were good. As far as I knew, Cheryl had never been one of them.

'Afraid to be alone with me in a bar at night?'

I blushed. She was a cop alright. 'No. Just noon would be better for me.'

'Noon it is. Good thing for you, I have tomorrow off. See you at the diner. And tell your "friend" to try and get some sleep.'

Shock threatened to set in as I logged off. I had actually agreed to meet her. Police help was the premise, but was that the only reason? I shook off the nerves and tidied up my computer—nothing really incriminating, just a little embarrassment removal. I spent the rest of the evening changing passwords. Then I took a drive to cool down. Then I went to bed, although I didn't sleep much.

Chapter Eight

I dozed fitfully; my dreams filled with lidless eyes. I woke well after my alarm was supposed to rouse me, starting a bad day that only got worse. Already late, I skipped breakfast and drove into full-blown rush-hour traffic; traffic I would have avoided at my usual start time. The gas tank that I'd been sure was three-quarters was in fact on fumes. Stopping at the Marathon ate up ten more minutes. Then, an accident blocked my regular route.

I tuned on the news hoping for a traffic report. Instead, I learned that the weather would be cloudy and muggy, with a high of eighty-five. I also learned that gold prices had risen another fifteen dollars per ounce. I had suggested to Cheryl that we invest in gold back when it was seven hundred per ounce; a suggestion that was met with a patented 'don't be an idiot'. Now, I took a certain perverse pleasure every time it climbed higher, passive aggressively calculating the riches I would have made and silently saying, "I told you so."

The guy behind me honked in frustration. I honked in frustration as well. A cop gave me a stern look of disapproval, then began directing traffic around the accident. I smiled at him as I passed, he gave me the facial equivalent of the finger in return.

As my speed climbed back to forty, I thought about my meeting today with Nancy, a worry I had blissfully ignored in my rush to get to the office. My preoccupied mind almost didn't hear the news bulletin. In some respects, I wish it hadn't.

"On the local scene, it looks like The Peeper has struck again. Another victim of this bizarre killing spree was reportedly found at a construction site off I-75 near Middletown. Police report that the middle-aged housewife from Midlothian was killed sometime between seven-thirty and eleven last night. This morning, a county employee discovered the body shoved into a drainage pipe. The police have identified the victim as…"

A shudder passed through me as I clicked off the radio. My mind snapped back to Parkersburg Road and the image of crow food with a staring eye. The image was still there when I pulled into the county municipal lot.

At first, everything seemed normal. I weaved along the front rows, but the best parking spots were taken; no surprise considering I was an hour late. I turned the corner, headed for a back spot, trying to catch a glimpse of Kirby the cat. But there was no gangly orange body to make me smile. Instead, I spied a cop car. Nothing unusual there considering the sheriff's office was just one building over. Only this cop car wasn't parked by the sheriff's office, it was parked wrong-wheel-to-curb in front of my building—and the wigwag lights were flashing. Parked just behind it was a brown unmarked car with familiar dings along the fenders.

I was glad I hadn't eaten, or I might have brought it up. For some reason I couldn't explain, I felt guilty. This in and of itself was not unusual; I've always felt guilty around authority figures, perhaps a residual from my strict upbringing. But now the feeling was stronger: the sweat of cold culpability dotting my forehead. This is silly, I thought, telling myself that I had nothing to feel guilty about; that the cop cars probably had nothing to do with me. That it was just another in a series of coincidences in the long line leading back to Parkersburg Road. But part of me wasn't buying it. I was reminded of vet school and Dr. Cunningham's law of veterinary parsimony. In my mind, I heard the gravelly voice of my old mentor chiding me to "tie two symptoms under the same disease until proven otherwise." Another form of Ockham's razor; the simplest explanation is the most likely. The knot in my gut tightened.

I guided the car toward the back, meaning to park and find out what it was all about. Then I glanced in the rearview and saw Garlicki come out of my building, a cop just behind him. The fat detective glanced around the lot, looking for something. I noticed that the uniformed officer looked ill at ease, a hand on his service pistol. Garlicki held something in his hand, a piece of paper, the folded, official-looking kind. Instead of parking, I pulled out of the lot and drove off, picking up speed as I went.

~ * ~

"Honk!"

I hit my brakes and swerved, barely missing a black mustang doing the same. My Buick slew into the curb with a "whomp."

"You went right through that stop sign, asshole! Doing fifty!"

A man in his thirties cursed a blue streak from the Mustang's rolled down window. I mumbled some kind of apology he wasn't prepared to hear, even if he could have heard through my unopened window.

"Do your sleeping at night, okay dickhead. I'd like to live to be senile like you." The guy's window hummed up and the Mustang drove off.

I popped the car into park, the soft tick of the gears lost in the rumble of the Mustang's engine. As the sound of the muscle car receded, another sound replaced it; a rapid clicking. I looked around, unable to place the sound. There was nothing outside except a row of houses and green street signs declaring 'Maple' in the direction I'd been traveling, Charest as the cross street. I'd come miles from the county municipal offices, yet I couldn't remember getting here; couldn't remember speeding here. I remembered seeing Garlicki in the rearview, the official-looking document clutched in his meaty fist, then I was screeching to a halt amidst the angered curses of Mr. Mustang. Still the clicking sound persisted.

What was it? I looked in the mirror, but there were no signs of pursuit. I looked at the moderately priced residences—no one had even come out on the porch to see what the screeching had been about. I looked around the cabin of my Buick but saw only the nicked plastic dashboard and an old napkin with a footprint on it—a small woman's shoe, probably Cheryl's. When had she last been in my county cruiser? I couldn't recall. But looking down at the dirty napkin on the floormat, the clicking sound seemed to grow louder. I followed it to where my hands rested on the steering wheel. I looked left to ten o'clock, my eyes locking on my wedding ring as it danced against the plastic of the wheel, clicking along with the rhythm of my shaking hand. I noticed the other hand start shaking silently. Then my whole body shook. I don't think I was breathing. I may have fainted.

~ * ~

The world swam back with a surreal flash of light and sound. Sun glinted off the windshield. A lawn mower started up, a sweaty guy with a cigarette drooping from his lips navigating it down a trailer ramp. There was movement across the street, a letter carrier trundling an old-style three-wheeled mailbag down the sidewalk. Inside, my car looked just the same, the nicks on the dashboard, the dirty napkin on the floor. I reached down and retrieved the soiled paper, shoving it into the pocket of my sport coat. I glanced back at the dash and did a double take—the clock, which had read nine-thirty when I pulled out of the municipal lot now read eleven fifteen. Almost two hours had passed. The sight of Garlicki and the folded paper must have affected me more than I thought. I still wasn't sure what was on that paper he'd held or who it was intended for, but that didn't help dispel the cold, nightmarish dread. It was like living in a Kafka novel.

I remember listening to something on the radio as I rushed to work. Something about the Peeper. I clicked on the AM news station. There was a commercial for financial planning, so long as you had at least half a million to invest, that is. Then a commercial about getting out of debt; this apparently directed at those without the requisite half million. Then national news, during which I learned the remarkable fact that the democrats hated the republicans, and vice versa. Finally, there was local news.

"The serial killer known as The Peeper has apparently claimed another victim. A middle-aged housewife from Midlothian…"

"Bleep! Bleep! Bleep!"

I held hands to ears to drown out the unexpected screech coming from the speakers, a sound somewhere between a cat in heat and fingernails on a blackboard.

"This is a required weekly test of the emergency broadcast system. The broadcasters of your area in voluntary cooperation with federal, state and local authorities have developed this system to keep you informed in the event of an emergency. If this had been an actual emergency, the Attention Signal you just heard would have been followed by official information, news, or instructions. This concludes this test of the Emergency Broadcast System serving the Midlothian Ohio operational area. We now return you to your regularly scheduled program. Bleep! Bleep! Bleep!

…Get out of debt fast…"

"Shit," I said, snapping off the radio. It was now eleven-thirty, which meant at least ten minutes of commercials before the news cycled through again. But I didn't have time to worry about that. I had just thirty minutes to cover the fifteen miles to Northfield if I was going to get Nancy Collingwood's advice. And something told me I desperately needed that advice.

Chapter Nine

Traffic was light, so I reached the diner with eight minutes to spare. A blue Prius was pulling out just as I arrived, giving me a spot almost directly across the street. I turned off the engine and thought for a minute how to proceed. Should I go in and look for Nancy Collingwood; grab a booth if she wasn't there yet? Should I wait a few minutes to see if she showed? I glanced back the way I had come but no Charlize Theron lookalike was walking down the street. Then I stared ahead, which is when I noticed the police car parked catty corner a half-block away.

Seemed like I was noticing cop cars a lot lately, which I chalked up to my current state of paranoia. Surely cops parking near diners was not unusual, I thought, especially at noon time. It might even be Nancy's car, assuming she was on duty. But this wasn't a Dayton PD blue and white, nor was it a Northfield PD black and white. This car was silver with gold trim; the distinctive combination belonging to Ohio Highway Patrol. Still not so unusual, but why wasn't he out patrolling the highway?

"You're being paranoid," I said aloud. Then I thought of the adage that being paranoid didn't necessarily mean they weren't out to get you. I cursed myself for not turning on the radio during the drive over. I had a feeling this all involved The Peeper's latest victim. Could it be someone I knew? Someone who'd filed an application complaint, like Suzanne Weider-White? Part of me didn't want to know.

That guilty feeling grew stronger. I stared at the OHP car, watching as a cigarette butt flicked from the open window. Some cop was inside, waiting. Waiting for me? The sense of guilty paranoia increased, like someone was looking over my shoulder. I glanced at the rearview and a familiar figure filled the mirror—a perky blond in workout shorts and a baggy sweatshirt that seemed too warm for the weather. She wore a Dayton PD cap, ponytail bobbing behind it in rhythm with her quick strides.

She looked both ways before crossing the street on a diagonal. I didn't know what to do. Soon, she would be in the diner, and I would have to go in to meet her. I would have to leave the safety of my Buick and cross the street in full view of the state cruiser. My heart throbbed in my throat as Nancy paused opposite my window to let a plumbing van cross in front of her. It was now or never. I hummed down the window.

"Hey, Nancy."

She stopped in the middle of the street.

"Nancy, over here."

She spun in the direction of my voice, hand dropping to the butt of a pistol on her hip. Then she beamed a smile that melted my heart even in my current state.

"Why, hello, there."

"Get in the car," I said.

Her smile vanished. "What?"

"Please," I pleaded, popping the button that unlocked the rear door, my eyes still focused on the Highway Patrol cruiser not one hundred feet away.

"What's this all about, Randy?"

She was right beside my open window, the smell of green apples and perspiration drifting into the cabin. I met her eyes. "Please," I whispered.

She hesitated for a moment, then slid into the back seat. I shifted my visor so it hid my face, then quickly pulled out of the spot, praying the statie up ahead wouldn't recognize me.

~ * ~

"So, my friend is getting pretty nervous."

Nancy cut me off. "Look, Randy. Let's lay our cards on the table."

She was now riding shotgun as we sat in the MacDonald's parking lot sipping large coffees and chatting like old friends. Thinking back on it, it was amazing how easy she was to talk to. I'd never even met this woman; oh, we had chatted online, flirted mostly, but never actually conversed face to face. Now, it was as if I'd known her forever.

"I'm a cop. You know that right?"

I nodded.

"Right?" she repeated.

"Right," I said.

"So, let's not insult my profession or my intelligence. We're talking about you, aren't we? Not some friend—*you*."

I nodded sheepishly.

"Right?"

"Yes," I said, feeling a bit annoyed at her bullying.

"So, are you telling me that *you* are The Peeper?"

I started to protest when she cut me off again.

"Okay, dumb question. Let's start over. The Midlothian cops questioned you, but they did not read you your rights. Correct?"

I started to nod, but instead said, "Correct."

"Nothing about you having the right to remain silent? The right to an attorney, even if you can't afford one? The fact that your words will be used against you? Nothing like that?"

"No. Nothing."

"You understand that you have those rights when you're talking to the cops, right?"

"Now who's insulting whose intelligence. They're repeated on every cop show and movie."

"Okay, okay. Just want to make sure you understand."

"Yes, Officer Nancy, I understand."

She smiled. "Okay. So, tell me again why you think they suspect you?"

"It's hard to explain. It's more a feeling than a knowing. But the way Garlicki asked his questions. His telling me to not leave town or clean house. The cop car outside my workplace. Garlicki holding some kind of official document, search warrant or something."

"How do you know it was a search warrant?"

"Or *something*. But it was the *way* he was holding it, like a process server ready to slam a subpoena in your fist." I gulped coffee, burning a mouth that tasted like cotton. "I just have the feeling it has something to do with The Peeper's latest victim."

"You know who that is?"

I shook my head. "I heard about it on the radio but couldn't catch the name."

"But you feel *guilty* about it?"

"Yes. Of course. The police have a way of making you feel that way. Even when you're not."

"Not what?"

"Not guilty."

She nodded. "But they must have *something* that says you are, or they wouldn't be after you, right?"

"How the hell do I know?" I didn't mean to get angry, but I couldn't tell where we were headed with these questions. I did know I needed to explain, to talk to a kind woman who was willing to listen and wanted to help. "It's like it's all a series of coincidences: my finding the body, knowing one of the victims, finding the panties from another. And then there's the comment on Weider-White's web page."

"The one that was changed? Are you sure *you* didn't write it? Maybe forgot?"

"It was changed."

"But you said it sounded like you."

"Changed by someone who *knew* me, my sense of humor. Someone with the skills to get on my computer, maybe as a joke. Someone who knew me well enough…"

"What," she asked, seeing something in my face.

"Nolan," I gasped.

"Your employee?"

"He's known me for years. And he's a bit of a prankster. And a computer hacker." I shook my head. "No, it couldn't be. Why would he want to get me in trouble?"

"To deflect blame?" she asked.

"What?"

"Deflect blame onto you. Is that what you're saying?" She put down her coffee and looked hard at me, blue eyes flashing. "Are you suggesting that this Nolan set you up? That maybe this Nolan is The Peeper?"

"That's ridiculous."

"Is it? Does he have an alibi for the other killings? For the killing yesterday?"

"I have no idea."

"What about you? What were you doing between six and midnight yesterday?"

"Me?"

"The cops are gonna want to know. So, tell *me*, six to midnight last night. What were you doing?"

I tried to think. It was only last night, but it already seemed years ago.

"I had a drink with Nolan until about six."

"Where?"

"Um, not important. Then…" It seemed hazy, out of focus. "I, well, worked on my computer for a couple of hours. Then, I drove around for a while."

"How long a while?"

I shrugged. "A few hours. I do that when I need to unwind, to think. I turn on jazz and drive."

"Think about what?"

"Things. You know, stuff."

"Drive where? Where did you drive?"

Where indeed, I thought. I tried to remember. "Nowhere in particular. I got on the freeway and just drove."

"Where? North, south, east, west."

"Not sure. I remember the sun over my right shoulder, so…"

"So south. South where?"

I found myself getting angry. "I don't remember. I just drove."

"Where was your wife during all this driving?"

"My *wife*? Why, Cheryl, was um, Cheryl was at some concert in Cincinnati. Was supposed to be anyway, if she wasn't in some guy's motel bed, that is." I tried to smile, but it became a grimace.

"Cincinnati is south."

"So?"

She looked at her watch, I thought she was going to say she had to be going. But instead, she flicked on the radio.

"What are you doing?"

"It's time for the news. I want to hear it. I think you should too."

The local news started as if on cue, no commercial preamble, no national rant.

"On the local front, The Peeper seems to have claimed another victim. The body of Mrs. Cheryl Corlane was discovered in a drainpipe near Middletown this morning. Police believe Mrs. Corlane was murdered between six and midnight yesterday. Authorities aren't releasing details of the killing, but anonymous sources inside the sheriff's office claim that the body held the telltale signs associated with the Peeper killings."

Something cold slapped my wrist. I heard a loud click as my hand was shoved forward. I tried to pull it back but was met with resistance and a clank of chain, as it jerked against the handcuffs tethering my two wrists to the steering wheel.

"Randal Corlane," Nancy said. "You are under arrest for the killing of Cheryl Corlane." She pulled up her baggy Police Athletic sweatshirt and held up a small digital recorder. "You have already indicated that you understand your rights, but I will read them to you again just to be certain. You have the right to remain silent."

"That won't be necessary." I looked into her blue eyes, which now seemed cold like a reptile's. "I trusted you."

She smiled. "And I caught *you*, Mr. Peeper."

Chapter Ten

I sipped coffee in what was referred to as 'interrogation room one'. It was like the ones you've probably seen on TV—bare walls, no windows, a set of molded plastic chairs, one on each side of the single metal table bolted to the floor. There was an eyebolt in the table, no doubt for attaching handcuffs—they'd removed mine, although my wrists still chaffed from the memory. Unlike the interrogation rooms on Cops and Law and Order, which always seemed spacious as the fisheye lens watched and recorded every move, this room was not much more than a walk-in closet, with an old-fashioned camcorder set up against the wall opposite my chair. They turned the recorder on only when asking me questions. My mind reeled with the questions.

Where were you on the night of such and such? What were you doing between the hours of seven and midnight on July so and so? Were you and your wife close? Were there problems in the marriage? When was the last time you had intercourse with her? Have you been seeing anyone else? Had she?

Mostly I answered truthfully. I don't remember. Driving. As close as other couples married twenty years, I suppose. Nothing unusual. I don't remember—not for a while. No, I have never cheated on my wife. Not that I am aware of. I didn't voice my suspicions; I didn't offer information. I'm no attorney, but I'm not stupid. Finally, when I could see they weren't satisfied with my answers but had no other suspects, I lawyered up.

Now I was waiting for my mouthpiece, Stanley J. Nuremberg, attorney at law, although I doubt if a man who made his living writing wills and trusts knew more about criminal prosecution than I did. Most likely, we both got our knowledge of the subject from TV.

The single metal door opened, and Stan came in.

"Well?" I asked.

Stan slumped down in the other chair.

"You're free to go."

"Bail?"

Stan shook his head. "No, charges dropped, at least for now."

My sigh of relief sent eddies into the air of the tiny chamber.

"Seems the arrest was premature. Some new evidence has come to light. And there were some process difficulties involved with your arrest." Stan put air quotes around process difficulties. "At least enough to give the DA pause about proceeding."

"Process difficulties?"

"Entrapment, for one thing. Officer Nagel hadn't made it clear she was speaking to you as part of a criminal investigation. That is to say, she should have formally read you your rights instead of tricking you into saying you understood them while she clandestinely taped you."

"Officer Nagel?"

"Aka, Nancy Collingwood. She's really Nancy Nagel." He giggled nervously. "Bet she was teased as a kid."

"You mentioned new evidence. What new evidence?"

"Well, it turns out that the latest victim..." He cleared his throat awkwardly. "I'm really sorry about Cheryl, Randy. You, ah, have my condolences."

I nodded.

"Seems that she had engaged in, that she'd been...there was semen in her. It didn't match the DNA in that swab they took from your cheek." He looked me square in the eye. "By the way, never agree to that without asking your attorney."

I nodded again.

"So, seeing as it wasn't yours, and since there was no, ah, boyfriend as far as anyone knew, they figured the semen must have been The Peeper's." He shrugged. "Ipso facto, you are free to go."

I grabbed his hand and squeezed. "Thank you, Stan. Thank you *so* much."

He smiled. "I didn't do much. And you're not off the hook yet."

"But I thought you said..."

"I said—for *now*. You're still on the suspect list. You are not to leave town, and I'm going to recommend a criminal lawyer friend of mine."

"But, but I don't understand."

"Seems that young Officer Nagel was a little overzealous, but she was not dumb. As my dearly departed dad used to say, she was one smart Lorna Doone."

"Yeah? How so?"

"Seems that the first victim was Karen Nagel."

"Any relation?"

"Her sister. That was another of the process difficulties. Cops don't like relatives of victims doing the investigation."

"So, how does her sister being a Peeper victim make her smart?"

"Seems that Nancy Nagel is quite the computer whiz. It also seems that her sister was very involved with social media. Quite popular, in fact. Five thousand friends, seven thousand followers, mostly lonely guys, like…" He cleared his throat as he looked sheepishly my way.

"Like me?"

"You said it, not me. Anyway, seems that Karen was fond of posting cheesecake shots. Bikini's, lingerie, workout outfits, that sort of thing. Real online tease. Sister Nancy started going through the list of friends, looking for ones that had made suggestive comments for said cheesecake shots."

I felt my face warm.

"Computer geek Nancy compiled similar lists for the other Peeper victims, then cross-checked for intersects."

"That's a lot of work," I said.

"Yep. Did it on her own time. Smart cookie and hard worker."

"And?" I asked.

"And…two names were friends with all but one victim. Only one name knew them all." He looked hard at me again.

My face warmed further. "Me?"

Stan didn't answer. He didn't have to.

"Which victim was it? The one that wasn't common to the other two?"

"A woman named…" He took a pad from his pocket and read. "Weider-White. Suzanne Weider-white." He noticed the surprise on my face. "Something?"

"That's um, that's the woman who, the one I went to meet, to investigate her complaint. When I found the…"

"Yeah, when you found the body. You also found blood-stained panties from the first victim, information that Dayton cop Nancy was able to attain from a brother agency. Hence, the sting operation."

"I don't understand." And I didn't. It was such a series of coincidences, as if the universe was setting me up. Or someone was.

"Sister Nancy also found the quip you made on Ms. Weider-White's post, something about circumnavigating hemispheres?"

I blushed crimson. "That wasn't me. Someone changed it."

"A comment very similar to the one you wrote on the second victim's lingerie photo. That one had something to do with 'exploring the heavens'."

I gulped. That one *had* been me.

"So, you see why I'm going to recommend a criminal attorney, and why I say you are not out of the woods yet." I stared at my hands while Stan stared at me. "Anything you want to tell me, Randy? While we are still under attorney-client privilege."

I shook my head, my face feeling hot and numb.

"Well, I suggest you keep a low profile and mind your P's etc. And stay off social media for a while. No witty quips or double entendre." He rose. "I also suggest you dig out your calendar and wrack your brain for alibis." Stan rapped on the steel door. "And one more thing, I wouldn't talk about this with people if I were you."

"Don't worry, Stan. I plan on saving myself the embarrassment."

"It's not just that," he said. "You don't want to sound like you're bragging." The door opened; a large cop framed in the entryway. "Or give away information that might get rumored about. Facts have a way of changing, getting blurred on the road to gossip."

Change, I thought. The one victim that I was solely linked to was also the only place where my comment had been changed. Who else knew about her? Realization struck me like a cold shower. "Nolan," I gasped.

"Huh?" Stan said.

"Nothing," I answered.

He held the door open. "You coming?"

~ * ~

It was late afternoon by the time I left the sheriff's office. With Stan's help, the cops allowed some extra phone calls: one went to my office, where I left a message telling Jan I wouldn't be in for a couple days (she should be expecting this after the news about Cheryl). I also asked her to pour some of the cat food in my desk over by Kirby's tree every day; no reason my troubles should be his. My other call was to Rossini & Sons Funeral Home. Mr. Rossini gave me his condolences and said they'd contact the morgue and handle all the details; he recommended a closed casket, perhaps the Eternal Ebony model. I mumbled my assent and said I'd be by in the next day or two to sign the papers.

Instead of driving directly home, I drove to Memorial Park, ten or twelve miles north of Midlothian. Cheryl's parents had gifted us adjoining plots there for our tenth wedding anniversary. You might think burial plots an odd anniversary present, and I'd agree; Joe and Dianne were an odd couple, although less odd than my own mother truth be told. I never knew my father.

During the drive, my mind buzzed with thoughts and emotions. Yet, I wondered why I didn't feel more grief about Cheryl. Was it just that we had drifted apart, or was I still in shock? A little of both, I decided. There was also worry about my own situation in the here and now.

My thoughts kept returning to Suzanne Weider-White and the altered comment. Nolan was the only one outside of Garlicki who knew about it being changed, and the only person I knew who might be capable of changing it (with the possible exception of Nancy Nagel). I grinned at her name, just as Stan had grinned, my brain concocting a youthful doggerel. Nancy Nagel ate a bagel, now she cannot poop. She left the potty in despair and squatted on the stoop. Yes, I thought, I'm still in shock.

The sun was westering as I drove slowly through the cemetery, a warm breeze coming through the open window, WJZZ coming through the speakers. Why would Nolan want to incriminate me? Nancy had suggested it might be to deflect blame, but she was just stalling, trying to get me to incriminate myself. And deflect blame for what? It wasn't like Nolan was The Peeper. Was it? This sudden thought travelled directly from my brain to my right foot stamping the brakes.

Stan had said that Nancy Collingwood, aka Nancy Nagel, had compiled a list of social-media contacts—two had matched all but Suzanne Weider-White. Those two hadn't been her online friends; apparently knew nothing about her. But Nolan did know about her; we'd discussed her at some length at the bar, although the specifics were a bit fuzzy to me. He also knew Cheryl; he had met her at county picnics and Christmas parties, had even complimented her appearance. He was also a self-proclaimed social-media guru. Was Nolan one of the two guys who knew four of the five victims? Nancy would know. And I had to know. I resolved to find out. Circling back to the front gate of the cemetery, I headed for home—and to my computer.

~ * ~

I skipped dinner, thoughts of eating last on my list of things to do. Grabbing a beer, I trod to my computer. I waited impatiently while it booted up, then logged into my account. Skipping the nine-plus notifications on my page, I jumped to messages. Not surprisingly, there was no new message from Nancy Nagel. I tried to banish thoughts of her eating a bagel (or squatting on the stoop), took a deep breath, and composed a reply to her last message agreeing to meet me. What to say? This was no time for double entendre or cute comments like 'Didn't know you were into handcuffs.'. This was time for something direct and serious. I hoped she wouldn't ignore me completely and typed.

'We need to meet. I have something to tell you.'

I sipped beer and waited. As I feared, there was no reply. She might not be online, or she might have been told by her superiors to cool it, or she just might be pissed. But before giving up, I tried again.

'I bear you no ill will. We need to talk.'

I sipped more beer. More waiting. Nothing but a blank screen and a message from some woman who liked my birthday greeting.

I logged off and went to bed, although sleep was a long time coming.

~ * ~

I woke from a nightmare involving the same lidless eye that had plagued me for days, an eye whose face kept changing; first the body I found, then Suzanne Weider-White, then Cheryl, then Nancy Nagel. The clock read quarter past seven. I knew sleep was over for this night, so I hit the bathroom.

Halfway through washing up, I remembered my message to Nancy. Rinsing toothpaste from my mouth, I headed back to my computer.

The system was updating so the bootup took longer than usual. I waited anxiously, forcing my hands away from the keys and off the mouse, not wanting to add inputs that might make it crash. I got dressed, but it was still updating. I decided to try and eat something, or maybe just juice, when my screensaver popped up. My mouse was flying before my butt hit the chair.

To my relief and dismay, there was a reply from Nancy. It was timestamped at seven-thirty this morning.

'My boss says to cease contact with you, and I agree. See you in jail.'

Not what I wanted to hear. I started typing.

'Sorry. I know you must be upset. But I have something to tell you that's important. And I need your help. You owe me that much.'

I hesitated before typing the last sentence. She probably didn't see it that way, but I was hoping to generate some guilt about what she put me through, what she put us both through.

I waited. I waited some more. She must be at work, I thought, and started to log off when her reply binged in.

'I don't owe you squat. Please leave me alone.'

'I'm glad you are there. I thought you might be at work or something.'

'Thanks to you, I have two weeks of unpaid leave. Now buzz off.'

And that is probably what I should have done but couldn't. I really did need her help. I was no computer whiz, and I could hardly ask Nolan's help tracking him down. Nancy had the information I needed. She'd already done leg work on The Peeper, and I needed to tap into it. Maybe I was way off base here, but something kept needling at me. Something about Nolan that felt so right (or was it wrong). I took a deep breath and typed again.

'I know how you must feel, but I need to talk to you. It's important.' I started to hit send, then added, 'I may have information about you know who.'

I didn't have to wait long.

'What kind of information?'

I smiled and typed. 'Not now. I think my computer might be hacked. Can't we meet? Please?'

There was another long pause. I could almost see her staring at her computer, pondering, a cute frown upon her face. I was hoping she was intrigued, intrigued enough to respond. And she might be eager to get something to redeem herself with her department, and maybe avenge her sister. Finally, she replied.

'Eleven-thirty today. Northfield. Hastings Park. The bench by the water fountain.'

I realized I hadn't been breathing and let out a long sigh.

'I can find it. Thank you. You won't regret it.'

'I already regret it.'

Chapter Eleven

It was muggy and overcast when I arrived at Hastings Park. The hovering clouds mirrored the dark thoughts in my head. Unanswered questions kept me edgy, hyperalert. Would she show? Would there be any funny business, like last time? The rational part of my brain repeated my mother's old adage, 'once burned, twice cautious'. Nancy Nagel had certainly been badly burned by her sting operation and was unlikely to make the same mistake twice. But I couldn't relax. Another part of my brain, the part where paranoia lived, etched anxiety onto my spirits like a tattoo needle spelling 'danger'.

I arrived early, stomach rumbling from the breakfast I'd been too nervous to eat. The park bench was empty. In fact, the whole park was empty—not unheard of for a weekday morning, but unusual enough to keep my paranoia company. Where was an old man feeding the pigeons? Where was the pickup game of baseball?

I scanned the street looking for police cars, surveillance vans, or any vehicles with folks behind the wheel trying hard to look inconspicuous. Nothing, just an unoccupied SUV parked at the curb and a line of crows staring at me from atop the swings. Still, I did not enter. Instead, I walked past then ducked behind a tree, a vantage point from which I could watch the park bench unobserved.

One of the crows took flight, but only to move from one end of the swings to the other. Swings, a slide, and monkey bars—all unoccupied on a summer morning. Not the same as when I was a kid, I thought. How things had changed with computers. Maybe it wasn't even technology's fault. Maybe the fault lay within us. Maybe we had too readily exchanged the pain of human contact for the cold sterility of the machine. I smiled sadly. My mother should have lived to see it; she was the poster child for cold sterility.

I ducked behind the tree as a car approached. Poking out only my head, I spied a blue Prius slow then pull to the curb. My watch said eleven-twenty-five. My heart rate increased. I held my breath. A young lady stepped from the driver's side. There was no PD ballcap, no ponytail, no shorts showing off shapely, tanned legs. This gal was dressed in business casual: chinos, a dark wrap-top, sunglasses. But Nancy Nagle couldn't hide behind the shades. I ducked back as she scanned the street, then stole a peek of her walking over to sit on the bench.

She had come. Now what? I found myself hesitating, frozen in indecision. What if this were another sting operation? I didn't notice anything unusual, but then I hadn't the last time either. What if she wouldn't help me? I was sure she wasn't my biggest fan right then (not that I had many). Then the biggest if of all—what if Nolan wasn't on the list of friends she'd compiled. I tried not to think about that. I also tried not to be attracted to her—but it wasn't easy.

People typically post old photos on social media; vintage shots from when they were young and fit. Nancy hadn't done that, hadn't needed to. Even in casual togs, her trim figure suggested taut, gravity-defying athleticism. The chinos draped neatly about her butt, not skintight, but well-tailored. The wrap-top snugged her slim figure, narrow in the waist, nicely tented on either side of the modest vee. There was no cap or ponytail to hide the shoulder-length hair hanging about her neck like a golden waterfall. But such fantasies were not helpful; I needed her assistance, not a date.

I kept thinking that I should approach her, get the conversation going. Instead, I kept watching. I watched her slow breaths send the wrap-top up and down. I watch as she flipped aside her hair to glance sideways at her watch. I watched her take off the shades and scan the park, ducking my head back behind a tree. I just watched.

This is silly, I thought. Yes, approaching her will be awkward. Yes, she may not help me or have the information I need. But I wouldn't know until I tried. Still, I observed instead of acted. Finally, as I watched her glance at her wristwatch and rise to leave, I knew I had to stop observing. I cleared my throat, tried to clear my head, and walked over before my brain could stop me.

She saw me almost as soon as I left the tree. I tried to smile. She didn't. She just sat back down and crossed her legs.

"Spying on me?" she asked. "Is that creepy or suspicious?"

"Suspicious, I guess." I tried to sound sincere. "Maybe I'm a little suspicious after, you know, what happened yesterday. I hope you didn't get in too much trouble for that."

"Let's get something straight, *Doctor*. We are not friends. So, let's cut out the pleasantries and get to business. What do you have to tell me?"

"I don't know how to begin," I said. I meant it.

"You said you needed to tell me something. Let's start there."

"Alright." I took a deep breath. "Stan, I mean, my lawyer tells me you are quite good at computers. You know, digging up information online?"

Her piercing blue eyes stared a hole through my head.

"Right. I'll get to the point." I cleared my throat. "Stan said you've compiled a list of all the social media friends of your sister. I mean, all the guys that were friends with your sister and with the other, you know, victims. That was real smart, by the way."

Another blue-eyed stare.

"Well, he said that I was the only one on the list that was an online friend with all the victims."

"So?"

"So, I understand why you might think I had something to do with it. You know, because of that."

She looked at her watch. "Get to the point, Doctor, or I'm leaving."

"Would you please call me Randy?"

"What's your point, *Doctor*?"

"Okay. Well, I was curious about the other names on your list, the ones that were friends with all but Suzanne Weider-White."

"Why?"

"Because, you see, I know someone who…Let's just say I need to know the other names."

She checked her watch again. "I am not at liberty to divulge those names. That information is part of an ongoing investigation. And even if I were at liberty, I don't think I'd give them to *you*. So, if we are done?" She started to get up.

I grabbed her hand; she snatched it back.

"Sorry," I said. "But please don't leave yet. I still need…" I thought fast. "How about this? I give you a name, and you tell me if it was on your list. That won't violate any police investigation, will it?"

She hesitated, unsure.

"Nolan Webster," I said quickly.

Nancy relaxed. "Bahmp!" It was the sound of a gameshow buzzer signifying the wrong answer. She stood. "Now, if we are done, I'm gone. See you in court." She walked toward her car.

I panicked; my brain froze. I'd been so sure it would be Nolan, Wizard of the keyboard. Wizard of the keyboard? The words struck like a Mike Tyson jab. I heard the electronic chirp of Nancy unlocking her Prius. Before she could get in, I shouted. "Wonder Webmaster."

Nancy stopped dead, her remote still pointed at the little car. "Where did you get that name?"

"That's it, isn't it? One of the other two names on your list."

"What if it is?"

"People use pseudonyms on social media. I mean a lot of them do."

"And?"

"And I'm betting *that* particular nom de guerre belongs to Nolan Webster."

She still stood by her car, but the remote had made its way back into her pocket.

"Who is Nolan Webster?"

"Someone I know." I looked around sheepishly. "Could you please sit down so I don't have to shout."

Nancy walked hesitantly back to the bench. When she was seated, she said, "Know him how?"

"He's, um, well he's a county employee."

"What about him?"

"He knew about Suzanne Weider-White. About my online friendship with her—attempted friendship anyway."

"How?"

"I told him. She complained to my boss about that lewd comment I made. Which I didn't make, by the way. Nolan knew all about it."

The cold smugness had left her pretty eyes, replaced by uncertainty and (I hoped) curiosity.

"So, why do you think this Nolan is Wonder Webmaster?"

"He told me. I asked him for help tracking down the person or persons that hacked my computer. The guy who changed my simple comment to the lewd one. He told me he was a social-media whiz and a computer hacker. Called himself Wonder Webmaster."

She pulled a pad and pen from her pants pocket.

"W-E-B-S-T-E-R?"

I nodded, she jotted.

"You say he works for the county?"

I nodded. "In my department."

She smiled up from her pad. It was a sarcastic smile, but I still found it striking. "Wouldn't happen to have his social security number handy, would you?"

"No, but I can get it for you." Giving out SSNs was a definite no no, one even government employees could be fired for. But if she was going out on a limb, I figured I could too.

"No," Nancy said. "I can dig it up. No sense getting you in trouble too."

For the first time, I sensed I was not necessarily the enemy. She spoke cautiously, as if she wasn't sure what I was, but not as if I was a presumptive serial killer. And she looked at me like a cop talking to a witness, not a woman confronting her sister's killer.

"I'll check him out," she said. "See what I can come up with."

"Thank you." I wanted to grab her hand but was smart enough not to.

"Don't thank me yet. You're still the best suspect. But maybe I do owe you a little due diligence." She rose. "I was lazy. I didn't check out the other names once I discovered you'd friend-requested all five victims. Seemed like too big a coincidence to be a coincidence. And…"

"And?"

"You were the only one who used your real name. Made it easy."

She looked puzzled, so I answered the question she was thinking but hadn't spoken.

"Used my own name, huh? Not the kind of thing a guilty man would do, is it?"

She shook her silky hair and left. But halfway to her car, without turning around, she said, "I'm sorry about your wife."

Chapter Twelve

I didn't hear from Nancy the next day, or even the day after. But I had long drives to fill the evenings and funeral planning to fill the days. Friday was the funeral and there were preparations to make. Rossini & Sons took care of all the burial arrangements and posting the obit, leaving me with lunch reservations and finding a parson to bless the proceedings and say a few words. Neither Cheryl nor I had been to church for years, but I found that if a few dollars changed hands (along with the promise of free food and booze), priests and ministers were more than happy to wax lyrical about the deceased.

As I collected the clothes she was to wear, a formality even for a closed casket, it finally hit me that Cheryl was gone. It hit even harder when Garlicki called to ask a few questions. Did she have enemies? Was she in the habit of picking up hitchhikers? Had new men been to our house recently: handymen, plumbers, strangers hanging around the street. How was our marriage? Was I aware of any infidelity? As at my own arrest, I answered honestly but curtly. Then I asked if it might be possible to forgo further questioning until after my wife's funeral. Garlicki replied (sheepishly, I thought) that it would be possible and passed on his condolences at my loss.

Thursday afternoon I was sipping a beer and looking at old photographs. I still didn't feel much grief, more a sense of emptiness, as if the house had suddenly grown too big or me too small. Shock I guess, the first stage of grief—disbelief. I tried to recall the other stages, but could only think of acceptance, which was last on the list. Then the phone rang, so I put down a wedding picture of Cheryl in off-white silk and answered.

"Hello."

"Dr. Corlane? This is Officer Nagel." Still formal, but at least I was Dr. Corlane instead of just doctor.

"Oh hello." I didn't know what else to say. 'How are you?' was out, as was 'Nice of you to call'. I settled on, "What can I do for you?"

"You can meet me at The Northfield Diner. I mean, if you would. I have some information you'll find of interest. And I have a favor to ask you."

I must admit to being surprised by Nancy Nagle wanting to meet with me, let alone ask me a favor. She'd been very hesitant before, made it clear she wasn't even supposed to talk to me. My threat radar went up, thinking of new tricks she might be playing. But, if it was true that she got in considerable trouble for her last sting operation, and a two-week suspension would suggest she had, then maybe I was being paranoid. Something else must have happened.

"Dr. Corlane, are you there?"

"Um, yes. Okay. My wife's funeral is tomorrow, but I guess…"

"Could you meet me now? Please?"

"Now?"

"Yes. It's kind of important." I hesitated, so she rushed on. "I'd be happy to buy you dinner. Just diner food, but they have a good menu." I noticed a smile in her voice—another first. I smiled myself as I thought of her eating a bagel.

"Well, I suppose. Thirty minutes?"

"Yes, that'll be fine. Thank you." She paused for a moment before adding, "Again, I'm sorry about your wife." Then she hung up.

~ * ~

I didn't wait outside the diner watching for her, as I had in the park. No more scanning the streets for suspicious vans or the loud, shabby jackets of plain-clothed cops. Something in her voice said she was sincere. Besides, you can't sting an innocent man. So, I arrived fashionably late (five minutes). As I entered, she waved to me from a corner booth. She was once again in business casual, the wrap-top replaced by a simple polo.

"Thank you for meeting me."

I nodded and mumbled something as the waitress approached with a menu. "Thank you, no," I said. "I'm not hungry."

"You sure?" Nancy asked. "My treat." She smiled.

I smiled back. "Just coffee, please." The waitress filled my cup and departed.

"I can understand you not being hungry," Nancy said. "What with everything that's happened." She looked down at her hands clenched white on the tabletop. "Sorry for my part in it."

I started to mumble no problem, but said instead, "Why the sudden change?"

"Pardon?"

"Two days ago, I was the murderer who killed your sister. Now, *you* apologize to *me*." I question-marked my eyebrows.

She cleared her throat. "Yeah, sorry. I kind of rushed to judgement there. I've had more time to research your history. And I've been able to look into your friend, Nolan Webster."

She took a manila folder from the seat beside her and slid it on the table. The folder was old and water-stained, the edges frayed. A piece of yellow tape along one edge had been ripped, the partial word 'confiden...' printed along it in bold black type.

"What's this?"

Nancy looked both ways, then whispered, "A juvenile record."

My older eyes met her flashing blue ones. "Should I be seeing this?"

She snatched it back and replaced it on the seat. "No. Technically, neither should I."

"Why...How did you get that?"

"It wasn't easy. Let's just say I made a deal with a guy in records." She blushed again, leaving me to wonder what this deal entailed.

"And?"

"Pardon," she answered.

I waved toward the folder. "I assume that is the reason you asked me to join you for dinner. Or am I wrong?"

She sipped coffee, looked around the room again, then leaned forward. "Our Mr. Webster had no record as an adult, except for a DUI five years ago. But there were juvenile arrests—records sealed."

"And you unsealed them?"

She nodded, then scanned the room again. "Young Nolan Webster was arrested three times, twice for window peeping: once at age thirteen and again at age fourteen."

"And the third arrest?"

"He did more than peep."

This got my interest. I leaned in. "Yes?"

"Seems fifteen-year-old Nolan was found in flagrante with a nursing-home resident. Specifically, his aunt."

"He raped his aunt?"

Nancy shook her blond hair again. "That's just it, we don't know. The aunt was suffering from early dementia. And it turns out that before senility set in, she was a bit of a cougar, young lovers, that sort of thing. So, there was some question as to whether teenaged Nolan took advantage of her diminished mental capacity or if she reverted to form and seduced him. The family wanted it covered up, as did the rest home, so they gave him probation and sealed the records."

I thought for a moment, sipping my coffee. "I'm not a psychiatrist or a cop, but I'm thinking this kind of behavior might suggest the beginnings of a sexual predator."

Nancy smiled. "That's what psychiatrists and cops think too."

I thought some more. "But sleeping with your befuddled aunt isn't rape and murder. Maybe he was just a horny teen. I know he's a horny adult."

"Yeah," she said, smiling a smile that would make any heterosexual man twitch a bit. "But you haven't seen the aunt." She dug a photo out of the folder beside her.

Looking at the picture, I could see how a young man might get seduced.

"Blond," Nancy said. "Leggy. Nice figure. Remind you of anyone?"

I nodded. "Suzanne Weider-White." A knot formed in my chest. "And my wife, Cheryl."

"And my sister," Nancy said. "It seems that young Nolan's type is also The Peeper's type."

"Well," I said. "I think attractive blonds are every man's type." Like Nancy Nagel, I thought, hurrying on. "Besides, that was when he was a teen. What about the fifteen years since? I mean, the Peeper dates back less than two months, not a decade and a half. Do these guys stop for long periods like that?"

"Sometimes," Nancy said. "On rare occasions. They mature, walling off the initial trauma until something sets them off again."

"Really? That's not what the cop shows say."

She smirked in response. "It may also be that he *didn't* stop."

"What do you mean? There's only been five cases."

"In Midlothian," Nancy said. "What about elsewhere?"

"I'm not following you."

Nancy shook her head. "You'd make a lousy cop, Randy." Add the word idiot, and I could have been speaking with Cheryl, rest her soul. "Think about it. These guys get smarter as they get older. Maybe smart enough to not get caught. Especially when they change towns a couple times." She put the photo back into the file. "How long has he been working for Midlothian County?"

"Three years," I said.

"Well, his last arrest as a teenager was outside Cincinnati. Webster's driver's license renewals list addresses in Muncie and Columbus before coming to you. Could be we'll find some unexplained rape-murders in those locations if we dig deep."

So now it was 'we', I thought. "Where do I come into this picture? You said you needed my help. What sort of help?"

Nancy huddled forward and spoke in hushed tones. "I think I told you that I got suspended."

"Yeah, fourteen days."

"Well." She sighed like long-suffering Job. "It's actually much worse. I always wanted to be a beat cop, on the front lines, protecting and serving. There aren't many of us on the DPD. The powers that be prefer to relegate women to desk jobs. I fought to get away from a desk, and now…"

I could hear anger and frustration in her voice. I wanted to give her hand a reassuring squeeze but didn't. "Now they're sending you back?"

"The precinct captain, a tight-assed, old-school son of a bitch—but you didn't hear it from me, suggested that maybe I don't have the judgement needed for patrol work. To quote Captain Bugliosi, I'd make a good candidate for community outreach, end quote." She shook her head in disgust. "McGruff lectures to school kids, meeting with neighborhood watches, that sort of thing. I can't let that happen. I've worked too hard. Not after what happened to Karen."

"And to keep from becoming McGruff, you need to do something big like bringing down The Peeper?"

"With your help."

I sipped my coffee and smiled. "I thought *I* was your *best* suspect."

Nancy's answering smile was more an apology. "I thought so too, until I backchecked your record." The shake of her blond hair reminded me of wheat on a Kansas prairie. "You are Mr. Clean. No DUI, disturbing the peace, soliciting a prostitute—nothing. I couldn't even find a traffic ticket. Then I tracked down your IP address." She blushed guiltily, before adding, "I'm a bit of a computer whiz."

I smiled. "Yes, Stan told me."

She stared at me, admiration in her eyes. "You may be the only man in America who doesn't surf porn. Do you have *any* vices?"

"Driving the speed limit while listening to cool jazz."

She nodded. "And casual flirting on social media."

I shrugged. "Pretty lame, huh?"

Nancy leaned back and drank coffee. "Probably par for the course for an old, married man." She grimaced, then reached out and squeezed my hand. "I'm so sorry. That was insensitive."

I squeezed back. "Apology accepted. How can I help?"

Chapter Thirteen

"My brothers and sisters in Christ. Let us remember the soul of Cheryl Corlane, taken from us too early. In times like these, it is difficult to know the will and mind of God. But be assured, that he has a plan, even if we don't understand it."

I sat in a front seat of the Rossini & Sons memorial chapel listening to the words of Father Charles McGonigle, a dyed in the wool, non-gay, non-African, Catholic Priest—one of a dwindling American breed. As far as I knew, he had never buggered an altar boy or pilfered church funds, but he could be had on short notice to provide a eulogy in exchange for five-hundred bucks, a free meal, and an open bar. As he read from his prepared remarks, I pondered my wife's casket.

The Eternal Ebony model turned out to be a shiny black box resembling a photon torpedo from Star Trek. The picture above this black box was of my wife of almost twenty years. I thought about using a wedding photo, a favorite of mine from a happier time, Cheryl resplendent in her off-white gown with ample cleavage. I chose instead a more recent shot, one taken I believe by one of her BFF League cronies (probably Elaine Miller). Cheryl was laughing, evidently having a wonderful time. As I stared at the photo, I was struck by how little she had aged. Oh, there were some lines, and the blond hair was more bleach than real, but she still had a beautiful face with a beautiful smile that the camera loved. I was struck by how little of that smile she'd shared with me over the years. Perhaps it was my fault, perhaps no one's. Perhaps it was just what happened when two people drifted apart.

I was still amazed at how little grief I felt. Was I still in the disbelief stage? Maybe I was still in shock. Or maybe we had grown even farther apart than I thought, so that the loss of my wife was closer to the loss of a comfortable old sweater than to a loved one of close to two decades. My morose ponders were interrupted by my name spoken in a slight Irish brogue.

"Now I would ask Cheryl's husband, Dr. Randall Corlane, to say a few words."

I looked at Father McGonigle, his eyes urging me forward. I looked around the room, all eyes on me, waiting. I cleared my throat, rubbed slick palms on the pants of my black suit, and approached the microphone.

As I passed, McGonigle whispered, "Just say what's in your heart, son." Easier said than done, I thought.

Friends, neighbors, and colleagues stared at me. I saw tears in the eyes of many of Cheryl's BFFL friends, mild boredom in the eyes of my coworkers. I noticed Irv Zimbauer look at his watch, his wife giving him an elbow poke for his trouble. But it was time for me to speak, so I stopped scanning the crowd and focused on the black bud of microphone directly before me. But what to say? I cleared my throat again.

"Well, first off, I want to, um, thank you all for coming." The microphone squelched at me. I tapped and it stopped. Somebody chuckled.

"I'm not really sure what to say. Father McGonigle said to say what was in my heart." I glanced at the good father, who smiled and nodded reassuringly. "But that's tough because I'm still having trouble dealing with this. I know that Cheryl is gone, at least part of me knows it. That part also knows how she died." I heard a sob from the back of the room. "But part of me is still numb. I don't know if it's shock, or just denial. You know how they say that's the first step of grieving." Many sad eyes nodded in understanding. Irv checked his watch again. "Anyway, I'm hoping for denial, because I know *that* eventually leads to acceptance; at least that's what the experts say." I didn't mention that I seemed to be skipping the other stages of grief entirely. "I'm hoping for the same for all of you, as well." Another sob from the back of the chapel. "I'm sure none of us will enjoy the anger and depression to come, but if it gets to acceptance, it'll, um, be worth it."

A lot of the faces in the crowd now held big, fat question marks. They probably wondered why I wasn't sobbing. Maybe they thought I should be talking about how much I loved Cheryl, rather than rambling about the stages of grief. But lately, I'd been wondering if I ever really did love Cheryl. I guess there was a time, although worship might have been a better term. Luscious Cheryl Labchuck was beautiful, smart, and confident—and she'd chosen me. It was like winning the lottery, reaching an unattainable goal. That's probably why I married her. And she probably saw a budding young doctor to give her the life she wanted. But I'd ended up a county employee instead of a rich practitioner. Once the dreams wear off, it's love that keeps you going. The kind of love you see in the movies, or read about in books, or see in the eyes of old couples holding hands in the park. That kind of love was missing, most likely always had been.

I realized people were still staring at me, but that I wasn't talking anymore. I felt embarrassed, but the faces looking back said they understood; people cut you slack at funerals. You've lost a loved one, so you're going to be in shock. You are going to ramble. I guess I was, so I did.

"Well, um, thanks again for coming. Please join me for lunch at Riverside Restaurant." Father McGonigle gave my arm a pat as I returned to my seat.

"Thank you, Ronny, for those…those heartfelt words." Like Irv, the good father looked at his watch. "Perhaps we should wrap things up and continue with our fond memories of Carol over drinks, I mean lunch."

~ * ~

My body stood in the back of the chapel shaking hands, giving hugs, nodding, and saying thank you. My mind was on the dark, oversized Tylenol caplet with Cheryl's picture on it. But I wasn't thinking about the laughing picture taken during a time of merriment. My mind's eye was focused on the picture I couldn't see, the one inside the box; the real Cheryl, or at least what she was reduced to. I hadn't had to ID her body, the identification in her wallet had been enough for that. So, I never saw what The Peeper had done to her. I had thankfully never seen the autopsy either, although my own necropsy experience painted a vivid picture. I had been spared those gruesome sights, but now I was suddenly curious. Rossini could easily hide suture marks with Cheryl's burial suit; her blond hair would conceal where the skull cap had been glued back on. But what about The Peeper's handiwork? Had Rossini managed to glue the eyes shut; created some artificial lids of latex and makeup? What else had been done to her? My mind was drawn by a curious compulsion, a fixation, an almost overwhelming desire to walk to the box and open it, if only just to see my wife one last time.

Maybe then the emotion I seemed to lack would come bubbling up.

"I'm so sorry, Randy."

I was engulfed in a bearhug by my tiny admin. Jan's trashy office attire had been replaced by a plain white blouse under a navy-blue sweater. Her makeup had changed from its cheery flamboyancy to dark, gothic smears, no doubt her gen Z idea of what was appropriate for a funeral.

"Thanks, Jan. And thanks for coming."

"Yeah, boss—bummer." Nolan was just behind her, dressed in a charcoal sport jacket over a tuxedo tee shirt. He held forth his hand. "I still can't believe she's gone." He seemed sincere and shocked. "She was good, I mean, she was a good lady." He nodded toward the coffin as we shook. "Quite a looker, what I'd normally call…"

"Nolan," Jan chided. "Shut your face."

"Um, yeah, right." He nodded. He may even have blushed. Looking at his loafers, he added, "Great lady."

I looked at my head inspector as if we had just met. Was this guy a serial killer? This guy I'd known for three years, this guy who hit on Jan almost daily, this county rat who gloried in goofing off, this man I had chatted with and drank with, could he possibly be The Peeper? Nancy Nagel, she who ate the bagel, certainly thought so. But then she had thought I was The Peeper. And what about Cash? No one had seen him for days, and he'd been in possession of soiled undies from one of the victims. I'd need to tell Nancy about that, in case Midlothian County hadn't shared this information with Dayton PD.

"Where's Cash?" I asked, perfunctorily scanning the room. "Couldn't he make it?"

Nolan shook his head. "I think we need to write off that boy. Went by his place—it was deserted, police tape over the door." He shrugged. "Probably skipped out on his rent after trashing the security deposit and then some. Landlord set the law on him."

"Are you alright, Randy?" Jan asked.

"As well as can be expected, I guess. Why do you ask?"

"I don't know, it's just, the way you asked about Cash out of the blue—at your wife's funeral. And that eulogy?"

"Yeah skipper," Nolan said. "That speech was…unique."

"Like I said, I guess I'm still in shock or denial or something. Everything seems a little off-center." I was crying now. I wiped my eyes and glanced at the black box, wanting (needing?) to lift the lid and take a peek.

Jan nodded and gave me another hug, then a kiss on the cheek. "I understand." She turned to leave, then turned back. "By the way, Irv said to take all the time you need before coming back."

"Probably glad to not have to record your time sheet for a while," Nolan said.

Jan nudged Nolan in the ribs, then said, "Don't worry about anything. We'll handle it."

"Yeah, piece of baclava," Nolan said. He shook my hand. I wondered again if this man was really my wife's killer.

Chapter Fourteen

"Sorry again about your wife."

Nancy and I were once more sipping coffee in a back booth of the Northfield Diner. She was dressed in denims that were tighter than her khakis, and a blue and white Police Athletic League tee shirt. Her hair was again ponytailed under a DPD ballcap.

"How was the funeral? Everything go, um, okay?"

I shrugged and waved *comme ci comme ça*.

"I thought about going," Nancy said. "But didn't know if I should."

"You would have been welcome," I replied.

She gripped my hand and wanly smiled. "I guess we share that now. Been to a Peeper funeral."

I suddenly realized that I had been an insensitive jerk. "That's right. I'd forgotten. Your sister." I squeezed her hand in both of mine. Her skin was smooth, but the muscles below firm and taut, like the hand of a marble statue. "I'm very, very sorry for your loss. And I understand."

She squeezed my hand in return and let go. "I guess you do. Few people do, but you're one of them." She cleared her throat. "So, how was our boy?"

"Nolan?"

She nodded. "How did he respond to the funeral?"

I more-or-lessed my hand again. "I didn't notice anything. Nothing like what you'd said might happen. In fact, he seemed genuinely touched."

"No nervousness?" she asked. "No distant eyes? No odd euphoria?"

"Just same old insensitive Nolan," I said. "Although I wasn't watching most of the time."

She frowned, then shook it off. "I guess not everyone fits the profile." She paused. "Or maybe they do."

I sipped coffee. "So, what now?"

"That's what I wanted to talk with you about. I have an idea how to proceed. It may be a longshot but just might work."

"Shoot."

"Tell me again how this Nolan knew about your dealings with Weider-White."

I put down my cup. "Like I said, he knew I'd been dinged by my boss for messaging her. That was all over the office."

"And he knew that the message, your message, had been changed?"

"Yep, I told him about that in the bar."

"Bozo's?"

"Yeah. We'd had a couple of beers. Well, more than a couple, and we discussed it. Then we discussed it again a few days later when I asked him to hack or counter hack or whatever you want to call it on my computer."

"That was also at Bozo's? That second discussion?"

"Yes, but don't get the wrong idea. The restaurant was Nolan's choice—both times. I just went along."

"Did you know The Peeper struck again last night?"

"Friday night?"

Nancy nodded. "Didn't you hear it on the news?"

I shook my head. "I took a drive, but I listened to jazz CDs, not the news."

"Yep," she said. "The evening of your wife's funeral." She looked at me and waited. Her eyes lit up as she saw the recognition in mine. "Maybe we got some reaction from old Nolan after all."

"So, you think he got all worked up...Wait. Who was it? When?"

"Between ten and midnight," she said. "A waitress—from guess where?" She waited again, eyes intently on mine.

"Bozo's?"

Nancy tapped a finger to her cute nose. "Bingo. Waitress named Shyreen Kolinsky."

"Shy? Shy's dead?"

"Shy?" Nancy raised her brows.

"That's what Nolan called her. Probably what everyone called her."

"I take it she waited on you?"

"Yeah," I said, "both times I was there. Nolan seemed particularly

95

taken with her. I was too. I mean, any guy would be—tall, blond, good figure."

Nancy smiled again at the recognition on my face. "Remind you of anyone?"

I nodded. "Several anyones."

"Including yours truly?"

I blushed in reply.

"And that's how we bait the trap."

"What trap?"

"The mantrap for Mr. Nolan Webster. Do you think you can wangle drinks with him at Bozo's again?"

"I guess. I can say I'm feeling low, maybe we could hoist a couple."

"Well don't have *too* many. I'll need you sober if this is going to work."

~ * ~

Nolan lifted his beer glass. "To Mrs. Randall Corlane. One of the good ones."

I clinked and drank, although good isn't a word I'd have used. Not bad either. Just…Cheryl.

"Kind of surprised you wanted to go out for a drink, what with the recent unpleasantness and all. Pleased, but surprised."

"Well, you know how it is. Something for a distraction." I held my glass up.

Nolan winked and did the same.

We were well into our second pitcher. I'd tried to pace myself, letting Nolan race ahead. Even so, I hadn't eaten much lately and was feeling the alcohol. Remembering Nancy's caution, I put my glass down without drinking.

"So how are you doing, boss?"

I waved my hand in the so-so gesture that was becoming my trademark.

"Anything I can do?"

I thought, faux concentration on my face. I brightened my eyes. "You could help me out with my computer, like we talked about."

He fist-bumped my hand sitting on the table. "Consider it done. No charge."

"No," I said. "A hundred bucks. A deal is a deal."

"Suit yourself." He drank beer and looked smug I thought; pleased with having offered and been refused.

"Yeah, I'm worried about this hacking. I ran an antimalware program but I'm still worried."

"Right you are to worry too." Nolan had the relaxed language of one sliding into boozy second. "Anti-virus software won't stop a hacker. It might find something he left behind, but even then, if he's good, there won't be anything to find." He winked again.

"Sounds like you've been there, done that." I smiled.

Another wink and the last of the pitcher poured into his glass.

"Yeah," I said. "I've just hooked up with a new friend on social media, but I'm afraid to chat because maybe the same thing will happen." It was an awkward segue, but he didn't seem to notice. "That would be, well embarrassing."

"Don't want another hemispheric circumnavigation sinking a budding *friendship*?"

I gave him thumbs up.

"Tell me about her." He waved to our waitress, Carly, a short African American lady with ample curves. She wore a black armband, as did all the waitresses, in memory of Shy Kolinski.

"Another pitcher, darlin."

"No more for me," I said.

Nolan thought a moment, then nodded. "Let's make it a twenty ouncer." He smiled at Carly, then turned to me. "What's your new friend's handle?"

"Handle?"

"Name, call sign, nom de guerre."

"Nancy," I answered. "Um, Nancy Proudfoot."

Nolan laughed. "Took that one right out of the Lord of the Rings. What's she look like?" The "what" and "she" slurred into "washee.

I stammered a bit. "Oh, you know." I smiled. "Can only go by her photos and those are probably from twenty years ago when she was a cheerleader. You know how people are on social media."

"Yeah, I know." He smirked. "Lots of bikini shots? Maybe some lingerie?"

I flushed, and not from the beer.

His smirk grew at my discomfort. "Let me guess: tall, blond, bouncy? Sounds like your type, you dog."

"Listen," I protested. "Nothing like that. I mean, Cheryl just passed. But, you know, I like to chat with her. I get lonely. We get along. She's new to social media, recently divorced, so we kind of have that in common."

"Just friends?" Nolan winked again, making me wonder if he had developed a tic. Carly brought his beer. He winked at her as well. He smiled. He drank.

"Right." I sipped some beer, paused a moment, then acted like I'd had a brainstorm. And 'acted' was the right word. It felt phony as hell, but I was hoping Nolan was too drunk to notice. "I have an idea. Why don't you friend her? She's new online, looking to build her friend list. And you could check her out, um, I mean check out her page. See if it looks, you know, legitimate."

Nolan laughed. "Want to find out if your sexy blond is really a fat construction worker from Patterson, New Jersey?"

"Something like that."

He gulped. He burped. He thought. He shrugged. "Sure. Couldn't do any harm. I can check for tells."

"Tells?"

"Telltale signs of phoniness. Hometown of Anycity USA. Birthdate that doesn't match the age in the photos."

"I don't think she posted a birthdate, at least that you can see."

"That *you* can see." Nolan tapped his head. "You're talking to Wonder Webmaster, remember. I can pull aside the curtain and reveal the wizard." He danced his fingers like a virtuoso of the keyboard. "Tell you what. I'll check her out tomorrow morning. See how the land lays." He grinned again as if with an inside joke. "Then I'll come over to your place tomorrow night and check out *your* computer. Howz bout dat?"

"Sounds great." And it would give me time to touch base with Nancy, the scrumptious bait for this mantrap. I hoped she knew what she was doing.

If Nolan was The Peeper, she was putting herself squarely in his crosshairs, with only a middle-aged county bureaucrat as a wingman. And said wingman was putting himself in the crosshairs as well. So, tomorrow night sounded great. Only the location was wrong; if the trap was to work, that is.

"How about I come to your place? You know, bring my computer to *you*?"

Nolan looked at me under one raised eyebrow. He was smiling, but it wasn't the old, affable, I-don't-give-a-shit, Nolan smile. This smile held something more sinister—perhaps a touch of venom just below the surface. It didn't last long, just an instant. But in that instant, I was looking into another face. One unlike the easy-going Nolan Webster I'd seen before. Was this the face of The Peeper?

"Don't want me at your house, huh?" His tone tried for humor, but it was forced. There was a strain to it, an underlying seething as if through clenched teeth.

"No, no. It's not that." This was the tricky part, but an essential part of Nancy's plan. "It's just that, well I'm sure you have software and stuff at your place. That is, I'm sure your setup includes anti-hacker software." I could feel myself muffing it. The sinister Nolan was again smiling at me. "You know, tools of the trade?" I had to sell it. "For the Wonder Webmaster?"

I must have struck the right complimentary tone, because the old Nolan was back inside his smile. "Yeah, I've got a few." He drank beer, pondering for a moment. "I could bring them over to your place."

I scrambled to come up with a believable excuse why that wouldn't work. I couldn't think of one. Fortunately, I didn't have to.

"But you're right," he added. "It'd be easier if you came to me. Not sure what I'll need. And I can tie into your laptop easier."

My sigh of relief was loud enough for him to notice, only he didn't. "If you think that's best."

"Name of Proudfoot?" He pulled a pencil stub from his pocket and jotted it on a bar napkin.

"Right. Nancy Proudfoot. I think she's the only one online."

Nolan grinned and burped. "Well, even if she isn't, with your description I'm sure I'll find her."

~ * ~

Nancy and I once again sipped coffee in the Northfield Diner. I wanted to ask if she wanted anything, perhaps a bagel? I wanted to ask her any number of things, from her favorite color to her preference in fabric softener. I wanted to say, 'we have to stop meeting like this. People will say we're in love.' The truth is, I liked talking to her. In fact, I found it comforting to talk to her, now that we'd eliminated the suspicions, hers and mine. I wanted to get to know her better. But I didn't say any of those things. I said only, "Maybe we should meet someplace else. Somebody might notice."

She looked around and smiled. "No one seems to."

Looking around myself, I saw she was right. Everyone was in their own little world, not ours.

"This is a good spot," she continued. "Halfway for both of us. Near the highway, so a lot of anonymous trucker business." She glanced over at the guy in ratty jeans and Peterbilt cap scarfing down pie at the counter. "Too far for Dayton cops to seven at. I'm guessing your wife's friends never ate here either."

The mention of Cheryl dug an empty pit in my stomach. "No. I don't think this is the kind of place favored by the BFF League."

She sipped her coffee, leaving little brown dregs at the corner of her lips. She had on an outfit like the one I'd first seen her in: shorts, ballcap, and ponytail. But instead of the baggy sweatshirt needed to hide the digital recorder, she wore a trim white polo, the kind with an embroidered alligator above the left breast; I watched the little critter rise and fall with each breath. She wore a bit more makeup as well. Part of me hoped she'd dressed up for me just a tad. Another part recognized this as delusional.

"So?" she asked. "Are we all set?"

I nodded. "I'm going to his apartment tonight—seven o'clock."

She smiled and upped her thumb.

"Is Nancy Proudfoot posted online?" I asked.

"Finished last night around one in the morning." She yawned and stretched, the embroidered alligator riding the wave of her chest. "The phony profile only took about an hour, but the photos took longer. I'm not very good at selfies. And I only have a few sexy outfits." She might have blushed under her make-up. "I'm generally just tee shirts and panties."

I quickly changed the subject. "I'm still not sure what I'm supposed to do. I doubt if the Peeper leaves souvenirs laying around his apartment for the taking, and I'm not much at snooping. What do you expect me to find?"

"I don't expect you to *find* anything. I expect you to *leave* something." She dug a small, black doohickey out of her shorts pocket. The thing was a bit wider than a flash drive, but only a quarter the length, excluding the metal sleeve that goes into the computer slot.

"What is it?"

"The world's smallest Wi-Fi transmitter. The signal only reaches about a hundred feet, but that should be enough."

"I don't understand. Enough for what?"

"Enough to reach the booster I'm going to install on his apartment cable box. It'll strengthen the signal and relay it to my computer."

"And?"

"And I will be able to see everything on Wonder Webmaster's PC. If he's been surfing snuff porn, we'll know it. Unusual interest in Peeper news stories—we'll know it. Online messages with Peeper victim's, we'll know that too."

I looked at the little gadget in wonder. "But what if all his computer slots are already used? Where am I supposed to plug it in? And won't he see it's hooked onto his PC?"

Her ponytail shook a negative. "Send him away for coffee or beer or something, then plug it into the USB he uses for his keyboard—he's bound to have one of those."

"Where do I plug the keyboard?"

"Same place, it fits right in the top." Nancy showed me that the Wi-Fi transmitter had a slot for another connector. "Leaves only a thin rim of rubberized plastic showing." She shrugged. "Unless he looks hard at this keyboard connection, he'll never notice."

"And what if he does?"

"We're busted. But by that time, I will have downloaded his PC onto cloud backup."

"What if he notices while I'm *there*?"

She smiled. "Run like hell. I'll be parked up the street."

I took some comfort in the fact that she'd be near, but I was getting nervous about the whole thing. Now that it looked like it was going to happen, I wondered why I had agreed to go through with it. Was it to avenge Cheryl's death, just as Nancy was trying to avenge her sister's? Or was it because Nancy wanted it?

"Are we supposed to be doing this?" I asked. "Without a search warrant or anything?"

"Technically?" Nancy said. "No. But then I'm not technically with the department right now, I'm suspended, a private citizen. You are and always have been a private citizen. So, as private citizens, we are technically only guilty of petty vandalism. Misdemeanor. Slap on the wrist at most."

"Will Dayton PD see it that way?"

She grinned. It was a rueful grin, but still looked great on her. "In for a penny, in for a pound. I'd rather be kicked off the force than be demoted to school safety seminars."

"Hopefully," I said, "neither of those will happen."

Her smile seemed a little brighter when she squeezed my hand.

Chapter Fifteen

I scanned Nolan's apartment as he banged away on his keyboard. I'd been looking around the apartment for three quarters of an hour, studying it, peering into nooks and crannies. I'd gone to the bathroom and studied that. None of it was as I'd imagined.

I'd expected some version of what I'd found at Cash's place, bachelor filth and disorder. But Nolan's small unit, one of four in the old building, was orderly and neat. Magazines were stacked on the table, books neatly stacked on the shelf; titles ranging from *Hacking: The art of exploitation* to *Of Mice and Men*. The carpet looked to have been vacuumed recently, and my view of the kitchen sink showed no stacks of dirty dishes. The bathroom towels were dry and clean, with no mildew odor. The air in the living area held a slight tang of burnt rubber, no doubt from the softly humming computer components piled onto his workstation, but there wasn't the stench of decayed garbage I'd noticed at Cash's place.

I also expected to see porn scattered about, maybe some racy calendars and posters tacked to the wall with plastic pins, maybe a Debbie Does Des Moines DVD atop the TV. But the only sign of the horny man I knew from the office, the guy constantly hitting on Jan and boasting of his sexual prowess, hung from the living room wall in the form of a three-by-four-foot print of a half-naked woman with short hair toweling off at an old wash tub. But even that print was tasteful; abstract colors that gave the illusion of sensuality without vulgarity. I wondered briefly if I'd misjudged Nolan, or if I was seeing just a surface view. The BTK killer had been a family man active in his church, Ted Bundy a law clerk, John Wayne Gacy a clown for children's parties. I wondered if this were true of Nolan; if deeper down, hidden under the socks and tighty whities, or more likely behind a hefty computer firewall, lay a collection of smut spanning the gamut from explicitly nude to sicko kinky.

The key clacks abruptly stopped, startling me into looking guiltily at Nolan. I half expected him to be staring back, eyeing me suspiciously, as if to say, 'what's so interesting about my place, huh boss?' But he was still looking at his screen. My laptop was still tethered into his elaborate system by a cable. We were still sitting in his living room, an office chair and kitchen chair flanking his workstation cluttered with computer components, cables, wires, and gadgets. Nolan was still hunched over the screen, concentration etched into his features, more concentration than I'd ever seen him produce at work.

"I don't know, boss. I'm not seeing any signs of illegal entry." He leaned back, eyes still on the screen, fingers ticking off his efforts. "I've run primo malware scans without finding any trojans, ransomware, or spyware. There's no signs of unusual disk activity. I'm not seeing any new or suspicious software, or any oddball prompts or updates for same. No backdoors or rootkits that I can find. No increased network activity or programs eating up bandwidth. Computer speed is good. Your firewall is tight. All your passwords seem solid and intact."

He sighed. "Either whoever hacked you is one of the best on the planet, or …" He looked at me, brow furrowed. "You sure you didn't write that comment to Wider-whatsis? Tried to be witty and didn't quite make it? Maybe forgot about doing it?"

I shook my head.

He looked back at the screen. "Well, I can't find any sign that someone else did it." He yawned and stretched, rolling his neck from side to side. "I don't know about you, but I'm ready for a beer."

Here was my chance. "Yeah, a beer would be great."

"All I got is Corona. That okay?"

"Sure, yeah, fine."

Nolan headed into the kitchen.

Even before his back had left the doorway, my hand was digging into my pocket, searching for the tiny Wi-Fi transmitter. But I couldn't find it. Panic kicked in as I poked my fingers here and there, feeling under my kerchief, atop it, inside it. Nothing. I was positive I'd placed it there, but still ripped my hand free to search my other pants pocket, feeling below the wallet. Nothing. I jerked my hand free again, jerked it fast enough to scrape the back of it. I rechecked the first pocket, fingers probing, pain lancing through injured cuticles that felt only linen and lint. I heard Nolan humming something in the kitchen, a tune I didn't recognize. I heard bottle caps being twisted off and tossed into the trash with a soft tinkle. He'd be coming out any second now. I tore my hand out again, my handkerchief floating free. I tried to think where the transmitter might be. My back pocket? In my car? On my dresser at home? As my mind stumbled through the possibilities, my peripheral vision saw the kerchief flutter to the ground, something else dropping beside it. It took my panicky brain a second to register the transmitter bouncing onto the worn beige carpet. Seeing the little gadget filled me with a sense of joyous release. I spun in my chair, then froze.

Nolan was staring at me from the kitchen doorway. I stared back, expecting him to point and say, 'What's that?' Instead, he cocked his head and said, "Hey, you want a lime wedge in yours?"

I started to breathe again. "Lime wedge? Um, sure. Great."

He winked and was gone.

I pounced on the transmitter so fast that I almost dropped it. Then I turned back to his computer system. Panic returned. I was staring at a nest of wires and cables resembling so many black snakes. But which one was the keyboard cable? My mind blanked. I used up precious seconds berating myself for not locating it while Nolan worked, rather than gawking uselessly about the apartment. Then a little voice spoke in my head, a little voice that sounded like Nancy Nagel. It said six words—just six. 'Follow it to the source, dummy.'

I grabbed the black cable coming off the keyboard, sliding my fingers along it. After a foot or so, it was intermingled with other cables of similar size, making it difficult to follow. I tugged frantically, separating the wires. After seconds that seemed like minutes, I spied a twitch where the keyboard cable connected to the USB port. I snatched the cable free and inserted the transmitter in its place, the little gadget tingling in my hand as it came alive. But in the meantime, the keyboard cable had slithered off the worktable onto the carpet. I frantically bent for it, banging my head.

For the next few seconds, all I saw were dancing stars. Then I heard Nolan's humming grow louder. Somehow, despite the flashbulb pops still blurring my vision, I managed to grab the cord by feel, then jam the metal connector into the transmitter. The click as it struck home sounded loud as a gunshot.

"What you doing, boss?"

Nolan stood before me holding two bottles of beer, lime wedges poking from the tops.

"Um, I, ah…dropped my handkerchief, then clunked my head on the table trying to pick it up." I rubbed the small bump on my forehead, grimacing with pain.

"You need to be more careful." He handed me a beer, then reached down and retrieved my hanky. "Here you go."

My fingers were shaking as I took the kerchief.

"Cheers," he said, raising his bottle.

I raised mine. "To better days."

~ * ~

I had to stop myself from chugging beer as I listened to Nolan wax on about computers, malware, backdoors, trojans, and firewalls. I wanted to get out of there but didn't want to look anxious about getting out of there. I'd come to him with a problem that needed solving, and it would look suspicious if I dismissed it too readily in my hurry to leave. Yet, I couldn't stop my eyes from staring at his keyboard connection, the little gadget that had come alive in my fingers, the unobtrusive rim of plastic that seemed so obvious now that I was looking for it.

"So, what can I tell you, skipper? I can keep trying, still one or two things I *might* try, longshots that are unlikely to find anything. But…"

"But?"

"That'd cost an extra hundred bucks." Evidently his offer to help for free had been forgotten.

"Another hundred, huh?"

"Fraid so." He swigged some beer. "Are you positive you didn't write that post? Maybe a senior moment?"

I started to shake my head then stopped. I wanted out. Maybe this was out. I tried to look pensive.

"Now that you mention it, I had been noodling a few witty posts. You know, funny but a little risqué? Double entendre?"

Nolan smiled.

"I thought I had discarded them and just gone with a generic pleasantry, but now I'm not so sure."

"And was circumnavigation part of those witty posts?" His smile had changed to a smirk.

I shrugged. "I frankly don't remember." I laughed. "As you say, maybe a senior moment."

Now Nolan laughed. "I hear you. Even I get them at my age from time to time."

"How old are you, Nols?" I don't know why I asked, I just did.

"I'm surprised at you, boss."

I started guiltily. Had he noticed the gadget on his computer?

"You already know that I'm twenty-nine. It's right in my employment file."

I sighed in relief.

"Right there with my A-positive blood type and medical clearance to wear a respirator."

"Oh yeah, I forgot." I downed the last of my beer in a single gulp, the cold brew bringing on an ice-cream headache. "Well, I'm glad that's solved." I looked at my watch. "Hey, it's getting late. I should be going." I rose and extended my hand. "Thanks for your help."

Nolan rose and shook my hand, his expression one of mixed humor and confusion. "Okay. I guess. You're welcome."

"And thanks for the beer." I handed him the bottle and turned toward the door.

"Hey, boss?"

The voice behind me sounded urgent; maybe accusatory. I froze. Then I turned, certain that Nolan would be pointing to his keyboard connection.

"Don't you want your computer?" He unplugged the tether, clicked my laptop closed, and handed it to me. "Be careful. Don't toss it around in the car, at least before it has had a chance to cool down. And don't forget to charge it when you get home."

My smile felt strained as I took the warm machine and turned. My hand was on the knob when Nolan spoke again.

"Aren't you forgetting something, boss?"

This was it, I thought. When I turned, Nolan would be holding up the little gadget, mischief in his eyes. I was certain of it. Like a cat playing with a mouse, he'd teased me into a false sense of security and was now going to spring the trap. Sweat trickled off my forehead. More sweat coated my palms. I hesitated, unsure if I should turn or make a run for it. I turned.

Nolan stood there with his hand out. "My hundred bucks?"

I hoped my relief wasn't as profound as it felt. "Oh, yeah. Sorry." I wiped palm against pant leg, then retrieved my wallet. The money compartment held exactly forty-two dollars, two twenties and two singles. In my worry over the pending evening, I had neglected to hit the teller machine.

"I, um, I'm sorry, but I don't seem... I can let you have forty now and..."

Nolan waved an aw shucks. "Don't sweat it. You can give it to me next time I see you. You gonna be in this week?"

"I, I'm not sure."

He winked. "I understand. Take all the time you need. I'm not going anywhere."

~ * ~

I almost fell walking down the single flight of stairs; leaning against the banister until the strength returned to my legs. Then I hurried to the bottom and out the front door.

As I stepped into the muggy evening, my first impulse was to seek sanctuary in Nancy's car. But my mind's eye saw Nolan staring out the window looking for me to do just that, his face barely visible in the crack of a drape. I decided to stick to the plan and headed to the small lot next to the building. Once inside my own car, engine running, I felt a little better. I turned on some cool jazz and rolled the window halfway open. Then I drove away, warm breezes and soft music soothing away the stress.

Chapter Sixteen

I waved to Nancy and headed to the back booth.

"Where the hell have you been?"

"What?" I replied. Her cheeks were flushed with anger. I thought of John Wayne telling Lauren Bacall that she had a fine color when she was on the scrap.

"I've been waiting for over an hour." She pointed at her cup, one finger striking the ceramic and skittering it two inches. "This is my fourth cup of coffee." She dropped her voice as the waitress brought me a cup, then amped up again when the waitress left. "I've been sitting here with caffeine nerves getting angry looks for taking up booth space. Did you get a flat? Run out of gas? Get lost?"

"I just drove around a bit to cool off. It relaxes me." I reached for my coffee.

"And by the way, if you're worried about people noticing we're here together, it's probably not a good idea to wave to me from the front of the restaurant."

"Well, *excuse* me. I was a little shaken up after playing 007 with Nolan. I half expected him to call me Mr. Bond, then cut me in half with a laser after finding your gadget on his computer."

At that moment, I realized we were having our first fight, if you didn't count the time she arrested me that is.

Nancy smiled. "Fine. Glad it worked out okay—Mr. Bond."

"How do we know it *did* work out okay?"

Nancy held up a tablet computer. Numbers and letters streamed across the screen at a dizzying pace.

"What are those?" I asked.

"Files copied from Mr. Webster's system to mine at home. In another half-hour, maybe less, I'll have everything. Where he's searched, who he's chatted with, downloaded porn—everything."

"And then?"

"And then, we start building a case against Mr. Peeper…and wait."

"Did you get Nolan's friend request?"

"You mean did Nancy *Proudfoot* get his request? Yes. I accepted and received a thank-you message that included a photo sans shirt, scrawny chest exposed, which I really could have lived without."

"You didn't tell him that, I hope."

She grinned and put down her mug. "Perish the thought. I sent him back an "OMG" and kissy emoji. Then added one of my lingerie shots—yuk."

"Don't overdo it. *One* of those pics would turn on any guy, Peeper or no."

Her smile now said the compliment was accepted. Not much maybe, but at least I had moved out of the pervert cubby hole in her cop brain.

"I can take care of myself."

"I hope so," I said. "If he *is* The Peeper, you're right in the crosshairs." I thought a moment. "Were his messages like this with your sis… the um, other victims?"

If Nancy noticed the reference to Karen, she let it pass. "System firewalls initially prevented me from searching private messages. I could see friend lists, which is how I know he was connected to all the victims, except Weider-White and your wi…"

Now it was my turn to ignore. "Couldn't you use police authority to search messages?"

"If I wasn't suspended and was part of an active, department-authorized investigation—yeah. But for now, we'll have to play it this way."

"So, if we don't know he was friendly like this with the other victims, how can we be sure he's The Peeper?"

"We can't."

"But you still think so?"

I watched her put down her mug, coffee moistening her lips, her blond hair bobbing.

"Just because he had social media contact with other victims and knew my wife?" I asked.

"Not *just* because he had social media contact with the other victims," she said, "but yes, because he knew your wife."

She must have seen my quizzical expression. "Did you know I have a master's in behavioral science?" she asked.

"Really?"

She nodded. "Minored in computer sciences."

"That surprises me. I wouldn't have pegged a street cop as a science grad student. They don't seem to go together, and you're kind of young."

"I graduated college at twenty-one, grad school at twenty-three." She smiled shyly.

"Overachiever?" I asked.

She shrugged. "And the two *did* go together, at least in *my* mind. A cop has to know human behavior, it's as important as knowing how to shoot well, more so."

She leaned back, assuming the attitude of a teacher giving a lesson.

"My thesis was on criminal behavior, specifically serial murderers. They are not a monolithic population, but they do have things in common. Tendencies." She ticked off fingers that had never seen a manicure but were still feminine. "They are white males almost invariably, although not all are heterosexual—Gacy for example. Most have a history of antisocial behavior that builds over time."

"Nolan's peeping?"

"Something like that. They also have a strong predatory instinct; they track and control their victims. A lot of them take trophies. They are impulsive but also smart, high IQs." She paused, then added, "And they seek sensation, love attention. Many taunt or play games with the police, just as they play games with their victims. BTK used to enjoy seeing people panic by shutting off their air with plastic, then cutting a small hole allowing them to breath, then taping the hole; over and over. And he used to tell them he was going to let them go, only to revel in the fear in their eyes when he didn't."

"In other words," I said, "they are twisted geniuses?"

"Let's say, twisted and smart. Logical thinkers who can see ahead, often several steps further than the police. Which makes them difficult to catch."

"This is fascinating," I said, and it was. "But what does this have to do with Nolan and The Peeper."

"It has to do with the fact that I believe The Peeper is playing games."

"With who?"

"With the police," she said. "And with you."

"Me?"

"I don't think it's a coincidence that his victims were taken from your social-media contacts, including Suzanne Weider-White. I don't think it was a coincidence that someone changed your post on her page just prior to her murder, who better to do that than Wonder Webmaster. I don't think it's a coincidence that Webster knew you liked that waitress from Bozo's, one that just happened to fit the type favored by The Peeper. And I don't think it's a coincidence that he also knew your wife and had admired her, nor that she also fit The Peeper's model." She paused. "Sorry."

I smiled shyly back. "To you as well. Your sister."

She took my hand and squeezed. She was doing this more frequently, I thought. I didn't mind.

"How is he playing with the police? Has he sent notes or left messages? 'Piggy' written in blood or anything?"

"No, nothing so overt. But don't you see, Randy, by setting *you* up, he set *me* up. I'm not saying he knew *I'd* be setting up a sting operation, but he thought maybe someone would."

"He left a clue," I said. "One imbedded in social media for the finding."

"Right. One that wasn't immediately obvious. One that required peeling away the onion."

"A sporting chance," I said. "For a worthy adversary."

"Exactly. And one that would implicate someone other than himself. Had the department not deep-sixed me, that could have been you."

I raised my brows and spoke like Boris Karloff. "Maybe I *am* The Peeper."

She laughed and squeezed my hand again. "Okay, don't rub it in. But you see what I mean."

I did see. It got me thinking about Nolan, the two sides of his coin; the loud, hard-drinking, easy-going horndog; the neat, studious, computer geek. The young man who took to window peeping and, perhaps, aunt raping. The twenty-nine-year-old with no wife or girlfriend in evidence. He talked a lot about sexual exploits, but never about dates. Was he all talk and no do, at least without the violence that fed his sickness? This struck a nerve.

"Stan, my lawyer, said that my wife, um, Cheryl had been, well there was evidence of semen. Not mine, that is."

She squeezed my hand again, then spoke softly. "Yes. That was one of the things that let you off the hook."

"I'm curious. Had The Peeper done that before? The news reports didn't say if he'd... You know, the other victims. If he..."

"Raped them?"

I nodded but couldn't meet her eyes.

"There was no semen found on or in the other victims. But there were traces of latex and lubricant, possibly deposited postmortem."

I looked up, startled. "A rubber?"

"Looks that way. Like I said, smart. And also telling—part of the game."

"So, why didn't he wear one for Cheryl?" I asked.

Nancy shrugged. "Who can say? Maybe a slip up. Maybe part of his game somehow."

A thought struck like a thunderbolt. "You've got his DNA." I almost shouted it. "I mean the cops have got it from his semen. If it *is* Nolan, all we need to do is get a sample from him."

She raised a cautionary hand. "But first we need to build a case before we can get an order to obtain his DNA." She pointed to her tablet still ticking off files. "Pictures of the victims would help build that." She pointed to herself. "Catching him in the act would be better."

Now I grabbed her hand. "Be careful."

She squeezed mine. "I always am."

Chapter Seventeen

I made a sandwich and grabbed a beer from the fridge. As I added ham to buttered bread, I absently wondered why Nancy and I never ate at the Northfield Diner—just coffee. Even when she'd offered, I'd refused. Maybe I thought food would have attracted more attention, although not eating at a diner was rarer. Maybe ordering food was too much like a date, which wasn't right—not yet. I sorted mail while I finished my sandwich, then headed to my room and my computer.

I still thought of it as *my* room, although the whole house was mine now. I could have moved into the master, but that was still Cheryl's domain. I pondered how that had happened, when it had happened? When had we split into separate rooms, separate lives? Why had Cheryl gotten the master, with the large closet, better mattress, and color TV, while I had been relegated to the guest room? I'd never even questioned it. I guess I had already become a guest in my own house. I shrugged and fired up my computer.

I no longer bothered with email or news feed; I went right to messages. To my surprise, there was one from Nancy Collingwood, aka Nagel. Odd, I thought, that I don't know her phone number or email. We'd met in person several times, but social media was still our only means of communication. I clicked on the message.

'I am an idiot! Contact me.'

I smiled. With Cheryl, I was always the idiot, never her. I put down my beer and typed.

'I wouldn't say that. What's up?'

She must have been sitting by the screen, waiting.

'There's been another Peeper killing.'

'When?'

'Sometime between six and eleven.'

'Tonight?'

'No, next week. If you'd listen to the news rather than jazz, you'd have heard about it.'

Sarcasm, I thought. We still hadn't exchanged numbers but were already sounding like an old couple.

'Right around the time I left Nolan.'

'No shit.'

'Why are you an idiot?'

'Because I should have been watching his place instead of drinking coffee with you in Northfield.'

'You think my visit set him off?'

'It would fit the profile. And the game playing we discussed.'

'What now?'

'Change of plans. We're going on stakeout.'

'We?'

'Sorry to drag you into it, but I can't handle it on my own. And help from the department is out, at least for now.'

'How do we proceed?'

'We'll start tomorrow night. We should be safe till then. He'll have sated his demons with this most recent one. You watch from six till midnight. I'll take over till six in the morning.'

'What about during the day?'

'Mr. Peeper has never struck during the day, so I think we're okay with twelve hours. Besides, doesn't Mr. Webster have a job?'

'Duh. ☺ Should we meet during the day to compare notes?'

'About what—what was on the radio? Don't you think sleep would be a better option for daylight hours? And I'll need time to go over his computer data.'

I felt disappointed. I guess I'd started to look forward to seeing her. Some people have that effect on you.

'Question? If I see him leave, what do I do?'

'Follow him but don't—I repeat do not—do anything else on your own. Give me a call and I'll come in a hot minute.'

I errantly wondered if she could come in a minute, or if it took longer. But it was too early in our relationship for risqué jokes, so I got back to business.

115

'How?'

'What???'

'How do I call you? I don't have your number.'

I waited for a reply. It seemed like I waited a long time, or maybe time was magnified by my wondering if she'd give it. Finally, after what was probably no more than thirty heartbeats but felt like more, a phone number appeared on the screen.

'That's my cell. I'll keep it with me.'

After a moment, an email and Yellow Springs address appeared as well. I smiled and typed in my info.

'Here's mine—just in case.' I paused and then added. 'I guess we officially trust each other now.'

She didn't reply to that. I'd hoped she would.

'6 till midnight tomorrow. Wait for my car before leaving. Night, Randy.'

'Night Nancy.'

I blew a kiss to the screen then went to bed…and dreamed.

~ * ~

I was walking up the steps of a house. It wasn't Nolan's apartment building, but in my dream it was. The place was eerily familiar, like I belonged there, like I should just be able to open the door and walk in. But it was Nolan's place in the dream, so I knocked. A feminine voice answered, "Who is it?"

I knew the voice but didn't know it. Such was dream logic.

"It's me," I said.

"Oh," she answered. "Come in, Randall."

No one had called me Randall since my mother. But that didn't seem strange here. I went in.

The room was like Nolan's, simple furnishings, neat and clean. But it wasn't Nolan's, it was some other place I remembered from long ago. The door entered onto a living room dominated by a large sofa, one my mother had called a divan, with an accent on the 'die'. Everything else around the sofa was blurry, but the divan was clear as Lalique (another phrase favored by Dolores Corlane). The center of that clarity was a sight to behold.

Nancy Nagel sat on the divan stark naked, legs crossed Sharon Stone style. Her body was exactly as I'd envisioned in my daydreams of her, taut, perky, well-toned. On her head was her old DPD ballcap. In her hand, a bagel she'd been nibbling. She held the bagel out toward me.

"Want a bite?"

"Yes," I answered. "But not of the bagel."

I smiled to myself, thinking I'd hit upon the right combination of funny and risqué.

"The old, double entendre, huh boss?"

I turned to find Nolan standing beside me, grinning.

"Want to do a little circumnavigating?" he asked. "You take north, I'll take south, we'll meet at the equator for a dip in the ocean." He winked.

"Do you have a tic?" I asked. "Seems like you're always winking."

He laughed. "I can take care of that."

Nolan raised his hand, which held a large pair of shears, the expensive kind used for sewing. With his other hand, he deftly pulled his eyelids out at a grotesque angle that made me cringe. Yet I couldn't turn away. I just stood there, dumbstruck, while he lifted the scissors and snipped through the upper and lower lids. His smile was now a lopsided grotesquery, eye squinted in humor on one side, staring boldly from the other. He held the scissors up to me, snipping them several times as if in invitation. I thought of some bully in grade school asking, 'You want some of this?'

I shook my head, wanting to backup. Wanting to leave, head through the door I'd entered. But I couldn't move, my feet two dreamlike blocks of cement. I tried to say something, maybe 'no thank you', but I couldn't speak.

Nolan cocked his hand to his ear, the one lidless eye glaring unnaturally at me.

I tried to speak again but produced only a strangled dream whisper.

Yet Nolan seemed to understand. He shrugged and turned to Nancy.

"Next?" he said, walking toward her. I could now see he was naked too. Naked and aroused.

Nancy sat up prettily, brushed crumbs off her upturned breasts, and obediently tugged her eyelids out.

Nolan laughed and headed toward her.

Panic rushed to meet me. The kind of panic reserved for dreams, the needing to act but not being able to do so. No, I thought. No, not her. Please God, not her. I wanted to tackle him, grab his arm, knock the scissors from his hand. But those cement pumps I was wearing froze my feet to the floor. I tried to call again, but even the dream whisper had fled, leaving only a soft scratching sound in my throat, like the static on an old-time record just before the needle hits the music. All I could do was watch, as if *my* eyelids had been sliced away so that I couldn't shut out the vision.

Nolan approached her slowly, steadily, laughing the whole time. Nancy sat there sexily; lids held obediently out for him. He raised the shears, their sharp blades snickering the air, the blades smeared with traces of his gore.

I tried to move. I couldn't. I tried to speak. I couldn't. My throat hurt with the effort to scream. The needle-like rasp gained a little volume, escaping my lips like a hiss of steam.

Nolan bent down, still laughing. He held the scissors on either side of Nancy's fingers, then moved them toward her face until they hovered around the outstretched lids.

He turned to me, still laughing, and winked his one good eye.

"No," I managed, the strangled cry a bit louder than before. The blades started to close.

Suddenly I had my voice back, but no breath to scream with. Bands of iron held my chest as tightly as the concrete held my feet. I fought for air, eyes bulging at the grisly scene, hands tightened into tetanic claws.

Nolan stopped laughing long enough to say, "Last chance, Skipper."

"No," I gasped. The iron bands broke, and I filled my chest with air.

Nolan turned back to Nancy and closed the blades.

~ * ~

"Noooo!"

I'm sure my scream was loud enough to wake Cheryl, had she been downstairs sleeping.

"Loud enough to wake the dead," I said aloud.

The imagery of the dream returned to me; I remembered every detail. I usually remember dreams, good and bad. That has been my curse and my pleasure. I shook with the memory, knowing that sleep was finished for this night. Sighing, I headed down to the kitchen to toast myself a bagel.

Chapter Eighteen

My early morning wakeup had been shared with a rerun cop show, the one with the bingy bell between scenes. As luck would have it, the TV detectives were on stakeout, so I learned some tricks of the trade. No coffee— that would require relieving myself behind a bush while night owls jogged or walked their dogs. Instead, I sucked on eucalyptus drops to keep my mouth moist. I didn't run the car's AC, which would produce engine noise and telltale exhaust. I just kept the window halfway down to let in the evening air. I dialed up some Yusef Lateef on the stereo but kept the volume low.

I was in my personal car, a Ford Flex. It was big but pedestrian, and I didn't think Nolan knew it on sight like he did my county Buick. I'd parked on the opposite side of the street from his apartment building, but with a good view of the parking lot. Nolan's Honda was there, so I assumed he was home.

Nothing happened for the first hour, except that my butt fell asleep. It was odd this didn't happen on long drives; it must be something about sitting still. Wiggling in the seat every five or ten minutes helped. I also developed a crick in my neck, something that sometimes did happen on long drives. Looking about the neighborhood helped with the crick, although there wasn't much to see: the occasional car passing, the occasional dog walker. One of the walkers was a tall blond, a few years past her prime, but still worth looking at. I thought of Cheryl, wondering briefly why she hadn't made an appearance in my dream last night. Then I caught a glimpse of someone exiting the apartment house and thoughts of Cheryl fled.

The evening light was fading into night, but I could plainly see Nolan saunter to his car. He whistled something, something not cool jazz. His old Honda coughed to life and backed out of the space. I ducked down in my seat as headlights raked my Ford then headed down the street.

I'd asked Nancy what to do if he left during my shift, but for some reason had never expected him to. Now he had, and I scrambled for what to do. She'd said to follow, she'd said to call her. I wanted to do both, but my cell was in the glovebox and Nolan was getting away.

"I'll call her when we get where we're going," I said to nobody in particular. Then I put the Ford in gear.

~ * ~

"I should have known."

I think I said this aloud, or maybe just thought it loudly. The large, feminine clown cutout with the strategically placed pompoms didn't seem to care as she watched over my parking space two lanes from Nolan's Honda.

It was a weekday night, so Bozo's lot was only half full, giving me a clear view of the suspect vehicle. I smiled at the cop talk in my head, then scrunched down in the seat. I thought about calling Nancy but dismissed it. Why bother her, when Nols was likely to leave in an hour or two and head home. Tomorrow was a workday after all. I'd call her only if he headed someplace besides the apartment house. The thought both frightened and excited me.

I watched the parking lot for a few minutes, maybe half an hour, then scrunched down in the seat further, trying to relax. That was supposed to be important in surveillance, relaxing, not fighting the boredom. I took some deep breaths, I rolled tension from my neck and shoulders, I shook my splayed fingers; all the relaxation tricks I'd learned in undergrad oratory class. I still felt tight, on edge. The problem was that my early morning was catching up to me. My eyes burned from fatigue. I'd just close them for a few minutes; get my second wind. Rubbing away the sting in my tired peepers produced flashes of bright light behind the lids. My mind wandered. Peepers. Eyelids. Last night's dream.

I tried to think of something else, latching onto the music coming from the speakers. Yusef's flute had changed to Wes's guitar softly strumming in the background. I remember thinking that Wes never used a pick; must have had quite the callous on his thumb. That was the last thing I remembered thinking before sleep took me.

~ * ~

I woke with the disoriented feeling of being in a strange place. It took me a second to remember where I was, the large clown cutout providing the proof to the pudding. I yawned, I stretched, I rubbed my eyes. I had to pee. I looked around for a good spot to go and noticed the space two rows down was empty. Nolan was gone.

"Shit!"

This I did say aloud, and loudly.

I reached for the cell in the glove box but stopped. What would I tell Nancy—that I'd fallen asleep on the job? Well why not? I'm no cop, and it was past my bedtime even if I hadn't woken early, all true. But still, my mind's eye conjured up anger and disappointment on her lovely face. Worst of all, she'd think less of me. I took my hand off the glovebox. It was past eleven. Nolan probably headed home, just like I thought he would. If he hadn't, then I'd call Nancy. I started the car and drove away.

By eleven-thirty, I was parked in front of his apartment building again, sighing in relief at the sight of Nolan's old car in its usual place. Nancy would be along in a half-hour or so. Nolan wasn't going anyplace. I stretched. I yawned. I still had to pee. I looked around for a likely spot and selected a large fir tree on my side of the street.

I stepped from my Ford, then darted back inside at a sudden flash of light. It took me a second to realize that I'd just freaked out at the dome light coming on in my own car. Chuckling into the night, I clicked the dome light to off and opened the door again.

There was a single streetlight two houses down, but the bulb must have burned out, probably sometime during the Clinton administration if I knew Midlothian department of public works, which I did. It was just as well, there was nothing much to see except the glow of a half-moon in the summer sky. The little residential street was deserted, as it should be at eleven-thirty on a weekday. I scanned the area a couple times to make sure, the darkness and my mission giving me the heebie-jeebies.

I never liked peeing outside, even when it was dark, and people couldn't see; especially when it was dark. The thought of standing in the shadows, not knowing what was around me or below me tightened up my sphincter like a dunk in an icy pond. Just my luck to piss off a hiding skunk,

I thought, heading toward the fir.

I didn't see anything in the shadows of the big spruce. I didn't smell any skunk, just pine tar and pollen. I felt like I had to sneeze, but it passed.

As I unzipped my fly, I tried to put my mind on something else, something other than darkness, skunks, and Peeper victims. Any mundane distraction that would ease the tightness, let the water flow. I thought about my office, Jan talking to a citizen on the phone. I thought of the parking lot at Bozo's. I still couldn't raise a drip. Then I thought of Nancy, her pretty face gazing at me across the booth, her strong fingers giving mine a squeeze. A dribble started. I sighed in relief. Then everything clenched tight as a beam of light bathed the area around me.

I quickly zipped up, painfully jerking netherworld hairs, then stumbled to the edge of the tree for a peek. A car was pulling up behind mine. My first instinct was cop; a big guy with a jarhead haircut pointing a flashlight in my face and asking what I was doing here indecently exposing myself at almost midnight. I think I told you that I've always had a thing about cops, any authority figure really: my mother, even Cheryl at times. It wasn't fear exactly, more like nervousness. They always made me feel a little guilty. I guess that's usual for most people, a lot of us anyway.

But it wasn't a police car. There was no bar of wigwag lights on a two-toned cruiser with 'protect and serve' on the side. It was Nancy. I recognized her Miata right away. The beams of the low-slung headlights flashed once, evidently my cue to drive off. Then she must have realized there was no one in my car. Her headlights clicked off. Her dome light clicked on. She exited.

She was dressed in black sweats and a like-colored pullover. She had what looked like a flashlight in her left hand, a dark shape in her right. Her body moved slowly, lithely toward my Ford. She looked briefly up and down the street, then placed the flashlight up against my window and clicked it on. I could clearly see the inside of my car for just a second, then it was dark again. She scanned the street again.

"Hey," I whisper shouted.

Nancy flinched and dropped into a low crouch.

I spoke a little louder this time. "Pfft. Over here."

She spun so quickly it made *my* head spin. I didn't know anyone could turn that fast. Her flash sparked to light again, bathing me in its glare. I protectively covered my eyes with the back of my hand, waving at her with the fingers.

"It's me."

The beam died, and she was suddenly at my side, grabbing my arm.

"What the fuck are you doing?"

"I, um, I just stepped out for some air."

I don't know why I didn't tell her my true purpose. Maybe because she might expect me to complete the assignment, forcing me to try and piss outside at night with her waiting on me; something I knew was an impossibility.

"Well, here's a thought." She still held my arm in a vice grip, flashlight tucked into her pit, her voice a murmur through clenched teeth. "Don't do that. Surveillance is about anonymity, not attracting attention."

"Sorry." I shook my arm free. "I'm new at this. And my butt fell asleep."

I couldn't see her face clearly in the dim moon light, but I thought she was smiling. She shook her head.

"Okay. No harm done I guess." I watched as she reholstered the dark shape of a blue-black automatic pistol.

"What are you doing here? Your shift doesn't start till midnight."

"Couldn't sleep. Nothing happening. So, I thought I'd head over. How about you?"

"Me? I wasn't sleeping."

"I know. I meant anything happen during your shift?"

I started to tell her about Nolan driving off. It seemed wrong somehow to lie to her. But then I'd have to mention I *had* fallen asleep. I imagined the disappointment on her face. I imagined the lecture I'd get. And after all, it was just a trip to Bozo's. And I still had to pee.

"Nope. Nothing."

She grabbed my hand and squeezed. "Okay. Why don't you head home and get some sleep? I've got this."

I returned the squeeze and walked to my car. As I drove away, I thought that I'd been wrong. A cop had indeed pulled behind my car. And I did feel guilty.

Chapter Nineteen

I slept well. If I dreamt, I didn't remember, so I'm guessing I didn't. I did remember the night before, but no longer felt guilty about lying to Nancy. She was maybe the first beautiful woman who hadn't intimidated me or kept me feeling guilty—not a lot, anyway. I smiled at the thought and headed down for coffee.

It was almost eleven when I finished breakfast. No sense going to the office. Besides, they'd understand if I took a few days, probably even expected it. So, I decided to go for a drive.

With Kenny Burrell on the stereo and a warm breeze through the open window I wandered north, no real destination. After twenty minutes I was at Memorial Park. I drove through the gate and parked in the first open space. Then I walked.

Cheryl's headstone was as ordered, the wording simple:

"Beloved wife. Rest in peace until the day of judgement."

I don't know why I added the last, the phrase just stuck in my mind. Probably something left over from my religious mother. But it was a sunny day, and I didn't feel like dwelling on painful, childhood memories.

I hadn't thought to bring flowers, had not even known I would be coming here, so I pulled a dandelion daisy from the edge of the road and tossed it on the fresh sod. I stood upon the empty plot on Cheryl's left, my someday resting place, and tried to dredge up a few tears. None came, I hadn't really expected them to. Then I drove home.

I hadn't checked my messages before my drive; Nancy was probably sleeping anyway and there were no other messages I cared about. Funny, I thought, how I used to look forward to my social-media time, sending birthday greetings, responding to random posts or sexy photos, answering each message. Now, I only wanted to hear from Nancy. And I did. Her message was brief and cryptic.

'Do you know her?'

There was an attachment that I assumed had to do with the 'her'. I clicked. To say the image on the screen was a shock was to say World War I was a little skirmish.

It was a woman getting out of the shower. A good-looking blond with a towel wrapped around her bottom half, her top half bare but turned strategically away. Her head was tilted back toward the camera, smiling a dreamy smile, the sexy type associated with either daydreams or posed pictures. Her face was plainly visible; a pretty face with a few wrinkles but otherwise handsome for a woman of forty-two. How did I know her age, you ask? That's easy, I knew the face. Had known it for twenty years. But I didn't remember that smile. It was one Cheryl hadn't shared with me.

I was numb, but my fingers moved of their own account, clacking out one line.

'Where did you get this?'

Somehow, I knew Nancy would be online, waiting. She was.

'From Nolan's photos. I started going through them today. Is it who I think it is?'

'How?'

'Good question. Is it one she gave you? Maybe a posed shot for Valentine's Day or something?'

I stared at the photo instead of answering. Nancy replied as if I had.

'Do you recognize the bathroom? Your house?'

Our house had two full baths. Cheryl always showered in the master, which was a walk-in with mosaic tiles. I showered in the main bath, a kit shower with sliding glass doors. The shower in the picture had a curtain, with a repaired crack on the unadorned, white splash tiles.

'Randy? You there?'

I came out of my stupor long enough to type one more line.

'Can we meet?'

I didn't need to say where; she didn't need to ask. It was our spot now.

'Two o'clock.'

It wasn't a question. It didn't need an answer. I logged off. For the first time, tears flowed.

~ * ~

We sat in our booth, sipping coffee. The waitress (Wanda according to her nametag) didn't ask if we wanted food, she knew our MO by now.

"You sure she never gave that photo to you? Maybe a couple of years ago?"

I shook my head and stared at my coffee. "I would have remembered."

"Maybe she was *going* to give it to you. For your birthday or something?"

I looked up suddenly. "It's in two weeks."

Nancy smiled. "She must have gone to a photographer and had it done."

I felt as if several hods of cinderblock had been removed from my chest. My relationship with Cheryl had lacked intimacy, as the psychologists say. Had lacked it for years. This gesture, this attempt to inject some spice, would have probably been too little too late, but it still brightened my heart to think she had made an effort. And it was better than the alternative I'd been thinking; what any man might think finding his wife's cheesecake photo on another man's computer.

"How did Nolan get ahold of it?"

"She probably had it on her laptop. A JPEG proof from the photographer. Maybe they were going to print it onto a birthday card. That's how lots of woman do it."

"But how did Nolan get it?"

"You mean Wonder Webmaster? Young master Nolan, the peeping Tom?"

"You mean?"

"Uh huh. I'm thinking yours wasn't the only hacked computer in the house."

"But Nolan couldn't find any evidence of my computer being hacked." I looked at her smile and realized how naïve I was being. "But what about the shower? In the picture? That's not our house."

"You ever been to a photographic studio, Randy? They aren't fancy, but they do have bathrooms. These bathrooms do have showers. These showers are used for just this kind of purpose. As are the big brass beds you'll find there."

"So," I asked, "this is a common thing? Posed sexy photos?"

"It's probably most of a modern photographer's business, along with weddings and baby pictures. You've been on social media. You think all those sexy shots are selfies?"

She had a point. Some were obviously self-made, cleavage blurred in the shaky foreground. Others looked posed, shot by gifted loved ones or professionals.

"Nolan finds it on her computer, gets his motor running. Downloads it to his own computer so he can look at it any time he feels the urge. Fits the pattern."

"A trophy?" I asked. It suddenly seemed so clear.

"What do *you* think?"

She unfolded a plain, black and white photo and tossed it on the table. It was a grainy print out, but the lady in question was clearly recognizable.

"Shy?"

"Ms. Shyreen Kolinsky," Nancy said. "Former server at Bozos. Recent Peeper victim."

"Nolan's computer?"

She nodded. "I also found one of my sister Karen but didn't print it out."

I grabbed her hand. She squeezed mine.

"I've only started going through his files, but I wouldn't be surprised if we find little mementos from all the vics."

The waitress checked to see if we wanted more coffee.

"Want to see a menu?" I asked. "On me."

Nancy hesitated, then shrugged. "I'm not that hungry. Maybe just a bagel."

I raised two fingers at the departing waitress.

"What's so funny?"

~ * ~

It was quarter past eleven and no sign that Nolan was going anywhere. The light in his apartment window had clicked off twenty minutes ago. I was trying to decide if I should head home or wait for Nancy when my cell rang. Or should I say buzzed, I'd learned enough about stakeouts to turn the ringer off. I'd become an old hand, I thought, as I looked at Nancy's number on the display.

"Hi. What's up?"

"Looks like Nolan's not our man. Why don't you head home?" She sounded disappointed, maybe frustrated, maybe, both.

"I don't understand."

Now she definitely sounded frustrated—at me. "You've got to start watching the news, or at least listening to radio other than WJZZ. There's been another one."

"Another what?"

"What do you think, Randy?"

"The Peeper?"

"You catch on fast. Last night, sometime between seven and midnight. While Nolan was sitting home under your watchful eye."

Seven to midnight. My mind raced. We'd gotten to Bozos around seven. Nolan's car had been back at his apartment by eleven-thirty. Over three and one-half hours, nearly three of which I'd slept through.

"So, no use wasting our time. Nolan's not the guy." I started to tell her when she interrupted. "Shit! I was so sure."

I wanted to tell her. I should have told her, right then. But I didn't. I felt too guilty. Another Peeper victim. On my watch, the easy watch, six to twelve. She'd be more than disappointed. She'd be more than angry. I needed time to think about this.

"Will I see you tomorrow? Regular place?"

"Not much point. I'll need to start from scratch. I won't need you anym...I mean, um, thanks for the help. Sorry to put you through all the trouble for nothing."

"It wasn't any trouble."

I felt eerie, out of body, as if I was floating. In the background, my brain was yelling, tell her, stupid. My mouth wouldn't cooperate. But I had to say something, or this would be it. The Peeper would keep on killing. And I'd never see Nancy Nagel again.

"How about the diner at nine for breakfast. One last meeting to discuss things. Maybe we can thrash something out." Nancy hesitated, umming and awing. "You know what they say about two heads?"

I could see her smile over the phone. "Okay, Randy. Nine it is. But this time, my treat. I owe you that much. Get a good night's sleep."

I clicked off the cell, but I didn't sleep. I stayed at Nolan's place, and watched, and thought. I'll admit I did doze off for a couple hours. But Nolan's car was still there. At six I drove home. But I didn't sleep there either.

~ * ~

"Two menus?"

"Please," I said to the waitress.

"You two finally moved past coffee, huh?"

She chuckled. I smiled.

I'd arrived early—ten minutes of nine. My brain felt sluggish, slow, like mush. But I had managed to reach a decision during the long night. I'd tell Nancy; let the chips fall as they say. I had to, there really wasn't any choice. I guess I'd known that all along, just needed time to come to grips with it. I'd tell her right away, even before we ordered.

I felt better, but anxious. I still felt anxious when nine o'clock came and went. My anxiety grew at nine ten, even more at nine-fifteen. The waitress came by with her coffee carafe. I waved my hand over my cup.

"Your girlfriend stand you up today?"

"She's not my…" I shrugged instead of finishing. Part of me said it wasn't worth explaining, another part didn't want to acknowledge the fact.

At nine-twenty, I pulled my cell from my pocket. Then I saw Nancy enter the diner and I put it back.

She plopped into the booth like a trucker and said, "I need coffee."

"You look like you do."

And she did. Bags the size of steamer trunks adorned her pretty blues. Her normally rosy cheeks were ashen. Her hair's lustrous shine was now straw bundled crudely under a scrunchie. Her sweats looked slept in; her shoulders sagged from lack thereof. Her freshly scrubbed smell of green apples had soured.

"Bad night?" It was all I could think to say and was better than the alternative 'you look like hell'.

"Nothing gets past you, Randy."

The waitress poured coffee into Nancy's mug, giving me a wink before saying, "I'll give you two a moment to look at the menu."

I thought about clutching Nancy's hand but held back. Her mood was raw, and I didn't want to set her off. Instead, I said, "What's wrong?"

She stared at her coffee for a moment, then smiled. "Had trouble sleeping; frustrated by the case, I guess."

I sensed more to come and waited.

"I was finally starting to doze off around one, when I heard someone trying to break into my apartment."

"Are you sure?"

She gave me that sarcastic gaze, the one that turned her from Officer Sexy into Jack Webb. "I'm a cop, Randy."

"Sure, I know. I just mean, you were tired, mind on edge. Maybe it was just a…" I shrugged. "Just a tree branch creaking. Or a squirrel or something running over the roof."

Nancy reached into her sweats and clanked something onto the table. The overheads shone off a thin metal rectangle about two inches long; one edge had a jagged curve.

"Squirrels don't use tools, not even in Yellow Springs."

"What is it?"

"A shim," Nancy said. "Probably part of a spackle knife. I found it wedged in my front door. "

I picked it up, almost cutting myself on the jagged edge.

"Burglars use them to jimmy locks. Fortunately, I'd installed a good deadbolt on my door."

I dropped the shim, wiping my hands on my shirt. "Did you see who did it?"

Nancy shook her head. "I saw a car drive off but couldn't make it out." She finished her coffee and signaled to the waitress. "Spent a half hour walking around the building with a flashlight, looking for clues, but came up empty." She smiled. "Neighbors probably thought *I* was a burglar casing the joint."

"Couldn't get back to sleep?"

She smirked. "What was your first clue?"

Wanda brought her carafe, Nancy pointed mutely to her cup, Wanda filled it.

"You two ready to order?"

"Um, just toast for me," I said.

Nancy chuckled. "You're a cheap date." She slid the menu away. "Two eggs over medium, ham, hash browns, toast with jam." She noted my surprise. "I eat when I'm frustrated."

Wanda left.

"The case getting to you?"

Nancy stretched. "It's pissing me off. A couple of days ago, this would have all made sense. Nolan kills this Rochelle person; then takes the social-media bait we planted and comes after *me*." She held up her hands like a departing blackjack dealer. "Now?"

"Well, maybe it still makes sense."

"How? Our Mr. Webster was home, snug as a bug, when Rochelle whatshername was killed. So, the chain is broken, one link as good as a mile."

I cleared my throat. "What, um, what if he *wasn't* home? You know, when this Rochelle what's her name person…"

"Kolodny," she said. "Rochelle Kolodney."

The name sounded very familiar.

"Right. What if he wasn't necessarily at home when she was killed?"

"What do you mean, *necessarily*? You told me…" She clunked her mug to the table and got back to Jack Webb. "You have something to tell me, Randy?"

"Well, what if Nolan didn't *stay* home that night, but went someplace instead?"

"Like?"

"Like Bozo's."

"Like Bozo's? And like how long might he have stayed at like Bozo's?"

"Um, at least half an hour?"

"At *least*?"

I closed my eyes so I wouldn't have to see her expression. "I must have fallen asleep."

She didn't say anything. I waited. I prepared. I steeled myself for the recrimination, the curses, the full-blown cop language that would compare me to a scum-sucking cocksucker of dubious parentage. Nothing happened. I opened my eyes.

She was smiling. "For how long?"

"A couple of hours, I guess. It was almost eleven when I came to. I drove right back to the apartment and his car was there, so I figured he just went home after a few beers."

"So, our boy was unaccounted for during the time in question. And he'd just been to Bozo's, which probably got his engine running." Her smile widened. "The world makes sense again. I just wish we'd had him under surveillance last night."

"We did," I said. Her brows tented. "I felt guilty not telling you I conked out, so I stayed and watched his place."

Her expression sank. "Did he go anywhere?"

"I, um, I don't know. I clunked out again for an hour, maybe two. But his car was there when I came to."

"When was that?"

"Maybe two AM or there abouts?"

She calculated quickly, eyes at the ceiling. "About thirty minutes to get from Midlothian to Yellow Springs; traffic is light that time of the morning. Thirty minutes back." Her smile reappeared. "It's doable." Officer Sexy was staring at me again. "Did you check the hood?"

"What?"

"Nolan's car. When you woke up, did you feel the hood of his car to see if it was warm?"

"No. But that would have been a good idea, now that you mention it."

She chuckled and shook her head. Her eyes were once again beautiful. Her complexion once again colorful. "When you screw up, you really screw up, I'll give you that, Randy."

I laughed a bit myself. "You're not angry?"

She took my hand. "Yes, you should have told me. But you're a stakeout virgin, so it's understandable." I felt the warmth of her hand in mine.

"Breakfast should be ready in a jiff," Wanda said, pouring coffee in our mugs. "Want me to bring your toast out now or wait?"

"Wait," I said. "I want to change my order." I smiled at Nancy. "I'll have what she's having."

Chapter Twenty

I sipped coffee and shrugged. "I don't know. I felt a sense of loss—shock, I guess. But not really the grief you're supposed to feel."

"No river of tears, huh?"

"I tried." I looked Nancy square in the eyes, seeing my reflection in a blue pond, but seeing no recrimination. "I actually tried. But?" I shrugged again.

We'd been chatting for over an hour. All through breakfast, then coffee. Chatting like old friends, not two-dimensional cyber friends, but real friends. Ones with shared experiences. Ones who could maybe become more than friends. Two friends at the beginning of something more.

Wanda poured coffee and smiled. I realized she saw it too. Two strangers who'd gone from sharing coffee to sharing their lives.

"If you have to try, you don't have any tears to cry." Nancy sounded as if she hadn't had to try to cry; tears had come easily after her sister Karen's death. She'd cried that proverbial river.

"I only cried once," I said. "And that was when I, you know, saw the picture you sent. But that wasn't grief. I guess, I thought…"

Nancy nodded. "Betrayal."

"Yeah." I put down my mug and sighed. "We'd been growing apart for a long time. Years. Funny, but I hadn't thought much about it at the time. It happened gradually, then it was the new normal. Now, I've had nothing but time to think about it. Now I know we were really living separate lives: mine work and social media, hers, gyms, spas, the BFF League. We were roommates working different shifts. Saw each other just five, six hours a week."

The enormity of that hit me. I'd seen my wife of twenty years for less than one hour out of every twenty-four. How long had that been going on? How many of those twenty years? A single tear rose to my eye, and I brushed it aside.

Nancy took my hand. She didn't squeeze, she just held it. It felt warm and good.

"I hadn't seen Karen for months, not since Christmas. Maybe if I had, well, maybe I could have talked some sense into her. Made her see that there were dangerous guys out there, guys you shouldn't tease, even if it was online."

"Don't blame yourself," I said. "That's par for the course on social media. Girls showing off, putting it out for everyone to see, showing photos they'd never show a stranger on the bus."

Nancy sighed. "The new normal?"

"Not the normal I grew up with," I said.

"Where did you grow up?"

"Town of Ridgeville, Ohio. You've probably never heard of it."

"Sure," she answered. "Near Cleveland, isn't it?"

"That's *North* Ridgeville. A booming metropolis by comparison. My Ridgeville is an unincorporated dot between Dayton and Cincinnati. What is referred to on the nightly news as a Midwest farming community."

"Bible belt?"

"I think we *wrote* the bible. At least my mother did. Wrote it and memorized it."

"Strict?"

"Severe. Beautiful and dogmatic and…let's talk about something else. Okay?"

"You folks want anything else?" Wanda smiled down at us. "We start serving lunch in ten minutes."

Nancy and I exchanged startled stares. Where did the time go? She smiled. I smiled back.

"No, just the check, please."

"Not so fast," Nancy said. "This is *my* party, remember?"

"Don't worry about it. You were a cheap date last time. I owe you after all the trouble I've caused you."

She chuckled. "You're a funny one, Randy. I have you arrested and falsely accused of murder, then I corral you into nightly surveillance, and *you* caused *me* trouble."

Nancy patted my hand, then slowly slid her fingers off the back of it. I felt the hairs on my arm stand to attention, the ones on my neck too. My face flushed warm.

"A shrink once told me I had a heightened sense of guilt."

Nancy raised a brow but didn't ask the obvious question.

I put my credit card over the bill and waited for Wanda.

"So," I said, more to fill the pause than anything, "what do we do now?"

"Well, tonight we go back on stakeout." Her smile now held a hint of shyness, something I hadn't noticed before. "If you're willing."

"I'll try not to fall asleep this time."

Wanda took away my card.

Nancy leaned back and closed her eyes, slowly rolling her shoulders and neck. I felt like a snake watching a charmer, her simple, sensual movements edging me toward a trance.

She opened her eyes, the trance held. "I'll head back to Yellow Springs and see you at midnight."

"All the way to Yellow Springs, then back to Midlothian? That's a lot of driving."

"Can't be helped. I've got to catch *some* sleep before tonight. And I don't fancy sleeping in the car."

Something came over me, something sudden. It wasn't quite a personality change, more like a momentary lapse. I found myself asking a question I'd never asked a beautiful woman, not even Cheryl; at least not after knowing said beautiful woman for a week and having one meal together.

"Why don't you crash at my place. You can get some sleep and won't have to drive thirty miles after dark."

"No. Thanks, but I think not."

"Come on. I've got lots of room. You can even have the master. I've been relegated to the guest room for so long, it's more like my room now anyway."

"I don't know?"

I could tell I was making headway. "Master has a walk-in shower; Showcr-Max spa head with six spray settings. Guaranteed to massage away those kinks."

Nancy started to say something, then stopped. She looked at me quizzically, not quite sure if this was a come-on or not. Her next words surprised me.

"I don't have a change of clothes."

My smile widened. "Clothes we got. Con gusto, we got, as the Mexican's say. My late wife was a clothes horse."

Now she smiled. "Mexicans don't say that."

"Okay, as *I* say. Well?"

Wanda brought back my card. I signed. No one spoke. I savored the silence. Bitter experience had taught me that the next words would dash my hopes. Nancy surprised me again.

"You lead. I'll follow."

~ * ~

"This is a nice place, Randy."

I tossed my keys in the bowl on the kitchen counter. "You like it? Cheryl picked it out, did most of the decorating. *All* of the decorating, actually."

"Didn't you get input?"

I chuckled. "I was allowed to live here."

It felt good to laugh. It felt good to feel good. I realized I had been living for a long time, years probably, without feeling good. Without feeling bad, either. Without feeling, period.

"Let me show you to the master. You'll probably want a shower."

"A shower would be nice. But seriously, the couch would be fine for me."

"We've had that argument. You lost." I pointed to the hall. "This way, Madam."

Nancy laughed. "Thank you, Jeeves."

I led her to the master suite. "The bed's been changed, no one has slept in it since, well, you know. The shower's in there." I pointed to the bathroom. "Help yourself to anything in here." I pointed to the dresser. "Or in there." I pointed to the walk-in closet.

"You sure it's okay? I feel a little funny wearing—you know?"

"Hey. It's either that or they go to Good Will. Cheryl won't mind; help yourself."

Nancy filled the awkward pause with a kiss on my cheek. Her lips felt soft. It'd had been a while since I felt soft lips, or a kiss with something behind it other than sarcastic routine.

"You're sweet. Thank you."

~ * ~

I got a couple of hours of sleep in the easy chair by the big screen but was up by four. Nancy was snoring blissfully from the master, so I fixed a sandwich for myself and another for her, wrapping hers in plastic wrap and leaving it and a spare key atop a note.

'Feel free to crash here this morning instead of driving back to YS. I've got plenty of everything and it'd be my pleasure.' I drew a smile face on the note.

That smiley face felt a little silly, but I needed to add something. A heart didn't seem appropriate—yet.

I was parked across from Nolan's apartment by five-thirty. Unfortunately, his parking spot was empty. This is something we should have planned for but hadn't. I started to worry, but only a little.

"I should have followed him from work," I said aloud.

I thought about calling Nancy for instructions but didn't want to wake her. So, I tried to relax into the routine of surveillance; not fighting the job as the cops said on TV. I sucked my eucalyptus drops. I listened to the radio, news instead of jazz. I stretched, I yawned, I wriggled life into my butt. But my eyes kept scanning the street, searching for the approach of his car.

By quarter of eight I was really worried. The Peeper had never struck before dark, at least I didn't think he had, so I only had another hour. And what if he was on his way right now? What if he was stalking some poor victim at this very moment? I thought about heading to Bozo's; there were lots of potential victims there. But what if he came home while I was gone. I picked up my cell to call Nancy when I heard an approaching engine, one that was old and in need of a tune-up.

I smelled Nolan's Honda before I saw it; the tang of burnt oil filling the air. I ducked low as he pulled into the drive, pulled in too fast and too wide for someone driving sober. When he got out, I could see that he'd had a few, probably at Bozo's, which seemed to be his hangout now. His steps had the controlled unsteadiness of the moderately inebriated, not so much of a stagger as a sway. He whistled something, a rock tune I didn't know. I scrunched lower, but he didn't take any notice of me or my Ford. He just fumbled with his keys, fumbled with the door lock, and went inside. A few moments later, the light on his apartment came on.

Did serial killers get tanked before stalking their victims? I didn't think so. I put my cell away and relaxed, settling into the job. I watched, I waited. The streetlamp blinked on about nine; I remember thinking it was odd it hadn't come on the other night. Nolan's light clicked off around ten. I listened to the radio, jazz now. I tried to remember the names of all the presidents in order, crapped out in the early eighteen-seventies. I hummed along to Misty on the radio. I didn't fall asleep.

Nancy's Mazda made its appearance at eleven-thirty-five. She blinked her lights. I thought about waving, then remembered not to. I started my car and drove home.

"Police work sure is exciting." The empty car thought so too.

When I got home, the note I left her was gone. So was the sandwich. So was the key. I smiled and went to bed. I slept. I didn't dream.

~ * ~

I woke to the 10 AM sun shining through the bedroom window. After cleaning up, I headed downstairs. Nancy's room was quiet; funny how I already thought of it as Nancy's room. I wanted to check in on her, but the door was locked. I guess we trusted each other, but not completely.

I didn't want to bother her, so I headed to the market for the fixings of a western omelet. I'd make us breakfast for lunch, and we could discuss surveillance notes over coffee. I felt oddly happy considering that my wife had recently been murdered and that I was initially arrested for the crime. I still had a sense of loss, but also a sense of beginning, rebirth. In a way, The Peeper had forced me from my humdrum inertia, had opened a whole new world of possibilities. And of course, Nancy was foremost among those possibilities.

I got home around noon and opened the door to the smell of Columbian blend. Nancy, dressed in Cheryl's shorts and tee, was sipping a cup at the kitchen table while looking at the paper.

"Morning," I said.

She waved back, head still in the paper.

"Did I wake you when I left?" I put my package down on the counter.

"No. I got up about a half-hour ago."

"You can't have gotten much rest. Why don't you take a nap this evening during my shift?"

"I'm fine. I don't need much. And I won't be here this evening."

"Oh?" I didn't like the sound of this.

"I'm going to head back to my place after lunch. I still need to go through Nolan's files."

"You could bring your computer here."

"I've got a lot of stuff—it'd be awkward. Besides, I need to be there. I'm the bait, remember?" She looked up from the paper and grinned. "Not much of a trap without the cheese."

"Yeah, I guess." I tried to keep the disappointment from my voice. "But with you gone all night, I don't see much point."

"I'm not going to be gone all night," she replied. "I'm going to be watching Nolan's apartment from six to midnight."

"But that's *my* shift."

She sat back in her chair with the confidence of one used to making decisions. "You no longer have a shift. I shouldn't have brought you into this in the first place."

"But what if he strikes after midnight?"

She shook her head. She must have showered because her hair glistened like harvest wheat.

"He won't." She tapped the paper. "I should have seen it all along."

I looked over her shoulder at a story outlining The Peeper's chronology. The headline read, "The Town that Dreaded Sundown'.

"Time of death for all his victims has been between six and midnight. *All* of them. I don't think he's likely to break his pattern now."

I thought about this. It sounded logical, except… "What about *your* place? Somebody tried to break into your place at one in the morning."

"That was probably a burglar. One to three is the most common time for break ins." She stuck her nose back into the paper. "We don't want red herrings leading us down the garden path."

"And a stich in time saves nine, but I don't think clichés prove The Peeper didn't come for you."

Nancy chuckled. "I like your sense of humor, Randy."

I smiled back. "I'm here all week." Then I had a thought. "Okay. You watch Nolan's place from six till midnight. Then I'll watch your place from midnight to six."

"What?"

"Just in case you're wrong."

She shook her head again; I recognized the orange-blossom scent of Cheryl's shampoo.

"That's nuts. And it's not necessary. I'm a light sleeper."

"Maybe. But you're exhausted. It's bound to catch up with you. God forbid it happens when Nolan comes to call."

"No," she said. It was a definitive statement, one intended to end the conversation. But she must have seen something in my eyes because she looked at me with a familiar expression, stern yet quizzical, serious yet amused. One I'd seen countless times before. I half expected her to say, "Don't be an idiot." Instead, she said, "What are you up to?"

I shrugged. "Nothing. It's just that you live on a public street. And there's no law against me parking on it anytime I want." I met her gaze unblinking, another Corlane first with either the police or beautiful women.

She folded the paper and leaned forward, continuing her good-cop-bad-cop stare. "You are stark-raving mad."

I smiled. "Have been for years."

Finally, she sighed. "On one condition."

I raised my brows.

"You stay inside my place not the street." Her semi-stern, semi-amused expression returned. "But you sleep on the sofa. I'm not giving up my bed for this craziness."

"Don't worry," I replied. "I'll be watching, not sleeping."

Chapter Twenty-one

I arrived at Nancy's by five. I knew she had a good forty-five-minute drive to Nolan's, and I didn't want to be late. I rang the bell three times before she answered.

"Oh. It's you. Sorry, Randy."

"Did I get it wrong?" I asked, stepping inside. "Wasn't I supposed to camp out here until you got back?"

The place reminded me oddly of Nolan's; neither feminine nor masculine, neat and tidy. The furniture was not quite Walmart, more Ikea-esque. As at Nolan's, a computer set up dominated the dining area. I recognized the telltale hint of burning rubber.

"I don't know why you didn't let me leave a key under the mat?"

"Well, McGruff," I replied. "That wouldn't have been very good security, would it? Leave a key the first place someone looks. What took you so long?"

"Huh?"

"To answer the door. I was going to start looking in windows."

"Sorry. But I was having a nice online chat with Master Webster." She pointed to her twenty-four-inch monitor. The tenor of the 'chat' was hard to miss.

'I'd like to start at the equator then circumnavigate both hemispheres.'

"Son of a bitch." My mouth dropped open as my eyes popped to the inspiration for Nolan's witty reply; a photo of Nancy sitting abed in a black teddy.

I cleared my throat. "Well, I have to admit, I'm a bit jealous. All you ever sent me was to jail."

Nancy clicked off the screen, the roses on her cheeks highlighting her blue eyes.

"I'll have you know that's a Dollar-Store negligée, bought especially for this occasion."

"Spared no expense, huh?"

Her blush deepened. "Smart ass. You recognize the quotation?"

"How could I forget. He planted the same one on my computer."

"He also found the Wi-Fi transmitter you planted on his, so be careful."

"How do you know?"

"The feed off his system cut out a few hours ago. Either that or the booster I planted on his cable box went kerplunk."

"Another Dollar-Store special?" She gave me an FU look. "I'm not worried. If he's the Peeper, what's he going to do, go to the cops?"

"And if he's not Mr. Peeps?" she asked.

"How do you accuse your boss of hacking you? Even in county government."

Nancy pulled a lightweight, long-sleeved shirt over her flimsy tank top. I could no longer see her nipples tenting fabric, which was a relief considering that I'd started to do the same. As before, she was all in black. She donned a black ball cap.

"Feel free to watch TV, whatever. Nothing much in the icebox but help yourself. I should be back by half past twelve." She pointed to the grey, parachute sofa. "That's pretty comfortable, if you want to sack out."

"I don't know. Might be tough after seeing you in all your Dollar-Store splendor."

I got another FU look.

She grabbed keys from a bowl on the kitchen counter. "See you later." She was halfway out the door, when she turned and said, "Stay out of my dresser drawers."

I put my hand to my heart. "I never enter a lady's drawers without permission."

This time, the FU look had a smile with it.

I thought briefly about asking her what I should do if Nolan showed up early? But then the door closed, and she was gone.

~ * ~

I'd gotten a pretty good night's sleep and had even taken a nap in the afternoon. So, I was as surprised as anyone when I woke suddenly on Nancy's couch. The room was dark, and it took me a moment to get my bearings. My fingers recognized the plush texture of the parachute sofa, which was as comfortable as Nancy had said. I recognized the now familiar scent of cooking computer components. A streetlamp penetrated the venetian blinds, casting dappled light over me, the threadbare carpet, and a wall-clock. I hadn't noticed the clock before, but I now saw it read ten-twenty-four. Still two hours until Nancy got here.

I yawned. I stretched. I discovered that it was easier to sink into a parachute sofa than it was to rise from one, at least once you passed forty. I reached over to turn on the table lamp, almost toppling it in the process. And then I froze. A noise broached the stillness, a sound of metal scraping metal. My eyes followed the sound to the front door, then shifted to the wall-clock. The clock definitely read thirty-six minutes to eleven, I could see it plainly in the slit cast by the streetlamp. Then my head jerked back toward the persistent scraping at the front door.

I froze, my mind darting through a thousand thoughts; the key one had to do with what to do? I cursed myself for not asking Nancy. I cursed myself for not knowing. I cursed the darkness. I searched for a weapon.

Someone muttered something on the other side of the door. I couldn't make it out, but it sounded angry. I imagined the source of that anger. My mind conjured up an image of Nolan, a new Nolan, Nolan Webster 2.0. A Nolan with crazed, bloodthirsty eyes. A Nolan with a demonic sneer. The Nolan behind the Nolan. A malware version. The Peeper.

The metallic sound resumed. I imagined a thin shim like the broken one Nancy had found, its jagged edge looking like a raw wound. The scraping stopped. There was a loud click as if the lock had given.

I found my feet moving, still not knowing where I was going or what I was going to do when I got there. The where turned out to be against the far wall, a spot that would be hidden behind the opening door. The what turned out to be striking out with a small statue I retrieved from the coffee table during my journey. I lifted the statue, a hefty bronze and wood affair, holding it like a batter ready to line a single. I held my breath, my other thoughts replaced by one sharp, cold, surge of adrenalin. The door opened. Someone spoke.

"What the…"

I pivoted around the door, swinging the statue. The base met flesh, producing a "woof" of expelled air. I advanced quickly against the intruder, but the intruder was quicker, shaking off the blow and grabbing my wrist in a numbing vice-grip that twisted the statue from my hand. I screamed in pain. The intruder screamed something from a kung-fu movie. Then I was on the floor, a hundred plus pounds pinning me, one of my arms behind my back, cold steel pressed against my temple.

"Move and you're dead."

I recognized the voice. I recognized the faint smell of orange blossoms. I could finally breathe again.

"Don't shoot officer. I surrender."

The gun barrel eased from my temple. "Randy?" Nancy slipped effortlessly off my back. "What the hell do you think you're doing? I could have killed you."

I rolled over, rubbing my shoulder. "*Me*? What do *you* mean coming back two hours early, unannounced?"

"What are you talking about? It's twelve-thirty-five."

"What? But the clock."

"Needs a new battery. Currently correct twice a day. Why is it dark in here?"

"I, um, I must have fallen asleep. And then I heard metal scraping at the front door, an angry grunt. I thought…"

"I dropped my keys. Took me a second to find the right one."

She stood staring down at me in the light from the open door, her eyes glowing like blue flames. I stared back. She smiled. I smiled. Then we both started laughing.

"You jackass," she said, holstering her pistol.

I raised fingers over my ears. "Hee haw."

Her laughter increased as she picked up the statue and shook it at me. "You were going to beat me insensible with my own Martial Arts trophy?"

"You are a martial arts champion?"

"Interdepartmental. Two years ago." She put the statue on the table, still giggling, and shut the door.

"Had I known known that I'd have hit you harder," I said. "And on the head."

Laughter struck her like a gale, bending her over with its force. "My least vulnerable spot," she gasped, holding her gut.

It was good to hear her laugh, and it was infectious. "Noted for next time."

"Next time maybe I'll blow your brains out."

"My least vulnerable spot."

We both roared like preteens at a slumber party; me on my back, holding my belly, her bent over, holding hers. After days of stress, lack of sleep, my arrest, her suspension, the murders of my wife and her sister, the sense of release felt wonderful.

As the belly laughs changed back to giggles, I held out my hand. "You want to help me up?"

"If I must." Nancy grasped my hand in both of hers. "On three. One. Two. Three."

I discovered that it was easier getting off the floor than off the sofa. I also learned that Nancy Nagel was even stronger than she looked. I literally flew into her arms, sending us both stumbling backwards. Her leg must have struck the edge of the coffee table because the statue fell with a clunk and we both went down, landing with a whoosh on the parachute sofa. Our laughter flared again.

We lay there holding onto each other, laughing. I felt the warmth of her under me, her body soft yet taut with muscles. I felt the tickle of her silky hair on my face; smelled its pungent aroma of orange blossoms and sweat. I felt her breath against my cheek, warm and moist, with hints of coffee. And then, I kissed her. I didn't think about it. I just did it.

At first her lips were unresponsive, surprise instead of passion. Then she kissed me back. We kissed once, then twice. By three, our tongues were exploring. Our hands followed suit. A few moments later, our clothes lay cluttered around the parachute sofa.

~ * ~

Nancy snugged into her ninja shirt then shook back her blond hair.

She looked good. She'd been good. Better than I'd imagined in my middle-aged fantasies. More than I'd imagined.

I thought back to my first time with Cheryl, at her trailer after a vet school party. She'd taken command, orchestrated the tempo, teased me, used me, almost made me beg. Nancy likewise took charge, they were in the same mold there, but with more sharing; a benign dictator who wanted to give as well as take.

"Listen, Randy." She pulled her black jeans on, head turned to the wall. "Maybe we shouldn't make too much of this. Think of it as, I don't know, a stress reliever. A lot's going on right now, and I don't…"

"Don't worry," I said, from my position on the bed. "Me too. Stress reliever. But one better than running or the Stairmaster."

Nancy shook her head. "Jackass." There was that smile again, just a little sarcastic crease to the lips. The same one my mother had had before delivering an affectionate rebuke. The same one Cheryl had had before deigning to make love.

I didn't hee haw. But I did smile back. And I had lied to her. Maybe she needed to worry. She may have seen it as blowing off steam with a tumble in the chaff, but I was falling. And I was smart enough not to say anything. Not yet. There was time. Time to let it build; let her come around.

"So, did anything happen during the swing shift?"

She grabbed a brush off the bureau and ran it through her hair. The bedroom, like the rest of the place, was neat and utilitarian, except for a few feminine, almost girlish touches: a stuffed dog, a prom photo (some guy with a tux so blue my eyes hurt), a framed picture of Kermit the frog in a police outfit.

"Nope. Master Webster came home at seven thirty and never left the house. Beddy-bye at nine forty-five." She smirked down at me. "And he didn't show up here, either. Not that you would have known."

I blushed. Truth be told, I hadn't been much of a watch dog. Then a thought occurred.

"Maybe we're going about this the wrong way."

"How so?"

"You're the bait, right?"

"Yeah."

"But you're never in the trap."

"Come again, Randall?"

I smiled inwardly. Cheryl had also called me Randall when she took charge.

"His MO, the time he stalks his victims, is six to twelve, right?"

She shrugged.

"You're not home then. You're watching his place. And I don't think he's expecting to find you in a car across the street."

She paused, as if I was making sense, something Cheryl rarely did. "But what about the other night, when he killed that Rochelle person?" The name again raised a twinkle, as if I should know it. "I was home, then."

"Yeah, but he hadn't focused on you yet. There were other fish to fry. But lately, judging from his reply to that sexy picture, you've moved to the front of the line. For all we know, he sat outside your door for a couple hours last night. Noted the lights off, no movement inside, no you coming back." I shrugged. "He gave up and went home. I certainly hadn't been looking out the window for him."

"I see your point. And another thing. We've been working under the assumption that Nolan comes home, gets whatever murder kit he has, waits for dark, then does the deed."

"Is that the assumption we've been working under?" I asked.

"*I* have." She smiled. "Jackass."

I smiled back. It wasn't idiot, but it would do.

"What if he leaves directly from work, or Bozo's, or whatever? He stalks his victim, waits outside her place or her work or whatever, then strikes?"

"In that case," I said. "Watching his place at all is fruitless."

"Exactly." She stood thinking, cute nose scrunched in concentration. "New plan. I stay put, bait in the trap. Maybe a couple more enticing messenger photos."

"Another trip to the dollar store?"

"No, Jackass. Not for you. You trail Nolan."

"Me?"

"Uh huh. You latch onto him at work, then follow where he goes."

"But I'm no cop. I've never trailed anybody."

"I'll give you some pointers."

"But what about my car? It's big and kind of obvious. Won't he notice me following?"

"You can use my car. I planted my address where he could hack into it on social media, but not my car description or license plate."

I didn't like it. I was no detective and had never followed anybody in my life. Oh, like everybody, I'd tagged after people who knew where they were going and I didn't, but not without their knowledge; not what cop shows called 'a tail'. Shows and movies listed all kinds of tricks for that, including block squaring, and paralleling, but those involved two or more cars. Doing it on your own was supposed to be tough, even when you knew what you were doing, which I didn't. I didn't want any part of it, but how could I say no to Nancy, especially after last night.

"Well, I guess, I could try."

She smiled. "Good boy."

"I could park at the municipal lot around three in the afternoon. Wait until he leaves work, then follow his car."

"Right." She slipped feet into her navy-blue running shoes. "Just stay well back. Turn when he turns. But well back. Let a couple of cars between you and him. But don't lose sight of him." She smiled. "Piece of cake."

My smile was less certain and more forced. "Right. Piece of cake."

Chapter Twenty-two

I got antsy waiting around, so I went to the county lot thirty minutes early. Almost immediately, there was a problem. I drove by where Nolan usually parked, and his beat-up Honda wasn't there. I circled the lot three times, but still nothing. Finally, I parked in a back row and called the office.

"Hello. Midlothian County Pesticide Control Program. May I help you?"

"Hi Jan. It's me, Randy."

"Hi Randy." She sounded sad and sympathetic. "How are you holding up?"

"Not too bad, I guess. Is Nolan around? Put him on, okay?"

"No can do. He's already gone."

"Already? It's not even three."

"He had an inspection at one, then said he was going home. I guess it was in his neighborhood. Can I help you?"

"No, no. That's okay. I was just hoping to catch him. Wanted to ask him something."

"You're lucky you caught *me*. I was just heading out when you called."

"When the cat's away, huh?" Like I said, there was nothing I could do about them leaving early, even when I was there. But I wanted her to know that I knew. I expected a smartass comeback, but not today.

"No. I have a funeral service to attend. It starts at five thirty. I'm gonna sing something, so I gotta go home to change and practice."

"Oh. I'm sorry to hear that. Anyone I know?"

"No." It sounded like she'd been crying. "You never met her. My friend, Rochelle. The one I told you about."

A light went off. That's where I knew the name. "Rochelle Kolodny?"

"Yeah. I guess you heard." She sighed. "I guess we have that in common now. You know, knowing someone who…." There was a hitch in her voice before she trailed off.

"Yeah. I guess. Can I ask you something?"

"If you make it quick. I really have to go."

"Sure. Did you, ah, ever introduce her to Nolan? Rochelle, I mean."

"No. I don't even think I talked to him about her. Nolan's okay, but he's not, you know, the kind of guy I'd hook up with a friend."

"He must have overheard Jan describing her to me," I mumbled.

"What was that?"

"Nothing. I just said, um, be careful driving."

"Sure." She sniffled into the phone. "Bye Randy."

Now what? Should I drive to Nolan's? Should I drive to Bozo's, his home away from home. No, I thought. Best to check in with the boss. I smiled and dialed Nancy's number.

Her cell rang five times then went to voicemail. Either she was busy or talking on it. Or? I tried not to think about her fighting for her life against a crazed serial killer. Besides, it wasn't anywhere near The Peeper's killing hours. And I remembered our scuffle, her atop me, pinning me down, in control; here was a lady who could take care of herself. No, I'd check at Nolan's first. If he went home like he said, I'd stand guard there. If he hadn't gone home, and something told me he hadn't, I'd head to Bozo's. This time of day, the lot should be sparsely populated and his car easy to spot. If he wasn't at Bozo's? Then, I'd drive to Nancy's. I felt better having a plan and headed out.

~ * ~

No car at Nolan's apartment, so I drove to Bozo's. The lot was only about a third full and it didn't take long to find his old Honda. I could almost smell the burnt oil as I drove by. I settled Nancy's Mazda into a space a few rows back then settled myself comfortably. I fired up some old-school jazz and rolled down the window to get a gentle, soothing breeze.

As so often happened, my mind wandered with the music. It drifted back to days gone by, now so many hazy memories. Things got murkier the farther back I fled, and more disturbing. Memory lane was not a friendly place. So, I tried to concentrate on the music; the Jazz Crusaders bopping along as young rabbits, then Andre Previn - Livin' Alone. I thought of the lyrics to the Previn song: 'So, I tell myself, that I like it on the shelf. But if the truth be known? I hate…"

Tap! Tap!

My head jerked up, eyes open, Nolan's car clearly visible through the windshield.

Tap!

I twisted suddenly to the passenger-side window, the source of the tapping. I didn't see Nolan's car, I saw Nolan himself, glassy eyes smiling at me across the partially rolled-down window.

"Hey, Doc. Fancy seeing you here."

I tried to think of something to say, but came up with only, "Um."

"Looks like you were falling asleep in there. Have one too many?"

"Um, no. I was just resting my eyes and listening to the music."

"Funny I didn't see you inside." He nodded toward the bar.

"Oh. I, um, haven't been inside yet. As I said, I was just listening. I, I love that song."

His smile clouded as if he couldn't understand my taste in music, then he shrugged. "I was just leaving myself, but if you want some company, I'll stand you to a round."

At first, I was going to refuse, but then thought, why not? There was no better way to keep an eye on Nolan than to keep an eye on Nolan. And he already looked two sheets to the wind. Why not add another sheet. A drunken serial killer was at least a clumsy one. And a passed out serial killer was no killer at all, at least for today. I hoped I could keep my wits about me as he lost his.

"Sure," I said. "But let me buy. I still owe you for that consulting." He started to refuse, until I said, "Just my way of saying thanks. You'll still get the whole hundred."

He smiled and shrugged. "You're the doctor."

~ * ~

There were no busty blondes in Bozo's that day. The barmaid was a cute black girl of maybe five feet height and twenty-two years. The hostess had red hair, a dye job to be sure, but not blonde. The waitress who served our beer, Bonnie, was a tall, very pretty brunette with minimal cleavage that needed the help of the pushup bra she sported. No likely candidates tonight, I thought, as I raised my beer glass.

"Thanks again for the computer help." We clinked. We drank.

"Speaking of that," Nolan said, "I found a Wi-Fi diverter tacked onto my system. You wouldn't know anything about that, would you?"

I tried not to look as shocked as I felt. "A what?"

"A hacking device. Sends my feed somewhere else."

He looked at me amiably enough, but with a keen interest. I couldn't help thinking he was baiting me, ready to let me dig a hole before he buried me in it. But the old saying was, 'deny, deny'. I denied.

"Never heard of such a thing. Never even knew they existed." Until a few days ago, I thought. I tried to smile. "But you know me. I've never heard of most computer whatchamagigs."

His look of keen interest disappeared with a chuckle. "Yeah. I had to ask, though. Only two people been around my system recently. You and a cable guy putting in a new modem." He shrugged. "I'd complain to the cable company but can't prove anything." He drank beer. "Been a friggin pain in the ass though. Had to redo all my passwords and perform a level three maintenance scan. Fortunately, I didn't find any malware."

I sighed and drank. "Guess you can't trust anybody, huh?"

"No, guess not." He winked. "Present company excepted."

His glass was nearing empty, so I waved my hand for our waitress. "How about another round—on me?"

"Well, if you're going to twist my arm."

Bonnie looked over and I twirled my hand over our table. She smiled and headed toward the bar.

"So, Doc. When are you coming back to work? Not that I'm complaining." Another shit-eating grin that said when the cat's away the mice would play and that he knew I knew.

"Oh, in a few days. Still a bit tough now that Cheryl is gone."

"Yep," Nolan said. He burped. "I'm gonna miss her." I raised a brow—he noticed. "I mean, I'm sure *you* miss her."

"You guys met, right? You and Cheryl? I can't quite remember."

He paused for a moment. Was that a look of panic? His answer came in kind of a rush. "Oh, yeah, sure. Bunch a times. I mean, there was that county picnic. She wore that sundress with the plunging… I mean, there was the Christmas party last year. *And* the year before." I thought maybe his color had increased, and not from the alcohol. "Why?"

I was onto something, I could tell. Maybe it was the alcohol working, but I decided to pursue it.

"Just something I'd been thinking about." I sipped my beer then nodded in faux recollection. "Yeah, the Christmas party." Nolan relaxed a bit. "You told some joke that really had her going. I remember her saying she thought you were funny—in a crude sort of way."

He was shit-eating Nolan again. "That's me. A regular Richard Pryor."

Bonnie brought our beers, smiled, then departed.

"So," I said. "What do you think of this Peeper?"

Nolan shrugged, a little too nonchalantly I thought. "Bad dude. Real sicko."

I nodded, studying him. "Seems to have a propensity for blondes, don't you think?"

"Never noticed. But now that you mention it."

The conversation seemed to be making him uncomfortable. I pressed on.

"Shyreen. Weider-White. My wife. Kolodny."

"Yeah. I guess. Who?"

"Rochelle Kolodny," I replied. "Latest victim. She was another blond."

He had the queasy look of the trapped animal. I continued. "Why do you think that is? Why blonds?"

"I don't know. Listen, mind if we talk about something else?"

"You look a little jumpy."

He gulped beer. "Well, sure. No fun talking about some nut job cutting up women. I mean, especially when one is, I mean was, you know, Mrs. Corlanc." I wondered about the sudden formality—Mrs. Corlane. "You must have come to grips with it, huh?"

"I guess," I said. "But it still upsets *you*?"

Nolan looked very antsy now. "Yeah. Sure. Listen. It's getting late, and I should be going."

"I'm sorry," I said. "No more morbid topics. Let's finish our beer." I drank deeply. I drank with satisfaction. "So, anything unusual happen since I've been out of the office?"

We chatted about the office for a bit. He told me Jan had been upset that a friend had died; didn't mention how. I pretended not to already know. He relaxed. I allowed him to buy me a beer, my third. I was feeling the alcohol, but he didn't seem to be. I remember thinking that it must really take a lot to get him to the state I saw him in the other day, wide turns in the car, a bit of a stagger. Long practice, no doubt.

Nolan burped again. "Well, Doc. I should be going. I hadn't intended on staying this long."

I looked at the bar clock: seven-thirty. Not as late as I wanted, but maybe good enough. I didn't think The Peeper would be working tonight.

I paid the tab and we walked to the lot, now three-quarters full. Nolan got into his Honda.

"You okay to drive?" I asked.

He winked. "I've made it home just fine with more buzz than this."

"Well, be careful," I said.

Nolan waved and backed out with a rumble of exhaust and oil smoke. His Honda jerked into first and he turned wide out of the parking lot.

I waved away the smoke and smiled. "No, I don't think The Peeper will be working tonight."

I felt good, relaxed, a weight removed. The steel bands were off my chest; I could breathe. The Peeper was foiled for tonight. No doubt Nancy would complain that I got the rat drunk instead of letting him come after the cheese. But she'd get over it. More importantly, she'd be safe—for tonight.

Chapter Twenty-three

Morning sun was in the window when I woke. First thing I did, after my usual morning ritual, was call Nancy to check in.

"Yeah," she answered, her voice groggy with sleep.

"Sorry if I woke you."

"Oh, um, Randy. No, I just, was just lazing around bed. What time is it?"

"Almost nine." I heard a voice in the background. "You got the TV on?"

She didn't answer right away, then mumbled something incoherent. I imagined her stumbling out of bed, maybe cursing as she stubbed her toe on the way to the TV set. I smiled at the thought of her in just tee shirt and panties. I smiled as only someone with such intimate knowledge can. Someone falling in love.

"So," she said. "What's up?"

"I need to tell you about last night. Is it okay if I come over?"

"Come over?" She sounded flustered. "No, why, why don't I meet you somewhere?"

"The diner for lunch? Noonish?"

She paused, then said, "Fine. No, let's make it eleven."

"Are you okay?" I asked.

"Me? Yeah, fine. I'm fine." She spoke quickly, in a hurry. "Eleven o'clock. I'll see you there." Then she hung up.

"Maybe she had to pee," I said to no one in particular.

~ * ~

I got to the diner at quarter of and settled into our regular booth. By my second mug of coffee, Nancy came through the door and headed over.

Her hair was mussed, as if she'd brushed it hurriedly. She wore only sweats and a tee shirt that read 'I invest in precious metals' above a drawing of a bullet. That's my gal, I thought.

"Hi," I said, sliding her a menu.

Nancy shook her head. "Just coffee for me."

I raised my cup to Wanda, who came over and filled our mugs.

"Didn't you sleep well?" I asked. She looked puzzled, so I smiled and said, "That's how I look with a hangover."

"Oh, no." She ran fingers through her hair. "I just…"

"Never mind. Let me tell you about yesterday." She sipped. I explained. She listened, nodding in the right spots. Yet, she seemed distracted.

"I know, I shouldn't have gotten him drunk, or should I say, drunker. That the plan was just to watch, give him a chance to go for the bait. But once he saw me." I raised my shoulders.

"No, fine. That's okay."

I'd expected a tongue lashing. Not getting one made me a bit nervous. Still, I pressed on.

"So, what's the plan for tonight?"

"Listen, Randy." Wanda came back over with her order pad.

"You sure you don't want anything?" I asked.

Nancy shook her head.

"Thanks, Wanda. Just coffee today."

When Wanda left, Nancy spoke again.

"I don't think there's going to be anything tonight."

"I know my surveillance method still needs work," I said. "But I promise to be more careful and just watch. We really haven't given this new strategy time to work."

"It's not that. It's just, well, I'm calling off Operation Peeper."

"Why?"

She shrugged. "I go back on duty next week. And it's probably best if I just report my suspicions to the higher ups. They can check out Nolan through official channels. If there's anything there, they'll find it."

To say I was surprised would be an understatement. "Why the change?"

"I've just been thinking that might be best."

"Okay," I said. "But what about your wanting to make detective and your boss wanting you to play meter maid?" I grinned. "Maybe we should noodle this decision a bit. How about I buy you dinner and discuss it."

Her return smile was more of a grimace. It was a smile I'd seen in my younger days; every time I'd heard the words 'It's not you, it's me'.

"Listen, Randy. I told you I had a lot going on. That maybe we shouldn't make too much of the other night."

"Yeah, I know, stress reliever. I get it. It's just dinner. We can decide if we want stress relief after we discuss this new strategy."

She chuckled. "It's not *just* that. The 'a lot going on' I mean. There's this guy. We were pretty close just before his overseas deployment. We kind of left things up in the air until he got back. And…"

"He got back," I finished.

She nodded. "Yesterday. So, we kind of picked things up where we left off. You know how it is."

I did indeed. Many times. "Was it his idea? This change in strategy?"

"Well, no. We discussed it last night after… I mean, we both thought it was best. The most rational thing to do. Also, the safest, least risky all the way around, for my career, for my safety, for *yours*."

"I see." I sipped coffee but didn't taste it. My disappointment must have shown.

"Look, you're a great guy. I like you a lot. It's just that…"

I held up my hand, stopping her. "I know. It's not me, it's you."

"I'm really sorry, Randy." She took my hand; I shook her off.

"Hey, no problem. Like you said, just stress relief." I slid my cup forward. "I gotta run. My best to you and what's his name."

"Brad."

The name brought forth the image of a jar-head haircut atop broad shoulders and bulging neck muscles. "Sounds about right." I spoke softly; I'm not sure she heard. I pushed my chair away and grabbed a five from my wallet.

"I've got it," she said, smiling that smile pretty women bestow on pathetic losers.

"No," I answered. "I invited you. You can leave Wanda something if you like." I tossed her car keys next to the five.

Nancy handed me my keys and I felt her skin for the last time.

"See you later?" she said, giving me her just-friends smile.

"Sure," I answered, knowing that would never be the case.

~ * ~

I drove home; tried to watch TV. I took a nap; the kind of long naps depressed people took, not so much rest as oblivion, zoning out. I looked in the fridge for something to eat but didn't have much of an appetite. I felt alone, really alone, for the first time since Cheryl's death. I also felt lost, not just because of the death of a budding romance, but loss of purpose. I'd been reluctant to take part in Operation Peeper, but now I'd miss it. It gave my life some meaning, something more than being the head of the smallest county department in Ohio's smallest county.

I stared at the blank TV screen and contemplated life. I didn't really have any hobbies besides jazz and driving; this had never seemed odd to me before, but now it did. I didn't have any close friends, mostly associates and colleagues, people you nodded to, not ones you told your troubles to. The only friend of that type I'd had lately was Nancy, which was maybe why I was so disappointed by a failed romance that was apparently doomed from the start. The next closest was probably Nolan, the guy I was trying to put away—The Peeper.

But was he Mr. Peeper? The more I thought about it, the less probable it seemed. Serial killers weren't usually functional alcoholics that hit constantly on office staff and bar maids. Were they? Weren't most serial killers solitary guys like Dahmer, or family men leading a double life like BTK? What about Bundy, my mind replied? He was an outgoing, charming, up-and-comer with a dark side. And what about Gacy, the killer clown? He was solitary, but also outgoing; performed for kid's parties. Maybe there was no one, single pattern.

Nolan fit the bill in other regards; Officer Nancy certainly thought so. He knew computers, was probably able to hack personal info. He'd found most of the victims from social media, knew Cheryl and Weider-White through me. He was solitary, at least appeared to be when he wasn't at work or hitting the bars. I never heard him mention a girlfriend, ex-wife, or even a date. No, that wasn't quite true. He had discussed dating. I dredged up something about that from talking with him somewhere, Bozo's I thought. Something about sage advice on how to score with women. Recall rose from the murky depths, his exact words floating to the top.

"It's okay to meet online, break the ice. But then what you want to do is talk to them. In person. Get a feel for how the land lays. Do your homework. Learn some things about her. Is she lonely? Where does she hang out, favorite restaurants, watering holes? Casually bump into her. Maybe buy her coffee or a drink. Ease into it, a little at a time."

None of it sounded sinister at the time, but now, remembering, it took on a creepy tone. Predatory. Tantamount to stalking. And then there were those childhood indiscretions. Window peeping. Banging his demented aunt, an aunt who'd been a busty blond. Weider-White, Cheryl, Shyreen; all attractive blondes. That sure sounded like a pattern.

I shook my head and rose to get a beer. I was no forensic psychologist who knew all this stuff. I wasn't even sure forensic psychologists really *knew* all this stuff. The only way to know for sure, was to catch him in the act. What Nancy and I had been trying to do. Now Nancy was out, convinced by hunky Brad to let the authorities handle it. Nancy was out. But did that mean I had to be? The thought hit home like a Louisville slugger.

Why couldn't I take over? After all, Nancy was still the bait, even if she no longer knew it. I was still the leg man, the tracker. Nolan was still the target, a target who didn't know my car on sight. This could work, I thought with a smile. OK, my stake-out skills were bad to start with, but I was learning. And if I took a nap during the day, I should be able to make it till the witching hour.

I smiled and put back the beer. I checked my watch. I had a half hour until quitting time. I'd head over and wait for Nolan. If he was still at work, I'd follow. If not, I'd head to Bozo's then his place. I had a plan. I had a purpose. And if it just so happened that I caught him? I wouldn't mind playing the hero—my fifteen minutes of fame. And Nancy might look favorably upon me; maybe decide that brains trumped brawn.

~ * ~

Luck was with me. I hit the municipal lot in record time and Nolan's junker was still in its grease-slicked section of asphalt. I drove past to make sure and then waited four rows back, near the exit, engine idling.

A few minutes later, I watched his lanky frame exit the building; three-thirty-five on the dot. Perhaps my running into him at Bozo's had done some good, at least as far as his putting in a full day. The old Honda coughed to life amid blue smoke, then rolled past me. I gave him time to hang a left onto the service road, then I followed.

Luck kept with me in the form of a pickup that pulled in between us, blocking my view of Nolan but his of me as well. He wouldn't notice the bulky Ford behind him as he turned onto Main Street, but I could still spot his smoke. As luck would have it, the pickup was going the same way, turning just ahead of me. I brought up the rear, pulling left of the pickup so I could keep track of the blue puffs marking the little Honda's passage.

I felt good, almost like a TV cop or maybe a private eye. I was tailing my subject without him knowing, staying a few cars back, just like Nancy had said. I thought of Nancy, how her body felt in my arms. How she took charge in bed. No doubt, hunky Brad wore the pants now, or took them off as the occasion warranted. It was clear that Brad had called an end to Operation Peeper. There had been no 'discussion', no matter what Nancy said. All of a sudden, I was out and the Bradster in, no doubt her fluttering heartstrings atwitter at bulging muscles and tales of martial heroism. Well, let's see what she thought when the headlines read 'County Official nabs Peeper killer!'. Yeah, old Walter Mitty was feeling good. It didn't last long.

Problems started when my Nancy daydream distracted me from seeing Nolan's turn signal come on. He was heading onto the freeway, the entrance-ramp just ahead.

"Shit," I muttered.

Traffic had picked up for the Midlothian rush, and I was still in the left lane, a line of cars preventing me from getting over. I tried to slow and wedge into the pack, but no way Jose. Cursing some flowery language, I signaled a left turn and entered the Midway strip-mall plaza. A few seconds later, I was pulling back onto Main, angling for a turn onto the freeway. What seemed an eternity passed before I'd merged onto the ramp. I just hoped I'd be able to spot Nolan, or at least follow his oil-smoke trail.

I rubbed sweat from my eyes as I squinted into the afternoon freeway traffic. At first, I looked at the vehicles immediately around me, but realized that was dumb. Nolan had at least a minute, maybe more, head start. I let my vision wander farther up the road but couldn't see jack. I said my new favorite word. "Shit."

A bit of panic crept my way as I turned on my left blinker and pressed the accelerator. Mercifully, the passing lane was clear. I pressed harder, watching the needle rise to seventy mph, then seventy-five. I needed to make up time, close with my quarry. My eyes strained for a hint of rusty brown or a puff of blue smoke. A wide space opened to my right, but I stayed in the passing lane, needle bobbing past eighty. All I need now, I thought, is a cop pulling me over for thirty over the limit. But I couldn't worry about that. I sped on, eyes searching, right foot heavy on the pedal.

Finally, as I passed a semi obstructing my vision, I saw something brown sending up puffs of smoke several cars ahead. I breathed a sigh and slowed, angling into the middle lane. The blue puffs slowed as well, then headed up the exit for Burkman Avenue. I angled further right and headed there myself. With a little luck, I could pick him up on Burkman. He'd never even know he was being followed. I was Sam Spade again.

The blue puffs turned to the right. I couldn't see more because a panel van was in the way. The van turned left just before the traffic light turned yellow. Cursing again, I gunned the motor of my Flex and spun a high-speed turn onto Burkman, my eyes searching, my nose following the telltale stink. I sped up to fifty, giving that hypothetical cop another thing to cite me for. I was close, any second now I'd spot Nolan's Honda, the source of the oily smell. "Yes," I shouted, as I passed a Prius and had a clear line of sight to the brown vehicle at the head of the oily cloud. "Shit."

I'd expected to see Nolan's Honda. Instead, I saw a beat-up Ford Ranger, brown with rust spots along the rocker panels. Looked to be from the early 2000s, and it was a diesel, hence the oily smoke. My disappointment changed to panic, which changed just as quickly to defeat. Nolan had a huge head-start now—an insurmountable lead. Dejected, I headed back the way I'd come. My one ray of hope was that Nolan hadn't been heading toward Nancy's; she lived in Yellow Springs, which was west, while Nolan had taken the freeway east. East wasn't the direction of Bozo's either; his apartment was reached most easily by surface streets. Wherever he was heading, it wasn't a usual haunt, at least not one I knew about.

I thought about going to his place to wait but decided to head to the freeway instead. I'd get back into the passing lane and hoof it for a few more miles, just on the off chance I could pick him up. I could always go to his apartment later, but even that seemed a waste of time. Needless to say, my originally buoyant mood had turned to buttermilk. I'd screwed up again, confirming at the very least my incompetence as a private eye. Maybe Nancy was right, let the authorities handle it. I chuckled in self-deprecation. Protecting Nancy was the whole reason for following Nolan in the first place, now I'd lost him, and she was no doubt safe in the arms of hunky Brad. The imagery made a knot rise in my gut, so I took a couple of cleansing breaths, punched some Winton Marcellus on the stereo, rolled the window down, and merged onto the e-way.

Chapter Twenty-four

I woke the next morning knowing two things. First, that a little man was running through my head with spiked shoes and a sledgehammer, and that he would soon be doing the same to my stomach. The second was that I drank too much the night before, this realization being predicated on the first. The rest was a bit hazy. I couldn't recall going to Bozo's, so I must have done the deed at home. I usually stick to beer, but when depressed I have been known to add a shot or two of bourbon. I recalled the pungent smell of Knob Creek. I also recalled the image of a lidless eye floating in the darkness, suggesting that the dream had returned after many nights of absence.

I managed to get my throbbing head into the bathroom for a quick pee and two extra-strength Tylenol. But before I could stumble back to bed, the doorbell rang. I waited, room tilting, head throbbing, to see if the purveyor of Girl Scout cookies or Jehovah witness pamphlets would go away, but after three rings I figured I better answer it. Donning a terry-cloth robe over my jockeys, I staggered down the stairs, that little man with the spiked shoes swinging his sledge with every footfall.

"Hold your horses." Raising my voice was my first mistake. Opening the door was my second.

"Yeah?"

"Hi, Doc. Mind if we come in?"

It took my foggy brain a moment to recognize Milt Garlicki in his rumpled splendor. Something grisly was again wedged into his toothy smile, causing that little man with the golf spikes to run to my stomach.

"Oh, hi Milt. Listen, it's not a very good time right now. Maybe later."

"Just need to ask you a few things. Won't take a minute." He brushed past me, followed by a blocky woman in a cheap pants suit who must have been his partner. "This is Detective Antonelli."

She smiled, scanning about the room. "I answer to Angie every time."

I closed the door, still not sure what was happening. "What can I do for you?"

"You can tell us what you were doing yesterday between eight and eleven," Angie said.

Now Milt gave the room the once over. "If you don't mind, Doc."

"*Last* night?" I asked.

Milt nodded. Angie held up a hand, still smiling. "Let's get the preliminaries out of the way first. Okay Milt?"

Milt nodded as Angie took a small card from her polyester pocket. "We're going to be questioning you about a capital crime, so I need to read you your rights."

The Miranda warning buzzed through my head, competing with mister spiked shoes for my attention. Angie finally stopped droning, and still smiling, asked, "You understand your rights?"

I looked at her, confusion stealing away my words.

"Doc?" Milt said. "Do you?"

"Um, yeah." I cleared my throat. "Yes."

"You want a lawyer?"

I thought about saying yes but thought maybe I should find out what this was all about first. "No, not yet."

Now Milt smiled. "Mind if we sit down?"

I pointed to the dining room table. Milt headed over.

"You wouldn't have any coffee made, would you?" Angie asked.

"Coffee? No, not yet."

"Mind if I make some? I could use a cup."

"As a matter of fact, so could I," I answered. "Let me show you where things are."

"Don't bother. I'll find it. You can answer Milt's questions while I make us a pot. Black okay?"

"Fine." She headed to the kitchen.

"Have a seat, Doc." Milt patted the back of a Queen Anne chair.

I sat obediently. "What's this all about, Milt?"

"Just need to know your whereabouts last night between eight and eleven."

"Um. I was home, I think."

"You think?"

"Well, things are kind of hazy. You see, I had a bad day, in fact, several of them."

"Yeah, sorry about your wife."

"Thank you. But I guess I had a drink. I guess I had more than one until time kind of slipped away on me."

"Time and memory?"

I smiled in reply.

"Was anyone with you? That is, can anyone corroborate you were home drinking?"

"Just the little man with the sledgehammer living in my head right now."

Milt chuckled. "That's good. I mean, did any neighbors stop over? Maybe a delivery man?"

"I don't…I don't think so."

Milt took a small recorder from his pocket and clicked it on. "You don't mind, do you?"

"No. I guess not."

"So, Doc." He recapped for the benefit of the recorder. "You understand your rights and have waived your right to counsel. And you say you were home alone drinking between eight and eleven last night. That no one else was with you and that no one stopped by. Is that right?"

I nodded.

Milt pointed to the recorder.

"Yes." I cleared my throat again, adding a bile-tainted burp to the kitty litter in my mouth.

"But you're not really sure, because you were drunk and have kind of forgotten. Right?"

"Um, yes, I guess so."

"Maybe we can jog your memory. Let's start with the last thing you *do* remember. What and when?"

He smiled patiently, the way a traffic cop smiles when giving you a ticket.

"Well, I was driving, I guess. At around four or so."

"Four in the afternoon?" I nodded. "Driving where?"

"I, I was on the freeway, headed east."

"Where were you going?"

I thought about telling him the whole thing. About Nolan. About my tailing him. About Nancy. But something stopped me.

"I was, ah, just driving. I do that sometimes when I'm stressed or sad or lonely. It's relaxing."

"Was anyone with you?"

"No."

"And how far did you drive?"

I grinned sheepishly. "I'm not sure." My stomach rumbled at the smell of ground roast. "That's when the hazy part starts."

"Take a guess. Ten miles. Twenty?"

"Probably more like ten…I think." I heard a clatter in the kitchen. "Need a hand?"

"No, I got it," yelled my new friend Angie.

"But you're not sure," Milt said.

"No. As I said." I mimed guzzling from a bottle.

"Were you drinking before your little drive?"

"No, I don't think…No."

Angie handed me a cup of coffee. It smelled great. As I was taking a sip, I saw she and Milt exchange looks as if he asked 'anything?' and she silently answered 'no'.

"This happen a lot, Doc? Getting drunk and passing out?"

"No," I said. "No, not a lot."

"But it has happened before, huh?"

"Listen." I cleared my throat a third time. "I've answered your questions. Haven't lawyered up as they say on TV. But now I need an answer. What's going on? Why are you questioning me?"

Milt nodded 'fair enough', but it was Angie who answered.

"Do you know a Nancy Nagel? Police Officer with Dayton PD?"

Both she and Milt were eyeing me the way a hawk eyes a rabbit. I thought about lying but knew that was stupid.

"Yes. What about her?"

"When was the last time you saw her?" Milt asked.

"Um, Yesterday. Around elevenish. For coffee. Why?"

Now it was Angie's turn. "Where did you meet her?"

I knew the way a tennis ball felt lobbed back and forth by two pros. "Northfield Diner."

"You ever meet her there before?" Milt asked.

"Yes. A couple of times."

"Waitress at the diner says more like half a dozen," Angie said.

I shrugged.

"Did you ever go to her house?" Milt asked.

"Yes. Once. A few days ago."

"How long were you there?"

"I ah, I don't recall."

"Neighbor said you stayed all night," Angie said.

"Well…"

"Were you sleeping with her, Doc?"

I looked at Milt, confused, head throbbing, not able to speak.

"Coroner said she'd slept with *somebody* recently."

"Coroner?"

"She was killed last night." Angie mimed cutting off her eyelid.

"Between eight and eleven, according to Doc Bowden," Milt said.

I think I said, "Um." That's all I could think to say. My stomach dropped. My heart fluttered. My face went numb. It seemed that my entire body was reacting in different ways that weren't helping my brain come to grips.

"But you weren't sleeping with her?" Angie asked.

"Well, um…" I finally dredged up something from left field. "Brad."

"Who?"

"I think she has a boyfriend. Brad somebody or other."

"Bradley Winston," Milt said. "We know about him. But there were other DNA traces as well."

"Matched your blood type," Angie said.

"What do you want to bet we'll get a DNA match as well?" Milt smiled that gotcha grin cops are known for. "Would you like to make that bet, Doc?"

The room seemed to take on an odd tilt. Or maybe my mind was tilting. "Well, I, ah, I mean, I…"

"You want to tell us about it?" Angie asked.

I hemmed, I hawed, I stammered, I grunted, I did everything but speak intelligently.

"What *do* you want, Doc?"

I cleared my throat a fourth time. This cleared my head as well.

"I think I want a lawyer."

~ * ~

"That's the whole of it, Stan. I swear."

My lawyer, Stanley Nuremberg, looked at his notes. We were back in the same little interrogation room, the room where I'd been questioned a week or so ago and where I'm sure I'd be questioned again, only this time with my lawyer present.

"Okay. Couple questions."

"Shoot."

"First, how much of this have you told the cops?"

"Well, I admitted to meeting Nancy at the diner several times. And I admitted to being at her house. But I didn't mention Nolan or my helping her surveille him."

"Did you admit to sleeping with her?"

"They already knew."

"But did you *admit* to it?"

I shook my head.

"Did you give them permission to search your kitchen?"

A lightbulb popped in my brain. "Is that what she was doing?"

"Did you *give* them permission?"

"Only to make coffee. Not to search."

He nodded. "Just one more question."

I waited. Stan looked me straight in the eye.

"What the hell did you think you were doing?"

"What?"

"You're a low-level bureaucrat for Christ's sake. You're no cop or private eye or James fucking Bond."

"Well, Nancy is. I mean was."

"Nagel was a Dayton police officer, not even a detective. A police officer on suspension I might add."

"Well, I just thought…"

"That it would be a good idea to tag along on her illicit, grief-driven, unauthorized undercover shenanigans?"

I grabbed Stan's hand in both of mine. I needed him to understand. "She made it sound *really* plausible. Like we had a chance of catching The Peeper. And besides, it was an opportunity, you know kind of a way…"

"To sleep with her?" He shook off my hands and slapped me; not hard, but not a love tap. "What's the matter with you? Your wife just died, was *murdered* in fact. And you're sleeping with some lady cop who had her sister murdered in the same way. And why didn't you consult Keith Bradshaw like I said?"

"Who?"

"The criminal lawyer I recommended. What am I doing here instead of him?"

My face still stung, more from his rebuke than his hand. "You said I was no longer a suspect."

"That was before your wife became a Peeper victim. And before you slept with Nancy Nagel just before *she* showed up dead." Stan shook his head. I cleared my throat, something that was becoming a habit.

"What happens now?"

"Now," Stan said, "the cops are going to try for a search warrant. They might not get it, given that they don't have much in the way of hard evidence. But from what you are telling me, they *will* get a DNA match. So, we better tell them about sleeping with Nagel."

"If you think that's best." I hoped I sounded contrite. I sure felt that way.

"And while you're at it, you better tell them about this Webster guy."

"About the stakeout?"

"About everything. Your suspicions. Her suspicions. They can go through her computer records. That should at least lend some credence to this whole dizzy affair."

"Do you think that will get me off the hook?"

"I think that will buy you time. Time to meet with Keith and figure out some kind of strategy. And it might keep you out of jail, at least for a while."

I reached for his hand, hesitated, then just patted his arm. "Thanks, Stan."

He shrugged and got up.

"Stan?" I called.

He turned.

"You know I had nothing to do with any of this. With the killings I mean."

"Sure," he said. But I got the impression that maybe he didn't mean it.

Chapter Twenty-five

I poured myself two fingers of bourbon. I needed it. It had been a long couple of days. I'd spent most of the first one being grilled by Garlicki and Antonelli, Midlothian's dynamic detective duo. I'd told them about sleeping with Nancy, at this point there was no reason not to. I told them about Nolan, about my suspicions, about Nancy's, as Stan advised, about everything. The only thing I didn't tell them about was Nolan's juvenile records; divulging that made me uneasy. Stan finally won my release without bond (so far), but I was told I'd be watched; I hadn't seen anyone watching yet, but what did that mean? I had an appointment in the morning with Keith Bradshaw, criminal attorney par excellence. Yep, I needed a drink.

By the time I'd poured my second drink, I was thinking about Nancy. By the third, I was crying, sobs hitching from my chest, tears and snot streaming down my face. I cried for Nancy, beautiful Nancy who would never become Detective Nagel. I cried for Cheryl; she hadn't been a great wife (nor I a great husband), but she hadn't deserved this. I cried for Suzanne Weider-White, for poor sweet Shy, for Rochelle Kolodny who I'd never met, and for Cash whom I had. I cried the river that had eluded me for so long. It didn't help much.

I finally got myself under control and stoppered the bottle; my hangover was gone but not forgotten. As I blew into my hanky, the phone rang.

I cleared my throat. "Hello?"

"Why hello there, asshole."

The voice sounded familiar, but out of context. It also sounded drunk. "Who is this?"

"Who is this? You don't know? You hack my computer, you stakeout my house, then you try to frame me with the cops and you don't know?"

"Nolan?"

"You win a cookie, *Randy*." It was probably the first time he hadn't addressed me as Doc, chief, or skipper. "Or should I say fink? Or maybe rat bastard."

I thought briefly about how much he must have been drinking, knowing how much it took to get him high.

"I'm sorry, Nolan. I had to tell what I knew."

"You *had* to? You sniveling weasel. What did they use, thumbscrews or bamboo slivers?"

"Listen, Nolan, you're drunk. And you shouldn't be calling here. For all I know, my line is tapped."

"Shut up and listen, ass wipe." I tried to imagine us having a working relationship now. I couldn't do it. "I called for just two reasons. One, to let you know that I knew it was you hacked my computer; knew it all along. You didn't fool me for a second."

"Fine. What's the other reason?"

"I wanted to tell you that this isn't over. From now on, you better watch yourself. You better look over your fucking shoulder. You better watch your rearview mirror. You're not the only one can do detective work. And you're not the only one can fuck with somebody."

"Fine, Nolan. I'm going to hang up now."

"You think you're gonna fuck me? No. I'm gonna fuck *you*! I'll clean your fucking clock. I'll make you wish you've fuckin' never been fucking born."

I suspect he went on for a couple more minutes, but I had already hung up. I downed the remainder of my third drink in one fiery jolt, then poured another. I thought about calling the cops, but what was I going to say? Besides, he'd vented his spleen. With any luck, he'd be passed out within the hour.

Yep. Rough couple of days.

~ * ~

I moved slowly, cautiously, carefully; body slipping imperceptibly forward. More swimming through syrup than walking. The surrounding air was dark and oppressive. Like being inside a cavern, or maybe a tomb.

I couldn't see much, but I could hear. A faint, barely audible sound of scratching. It might have been wind-blown branches creaking against the house, but something deep inside me said it was more ominous, a sound associated with dungeons or premature burial. I followed the sound.

I moved down a short corridor that was foreign yet familiar. I knew that one end of it held a bathroom, the other a living room. I slipped slowly toward the living room, my movements drawn and sluggish, as in a nightmare.

Something waited in the living room, the source of both the ominous scraping and the phosphorescent glow that had begun to seep vaguely into the hallway. The glow intensified as I edged forward, growing from barely noticeable to undeniable. It was just ahead at the end of the hallway but seemed to take forever to reach. Finally, after many beats of my hammering heart, I was there. I turned the corner.

The room was more familiar than the hallway, but still hidden behind a repressed memory, a thin veil of forgetfulness ready to pop like a soap bubble. I recognized the windows sending thin slivers of light through partly open blinds, their narrow bars coating a coffee table, rug, and a sofa; the parachute kind that was easy to sink into but hard to rise from. The light coated everything except the source of the glow, a glow that devoured the light, absorbed the light, transformed it to an eerie, pulsing radiance. My eyes didn't want to look, but they did, seeking out the glow the way a tongue seeks out a chipped tooth.

The source of the unearthly glow sat upon the end of the sofa; one curvy leg casually crossed. I recognized the blond hair trailing lazily over the back cushion, as if prearranged. I recognized the face, its mouth stretched into a rictal grin. Mostly I recognized the eyes, the bright blues staring unblinkingly at me. A scream formed in my throat but would not come. Then, as if on cue, the scratching sound resumed, the sound that had led me here but that had evidently stopped as I approached.

The source of the scratching became obvious. Not quite fingernails on a blackboard, but fingernails none the less; trim, feminine nails that trailed along a framed Kermit the frog photo. My mind realized the picture was out of place, but only as an abstract memory coming from a dusty corner. The rest of my mind was occupied with the sight of a topless Nancy Nagel, one breast changed into a raw wound, an unearthly glow pulsing from the lidless eyes. The scream that wouldn't come found its voice.

~ * ~

I bolted upright in bed, sweat drenching my hair, shorts, and tee shirt. I thought I heard an echo of my scream play faintly across the spare bedroom (my room), but it may have followed me from sleep, a residual fragment of the nightmare. The scratching may have followed me as well, but I didn't think so. Something told me that the dream subsumed the scratching, the way dreams incorporated the reality of a buzzing alarm or need to urinate into dream-world props. I listened to the darkness. No scratching. No nothing. Just my own ragged breaths and slowing heartbeat. Yet still I sat there listening, unconvinced. After many breaths and many more heartbeats, I decided I might as well investigate, no more sleep tonight.

Donning the same robe I'd worn to greet Milt and Angie, I moved into the hall—no scratching. No scratching at the head of the stairs. No scratching at the foot of the stairs. No scratching at the front door. No scratching in the kitchen. I turned on the kitchen lights, their fluorescent glow playing off the stainless-steel appliances but revealing nothing unusual.

I was about to turn off the lights when I saw it, an out of place glint. I approached it slowly, as I'd approached the glow in the dream. There, at the base of the backdoor sat a shiny strip of metal. What Nancy had called a shim. I picked it up, almost cutting my finger on the jagged edge, the same finger I'd almost cut on the shim that Nancy had found. I dropped the metal back down to the floor, then checked the back door. Faint scrape marks were plain along the inside edge. They looked fresh.

"Nolan?" I asked the empty kitchen.

~ * ~

The door was open, but I knocked anyway. I didn't know what the protocol was with the county detectives, but better to be safe than guilty.

"Yeah?"

I popped my head into the doorway, smiling but trying not to look sheepish.

"Why hello there, Doc. Come on in."

Milt Garlicki was sitting at his institutional metal desk covered with institutional forms and files. His checked jacket was hung over the back of the institutional office chair on which he perched, the old metal creaking under the strain. The sleeves of his greying white shirt were rolled past the elbows, pit stains visible higher up. His smile wasn't sheepish, more like the wolf in Red Riding Hood.

"Wasn't expecting you today, Doc. You were lucky to catch me. Busy busy." He flashed his teeth. Today's food wedge looked like lettuce. "Have a seat."

He pointed and I sat in the same institutional metal chair I'd sat in before, the same stain gracing its worn fabric.

His smile broadened. "Here to confess?"

I smiled back, again trying not to look as sheepish as I felt.

"No. I want to, well, I guess I want to report something."

He leaned back, hands behind head, pit stains in full flower.

"Something like what?"

"I'm not sure. I guess something like someone trying to break into my house."

He leaned forward again. "When was this?"

"Not sure. Maybe two or so this morning."

"Not sure? Was it two, or wasn't it?"

"Well, you see. I was, I had just woken up from a night…from a dream and I thought I heard something. A scratching noise of some kind."

The arched wooly worms over his eyes told me to continue.

"So, I got up and looked around."

"Could you still hear the scratching?"

"No. That's why I'm not sure exactly when it happened. When somebody tried to break in, that is, because it may have been part of the dream. I mean, I may have heard it in my sleep and incorporated it into the dream. You know how that is."

His smirk said he didn't. "So, you heard scratches. Why do you think someone tried to break in?"

"Because I found this." I pulled the plastic baggy containing the shim sliver out of my chinos and dropped it on his desk. Milt picked it up.

"Where did you find this?"

"By the back door. I checked the inside edge of the door and thought it looked scratched up."

He held the baggy to the light.

"It's a shim, isn't it? A burglary tool."

Milt turned it over in his hand, still holding it to the light. "You hear that on a Cops rerun?"

"No. It was something Na… No. Is it?"

He shrugged and tossed the baggy on his desk. "Did you handle it? Without the baggy that is?"

Now I really felt sheepish. "Yes."

He looked as if he'd expected that answer. "And this door, the back one with the scratches. They were new? The scratches that is? Not there before?"

"Well, I don't know. I think so. How often do you look at your backdoor jamb?"

Another shrug. "Is that it? Anything else?" His eyebrows arched again.

"I think I may know who tried to break in."

His wolf smile was back. "Well don't keep me in suspense."

I cleared my throat. "Nolan Webster."

"Because you think he's The Peeper, so naturally he tried to break in."

"No. Well, yes. But he called me."

Now Milt seemed interested. "When?"

"Yesterday, about seven or so in the evening."

"And?"

"He was angry. And, well, drunk."

"What did he say?"

"That he knew all along that I'd hacked his computer. Although I don't think he did."

"Anything else?"

"He called me a few names. Said I ratted on him."

"Did he threaten you?"

"Yes. Said he was going to, um, fuck with me. That I should watch my back."

Milt seemed satisfied. "I'll have a talk with him. Okay if I come over to your place, check out that back door, maybe look around?"

I smiled. I was no detective, but I was starting to recognize detective tricks. "If you've got a search warrant."

Milt raised his hands as if taking offense. "Just trying to help. You're the one making the complaint."

"Of course. But I don't think Mr. Bradshaw would approve of any informal snooping."

"*Keith* Bradshaw?"

I was glad Milt had heard of his reputation. "Yes. He's my attorney now."

"He's a good one." Just like that, we were back to cop and plaintiff. "Anything else before I have my talk with Mr. Webster?"

He obviously expected me to say no. Instead, I said, "I think he followed me."

"When?"

"On my way here. There was a brown car that moved when I moved, turned when I turned; everyplace but into the municipal lot."

"It was Webster?"

"Can't say for sure. He hung well back, couldn't get a positive ID on his car."

Milt was losing patience. "Are you sure you haven't been watching too many spy movies?"

"Maybe. But I kept thinking about another thing Nolan said on the phone. That I wasn't the only one who can play detective."

"Fine. I'll ask him about that too. Meanwhile, I don't want to catch *you* playing detective anymore. That's my side of the street."

"You can have it."

~ * ~

I thought about going into the office, which was just across the parking lot, but didn't want to run into Nolan. I saw no brown Honda in the parking lot but didn't want to take any chances after yesterday. So, I called instead.

"Hello. Midlothian County Pesticide Control Program."

"Hi Jan. It's me."

"Hi Randy. How are you?"

"Fine. Fine. Is Nolan around?"

"Un uh. He phoned in sick yesterday. Hasn't shown since."

No doubt hung over, I thought. Though not so hung over he couldn't follow the boss.

"Wanna leave a message?"

"No. That's okay. I'm in the neighborhood so I'm going to stop by for a bit. Catch up on some paperwork."

"On a Friday afternoon? A county employee?"

"Yeah. I know. But you know what they say about work taking your mind off things."

"I guess." Her tone held some of that sympathy she hid behind sarcasm and sexual titillation. "How are you holding up?"

"Okay. And you?"

She sighed. "Better."

"Great. I'll see you in a bit. Bye."

I killed the phone then spent the next little while listening to WJZZ. When I thought I waited long enough to not appear to have called from the parking lot, I walked over.

The building held a tomb-like quality, my footsteps startlingly loud on the old linoleum. Unionized county rats could legally jump ship one Friday out of every two, but that didn't stop the rest from using the numerous sick days and personal days they gave us (in lieu of money) to hurry up the weekend. 'Skeleton crew' was the phrase that came to mind, a skinny one at that.

Jan's attire fit right in with my thinking. She was dressed in black bicycle shorts and a black skeleton tee, the white bones tented over her pert bosom. No doubt mourning attire for her late friend, Rochelle.

"Hi Randy." She got up and gave me a hug. I could feel the nipple ring through my shirt, so mourning must not include a black bra. "Get you some coffee?"

I looked at the empty carafe in the Mr. Coffee.

"I'll have to get it from the break room," she added, "but I don't mind."

I tried not to look shocked, even though Jan never poured me coffee, let alone walked over to the breakroom for it.

"Why, thank you." I reached into my pocket for a quarter for the communal coffee can.

"I got it," she smiled. "One sugar?"

"Please."

"Wonders never cease," I mumbled as I fired up my computer.

I immediately checked the complaint log, noting that seven were outstanding, one from more than a week ago. While I was away, Nolan definitely did play, or at least he didn't work. I briefly considered leaving to inspect overdue complaints but felt my Friday PM efforts were best spent tackling the two-hundred-seventy-four emails that had accumulated during my absence. I was well into the tenth one when Jan brought my coffee. My thoughts that she was being extra-nice to me because of Cheryl were soon disabused.

"Thanks."

"Is it alright?"

I sipped. "Yes. Fine. Thanks."

"My pleasure." She beamed. No sarcastic, long-suffering smirk; an actual toothy smile. "It's easy to be nice to the world's greatest boss."

I put down my cup and leaned back. "Let me guess. You have a hot date tonight and want to leave early."

Her face lit with amazement. "See what I mean? Not only are you a pleasure to work with and for, but you're also clairvoyant."

"It's in the job description." I held my hands as if framing a job posting. "Wanted. Manager for the smallest program in the state's smallest county. Must be great to work for and with, clairvoyant, and a pushover."

She bent down and kissed my cheek. "They found their man."

"When do you want to leave?"

"Two-thirty?"

I looked at the clock. It was two-fifteen. I shook my head and waved. "Go."

"Don't work too late," she called as her cute ass rounded my partition. "See you Monday." echoed down the hall.

~ * ~

I hadn't realized I'd been missing going to work. Or maybe I just missed something to occupy my time now that Operation Peeper was defunct. I shuddered thinking that Nancy was also defunct. How had it happened? She was a savvy cop and a champion martial artist. Had Nolan slipped up on her while she slept? Where was hunky Brad? I sighed and rubbed my eyes. There were no tears, but there was grief, if not for Cheryl, then for poor Nancy. No more Brad. No more dreams of being supercop. No more bagels.

I spied a streak of orange outside my window and smiled. Kirby was looking fit and frisky as a kitten. He crouched low, then pounced, sending a grasshopper skyward. I'd have to thank Jan for feeding him.

By email ninety-six, I heard the night janitor vacuuming the hallway. I thought about telling him to skip my office, but I was right in the middle of answering a technical question from Ron's Pest Control, and there wasn't much chance that Deshawn the janitor would disturb me. Jan once dumped a pile of paper punch-holes next to her desk, betting me that it would take Deshawn at least three days to vacuum them up. On the fourth day, I paid my dollar and swept them up myself.

Around email one-sixty, a memo from Irv about the governor's new directive on politically correct speech in the workplace, I headed to the breakroom for more coffee. While nuking the dregs, I rinsed the fifty-cup urn and set it by the sink. Thus fortified, I headed back to my office to tackle email one-sixty-one.

By email two-hundred, sunlight had faded away; the view of my tree was now lit by klieg lights from the parking lot. I had actual hope of finishing before the witching hour, then locking up and heading home.

The building was officially deserted, not even a security guard; such humans having been replaced by burglar alarms long before I took up government service. I never realized how quiet the old place got at night, the click of my keys pealing like Big Ben. I thought briefly of the old Gilbert and Sullivan ode to a fly's footfall. I paused to sip some coffee and wonder if the alarm had been set, or if I was supposed to do that when I locked up. That's when I heard it.

It wasn't so much a distinct noise, as a break in the pattern of the silence. A less-quietness, as if someone were sneaking down the hallway, pausing now and then. Regularly irregular, as we used to say about some heart arrhythmias back in vet school. I listened, cup almost to my lips. Was I hearing this, or was it my imagination; autosuggestion from thinking about the emptiness of the building and uncertain alarm status? Suddenly I thought of Nolan, a problem that had been blessedly absent from my mind for the past seven hours devoted to work. I listened more intently but could no longer make out anything over and above the pounding in my chest and ears.

"Is anyone there?" I yelled. Only my echo answered.

I thought of other things to shout, such as, 'I've called the police,' or 'I've got a gun.' All seemed senseless. I looked about for something to use as a weapon. I thought of that first night (only night) at Nancy's, trying to bludgeon a martial arts champion with her own trophy. There were no trophies here. Nothing but a few pictures, notices on the bulletin board, some push pins, my laptop, and the empty coffee carafe. No, I thought, that's not exactly true. Carefully, I slid open my desk drawer, the old metal screeching God's own howl, and withdrew the letter opener that I rarely used. It wasn't very sharp, but otherwise it functioned as a knife.

I thought briefly of yelling, 'I've got a knife,' but instead rose slowly. Like the Gilbert and Sullivan pirates, I moved with cat-like tread around the partition. I still couldn't hear much beyond the pounding in my ears, but something, something deep inside, said that the noise in the hallway had resumed, the regularly irregular break in the silence. I edged slowly past Jan's desk, heading for the open hallway door. I swung the letter opener forward, flinching when it clanked against something, then flinching more at the sound of broken crockery. I looked down at a smashed mug; 'I heart nasty boys' written on the largest piece. I almost laughed aloud, but then the noise was back, louder, now regularly regular. Someone was running, the footsteps dopplering away instead of toward me.

I dashed forward and peeked into the hall. Nothing. Perhaps the echo of footsteps, but that could have been my imagination. What I didn't think was my imagination was the soft whooshing sound that a pneumatic door-closer makes upon exiting. I stood for a moment, letting my heartbeat settle and my eyes adjust to the dim light of the hallway. Then, with my trusty letter opener held before me, I glanced both ways before heading down the empty hall.

I started walking slowly and carefully, but after a few steps, I was running. I don't know why I ran, or what I planned to do when I reached the building exit. After what seemed more than the thirty-seven paces I knew it to be, I slid to a stop in front of Peggy's empty desk. I peered outside. Nothing but the glare of the kliegs. Nobody running. No car pulling away. I sighed in relief, then wiped my shaking hand across my sweat-slicked brow. I stopped, hand on forehead, at a new sound—the screech of tires turning sharply, the low-throaty cough of an engine in need of a tune-up.

Chapter Twenty-six

"Can I help you, sir?" the guy behind the counter asked. He was a young man with an old-man's scraggly beard. His tee shirt sported the don't-tread-on-me flag and snake. The nametag on his shirt said his name was Trey.

"Yes, um, Trey. I'm looking for some basic self-defense. I mean, a firearm for basic self-defense."

"You came to the right place." His smile was reassuring; it said he was proud to help someone who 'got it'. The weapons of various kinds lined up behind him were dark and threatening, and a little intimidating.

I waved at the counter and the row of guns. "I'm a newbie to all this. Can you help me sort it out?"

"Sure." Now he was in his element, instructing a rookie in the basics of what he loved. I suspect Trey also saw a hot prospect and a sales commission. "Tell me a little about your situation."

I hadn't thought much about it myself; I was here more from reaction than from reason. I thought about explaining, about telling this guy how my wife was killed by The Peeper and that now I feared I was being stalked as well. I imagined the look on his face, a mixture of 'Oh Jesus,' and condescension. I thought about these things for maybe a second and a half, before settling on a verbal equivalent of Occam's razor—the simplest explanation being the best.

"I'd like something for self-defense. Something easy. Something I can handle without much practice."

He nodded. "Nothing complicated."

I smiled. "Exactly."

"Personal defense at home?"

"Yes. Or in the car."

Trey grimaced. "In the car, or on your person, requires a CCW permit."

"CCW?"

"Concealed carry. That's not a problem, but you gotta take a class, fill out a form, get background checked and fingerprinted." He smiled again. "And pay the county a fee of course."

I smiled back. "Of course. Can't forget that."

He winked. I thought briefly of Nolan. "If it's just for home defense, can't go wrong with one of these." He pulled a shotgun off the rack, worked the pump and handed it to me."

"Is it loaded?"

He laughed and waved to the rack "None of them are. But when it is, it'll get the job done. Jacking the pump alone scares the shit out of burglars."

I hefted it and was intimidated by the cold weight of metal. "It's kind of big and heavy."

"Yeah, but not complicated. Just rack the pump and pull the trigger. Go ahead. Try it. All the way forward, all the way back."

I obeyed instructions, but the trigger wouldn't move. "Am I doing something wrong?"

"Forgot about the safety," he said, snapping his fingers. "Keeps it from going bang until you need it to go bang. That little thingy up top—just push it forward.

I did. The trigger clicked.

"What do you think?"

"I think I'd probably forget to push it forward when I needed it to go bang. Then I'd drop it on my foot." He grinned. "What about one of those?" I pointed to a pistol in the case. "What's that?"

"Glock nineteen," he said, placing the shotgun back in the rack. "Same as this." He pointed to the pistol on his right hip. "Good weapon. Light. Fifteen rounds of nine-millimeter hollow points." He squinted, reminding me of the old granny from the Lil Abner comics. "You ever fire a semi-automatic pistol?"

"Um, no. I've never fired anything."

He laughed again. "Okay. I'm zeroing in on what you need." He reached into the case and pulled out an oddly shaped black revolver. With a flick of his thumb and wrist, he opened the cylinder, revealing five dark holes that looked evil even when empty. "Smith Bodyguard. Just pull the trigger and you get five sure shots."

"No, what you call it, safety?"

He shook his head. "Trigger is the safety. Got to pull it like you mean it." He snapped the cylinder closed and handed it to me. "Here. Give her a try."

I took it gingerly but liked it almost at once. It was light. It didn't look complicated. It felt good in my hand, the slightly rough texture of the handle, the smoothness of the trigger. Trey noticed my smile.

"Falling in love?"

"Can I pull the trigger a few times?"

"Sure. It's not loaded."

I tightened my grip, then almost dropped the pistol as a red light flashed across the counter. "What the..."

Trey laughed. "Laser sighting. Little red dot beams out when you grip it ready for business."

I pointed across the counter and the red light danced among the arranged long guns. "And that's where the bullet goes?"

"Yup. Just place the red dot on what you wanna shoot. Even at night. Couldn't be simpler."

"Does it have much of a, what do you call it?" I jerked my hand back as if shooting.

"Recoil? A bit, but it's controllable. Not a magnum. Just takes thirty-eights. Or you can use plus P; extra power but more kick."

I hefted it in my hand. I danced the laser across the room. I pulled the trigger. If it had tires, I would have kicked them.

"I'll take it."

Trey winked. "Just need to fill out a little paperwork first." He grabbed a form from behind the counter.

"How long is the, ah, waiting period." I'd heard that on Law and Order.

"Oh?" He squinted into the distance. "About fifteen minutes." He chuckled at my surprise. "This ain't New York or Caleefornia. Just an electronic background check and pay your money. Course, like I said, more complicated if you want to carry it." He slid the form and a pen over to me. "Just fill in the top, answer the questions, then sign on the next page. No abbreviations. Oh, and I'll need a driver's license for the instacheck."

I dug the license from my wallet. "What if you put it in your pocket or the car without the, what you call it, carry license?"

"The cops take it away and slap you with a fourth-degree felony." He winked again. "*If* they catch you."

I nodded. "I'll need some bullets too."

"For practice or protection?"

"Um, protection, I guess."

Trey reached behind him and plunked a box on the glass. "Soft-head hollow points. Mushroom open when they hit." He splayed his fingers and popped his lips. "Does more damage and prevents it from going through the wall to the neighbor's house."

"And that will stop somebody, you know, attacking you?"

"If it don't…then you got real trouble."

Chapter Twenty-seven

Pain lanced through my finger. "Damn it!" A small bleb of blood slicked my fingertip, which I wiped on my tee shirt. I pried open the cardboard lid, dodging a staple that popped free and flew onto the floor. I managed to poke myself again picking it up.

"Son of a bitch!"

I may have told you that I'm not very mechanical. I may not have told you that I'm also a bit of a klutz. I again wiped my finger on my tee as the doorbell rang. I stared at the offending digit, which had already stopped bleeding. The bell rang again.

"Hold your horses. I'm coming."

I clicked open the door. Milt Garlicki and his partner Angie stood before me. They were dressed much as before—frumpy, out-of-fashion, business attire.

"Hey, Doc. Cut yourself shaving?" He pointed at the blood smears on my tee.

"Trouble opening a box."

"Mind if we come in?"

"Um, okay. I guess. What brings you by on Saturday evening?" I tried a friendly smile. "Don't you guys get a day off?"

"Peeper keeps us hopping," Angie said.

"Oh my God. Was there another one?" I asked.

"Not unless you know something we don't," Milt replied. "Mind if we ask you a few questions?"

"I'm not sure. Shouldn't my lawyer be present?"

"You can call him if you want to," Angie said. "But they usually charge double for the weekend."

"Yeah. Real high-priced sharks," Milt said. Then he shook his head. "Actually, this isn't about The Peeper. It's another matter."

"Mind if I use your bathroom?" Angie asked.

I almost said yes, then caught the sly look she gave Milt. "Yes, I do mind. I'd prefer you didn't make coffee either."

She smiled. "I guess I can hold it."

"What you been up to the last couple of days, Doc?"

"I thought you said this wasn't about The Peeper."

"It's not," Milt said. "It's about your friend, Carter McCall."

"Cash? What about him?"

"He showed up dead behind a Walmart in Northfield," Angie said. "Head bashed in."

"Oh my God. When?"

"This morning," Milt said. "Homeless guy stumbled onto him. That diner you met Nagel, that was Northfield, wasn't it?"

"So? Lots of things are in Northfield."

He shrugged. "Body was kind of messed up, animals got at it. But preliminary forensics based on decomposition suggest he may have been killed within the last seventy-two hours."

"Mind telling us what you were doing between noon Wednesday and this morning?" Angie asked.

Keith Bradshaw would probably say 'yes I do mind', but I wanted to answer because I could detail my whereabouts for a change—more or less.

"Not at all. I spent most of Wednesday with you and Stan Nuremberg. Then I went home. I don't remember going out again until Friday. I met with Keith Bradshaw at ten, then stopped by to see you to complain about Nolan; he called Thursday night, remember?" Milt nodded. "After that, I went into the office to catch up on paperwork."

I didn't mention the noise, or lack of it, I'd heard at the municipal building.

"I left about ten, got home by ten thirty. Neighbor was walking his Scottie, Benjamin Martin from down the street."

"The dog's name is Benjamin Martin?" Angie asked with a smirk.

"Ha, Ha," I said. "I waved to my *neighbor* Ben, he waved back. You can ask him. Today, I did some shopping. I stopped by a..."

I was going to lie here but decided I better not.

"I stopped by a gun shop. Then I went to Computer City and picked up that." I pointed to the box.

"Safe-at-home security system," Angie read from the box. "Those things easy to set up?"

"Supposed to be," I replied. "Or I'm in trouble."

"What gun shop did you stop at, and why?" Milt asked.

I cleared my throat, which had suddenly gone dry. "I don't remember the name. It was on Main and Sixth, or maybe Fifth."

Milt pulled a pad from his breast pocket. "You stopped at The Armory, Main and Fifth, between nine-fifteen and ten-oh-six." He smiled at my surprise. "We've had you under surveillance since early Thursday."

"If you already knew, then why the hell did you ask?" I was getting angry, but not angry enough to call for Bradshaw—not yet.

"Just wanted to see if you'd lie to us," Milt said.

"You wouldn't, would you?" Angie asked.

"Listen. I don't think I should say anything else without my lawyer."

"What'd you buy at the gun shop, Doc?" Milt asked.

"A gun of course. Anything illegal about that?"

They both shrugged.

"I have a right to keep and bear arms, don't I?"

More shrugs. "How come you suddenly wanted a gun? Still worried about Mr. Webster?" Milt raised his eyebrows.

"That's my business. And I think that's the end of this conversation."

"What are you getting hot about, Dr. Corlane?" Angie smiled. "We're just asking questions."

"And I'm done giving answers. Unless we call my lawyer. Should I give Bradshaw a ring?"

"That won't be necessary," Milt said, putting away his notebook. "There's a few missing hours Wednesday, but Bowden thinks time since death was more like forty-eight than seventy-two hours, so I guess we're good."

"Fine. Can I get back to setting up my security system?"

Milt waved. Angie said, "Thanks for your time, Dr. Corlane. Have a good weekend." She smiled again, as if that made it okay.

"Oh, Doc. One more thing," Milt said.

I thought of Detective Columbo from TV but answered anyway.

"Yes."

"Speaking of your pal Webster, we checked up on him."

"And?"

"Couldn't find him. Car was gone. Apartment locked. Neighbors haven't seen him in a couple of days."

"Did you check Bozo's?" I asked with a smirk.

"We did," Angie said. "They haven't seen him either."

"You were probably the last person to talk with him," Milt said. "That was Thursday night, as I recall."

"So?"

"But you haven't seen him or spoken to him since?" Angie asked.

"No," I snapped. That was technically not a lie. And I was getting hot enough to be rude. "Now, please leave unless we call Bradshaw."

Milt held up his hands in surrender. "See you around, Doc." Angie only smiled.

I closed the door and locked it, noting that my hands were shaking. I walked into the kitchen and poured myself a bourbon, wondering if Nolan had made me his full-time hobby.

"Yep, rough couple of days."

~ * ~

A lidless, crimson eye stared at me in the darkness. I sat up with a start before I realized I was looking at the light of the ever-vigilant smoke alarm on the ceiling; a government-mandated fixture in every bedroom, including the guest room, my room. My breathing slowed, but my heart kept racing, mind fixed on the imagery that carried over from my nightmare.

For most people, dreams fade away even before they can evaluate them. But I think I told you that I tend to recall details for a lot of dreams, usually nightmares. It's been a curse as long as I can remember. So it was now, my mind's eye replacing the red eye on the ceiling with images of staring eyes. Female eyes that belonged to Cheryl, Nancy, Suzanne, Rochelle, the woman in the ditch (I couldn't remember her name), my mother (odd that she should be there). The eyes kept changing colors, shapes, ages, but they were strangely the same; one composite lidless eye staring, accusing. Why would they be accusing me? I knew immediately. Nolan. They expected me to do something about Nolan. But what could I do? I'd told the police. *Yes,* said the unblinking eyes, *but not everything.* My efforts at detective work had failed. *But had you really tried?* I pondered these questions, these accusations, sitting up in bed staring at the smoke alarm, listening to the night wind.

That's when I heard it. That strange change in the quiet. The same regular irregularity that I'd heard at the office, if I *had* heard it at the office. But deep inside I knew I'd heard it then. And I was sure I was hearing it now. Not quite a noise, more a sensation of movement, stealth, creeping; not outside, but inside. This is ridiculous, I thought. It's just autosuggestion. I'd set my new safe-at-home before I went to bed. At least, I thought I had. Memories from the night before were a bit fuzzy, as was my head, as was my mouth; no doubt courtesy of that fourth bourbon. Still, I thought I recalled clicking the switch and seeing 'system armed' LEDed across the plastic. I could even recall the disarmament code—2244, an easy one to remember. The alarm should have warned me of an intruder. Why hadn't it? Because maybe you didn't set it, my mind answered. But I remembered, I replied. I shook my head.

"Not going to go in a circle on this."

My own whisper sounded loud in the stillness. But not quite stillness. There was that strange change in the quiet. That almost but not quite noise.

I slipped my legs quietly outside the covers and sat on the edge of the bed. My bare feet found the floor, its chill sending a shiver up my spine. I started to stand but remembered something. Feeling along the bedside table, my hand met cold, hard steel. I gripped the Bodyguard pistol, its red laser light dancing across the closet door. Thus armed, I stood quietly and went into the hall, cursing myself for not including a flashlight among my bedside tools.

The noise that wasn't a noise may have stopped, or my mind may have simply stopped dwelling on it. Regardless, I heard nothing as I found the steps in the darkness and headed down. I squeezed nervously on the pistol's rubber grip, sending dancing red light ahead of me like a beacon. Loosening my grip, the light went out and I descended silently.

The foyer was empty. The living room was empty. There was no sound, regularly irregular or otherwise. I shuffled slowly, carefully to the front door and turned on the light.

The sudden flare blinded me, my hands instinctively flying to my face, the pistol's hard metal raising a painful welt on my forehead. I forced my gun hand away and, using the other hand to shield my eyes, scanned the room. Nothing. No sign anyone had been there, not even a lingering, telltale odor from Milt Garlicki's BO.

Lowering the revolver, I walked over to the command unit of the security system, its white and red box just where I'd left it on the table. I tripped over no wires as I passed. Wires were passé, a fugitive from my childhood. Nowadays all was wireless. The sensors I'd adhered to either side of the door jamb fed wirelessly into the command unit, which fed wireless into the window sensors I'd attached around the first-floor glass.

I looked down at the unit. 'System Armed' stood out plainly through the plastic. But two other things caught my eye. Next to 'Armed' was the word 'Silent.' I recalled the two modes, the silent one emitted no klaxon blare when triggered, just a quiet alert to the police, if one paid the thirty-three-fifty per month to have the cops linked into one's safe-at-home system, which I had not. The other thing I noted was that the 'Silent' was flashing. That meant the alarm had been triggered. Someone had entered after I had turned it on.

I scanned the room again, jerking the Bodyguard around the perimeter, its red light dancing off pictures, wallboard, and ceramic tile. Nothing. How could that be? I thought I knew. My fuzzy brain remembered putting the alarm in silent mode to test it, not wanting the blare to wake the neighborhood. What I didn't remember was whether I'd reset the system before going to bed. I looked for a timestamp that might say when the alarm had triggered, but then recalled that was only on the higher-priced models. Of good, better, best, I had chosen good, saving myself twenty dollars but robbing my peace of mind.

"Penny wise, pound foolish," I muttered. Another of Dolores Corlane's pet phrases. I tried to ignore the chill winds on memory lane and reached down to click the switch from silent to audible. Then I checked the door lock. It was unlocked, so I turned the deadbolt. Satisfied, I gave the area another scan, turned off the light, and went to bed. If I dreamt again, it was one I didn't remember.

~ * ~

I spent a restless Sunday, starting with a minor hangover and ending with major insomnia. When I did sleep, the dream crept up again. More staring eyes. More accusations. Around four, I resolved to do something about it, first thing tomorrow. This made me feel better and I nodded off till seven.

After a hurried breakfast of dry toast and coffee, I grabbed keys and headed toward the front door. It was almost eight, which should get me to the municipal building around half past. If I was still too early, I'd wait for Milt, or I'd talk to Angie, or I'd leave a message. I wouldn't put it off. This time, I wouldn't hold anything back.

As I opened the door, I almost walked into Milt Garlicki standing on my stoop, finger raised to press the bell.

"Jesus, Milt. You almost gave me a heart attack."

He chuckled. "Sorry, Doc. Didn't mean to startle you. May I come in?"

I started to mention Bradshaw, but I shouldn't need him. I'd resolved to spill the rest of what I knew, and this was my chance.

"No. Come on in. I was just coming down to talk to *you*."

"Great minds, as they say. Why don't I go first?"

I nodded and pointed to a living room chair.

"I've got good news. *Just* got it in fact and wanted you to be the first to know?"

"I'm listening." I wondered if good news for him meant bad news for me.

"What you told us initially wasn't enough to do more than ask around about Webster. But his threats against you gave us cause for a search warrant. Angie and I served that Friday.

"Friday?"

"Yep. Before we talked to you." He waved off my mounting anger. "Don't get your jockeys in a knot. There was nothing you needed to know, not then anyway."

"So, did you find any, what do they call them, souvenirs? I hear that these Ted Bundy types tend to keep little, well mementos."

Milt chuckled again. "That's what they say in the movies. But no, we didn't find souvenirs. But we did find a hairbrush with quite a few ripped out follicles."

"So, Nolan was losing his hair?"

"No, Nolan was shedding DNA. Hair follicles have DNA. Sent a sample to the lab and asked them to rush it. Results came back this morning."

"And?"

"And they match the semen we took from Mrs. Corl…one of the victims."

I silently thanked him for his tact.

"So that means?" I couldn't imagine it was true, even though it was what I'd thought all along. Somehow, I'd hoped I'd be wrong about Nolan.

"That means, Mr. Webster moves to the top of The Peeper list."

"So, I'm off the hook?"

"Let's say you're out of the pail and back in the water. You haven't slipped the hook yet, but right now we've got bigger fish to chase. So, don't go anywhere." His crocodile smile was back. Even so, I think I smiled in return.

"Sure Milt." I suddenly felt generous. "Want some coffee? There's half a pot."

He shook his head and tapped his belly. "Indigestion." Then he switched gears. "What's *your* news?"

"Mine?"

"What were you coming down to tell me?"

"Oh." I suddenly wondered if I still needed to. But those lidless eyes started talking again. "Yeah. I um, I guess I didn't tell you everything before. About Nolan that is."

He raised his brows.

"I told you that Nancy, I mean Officer Nagel, had suspicions about him because of his social media ties to the victims. Me too for that matter. But there was more than just that."

"Such as?"

I told him the rest, about Nolan's peeping-Tom arrests and his dalliance with his aunt. I told him about Nancy unmasking sealed records. About the resemblance between Nolan's aunt and the peeper victims. I don't know why I hadn't spilled it before to Milt or to Stan. I guess I didn't want to get Nancy in trouble, to taint her memory. But now it felt good to get it off my chest.

At first Milt just listened. Then he took out his pad and pen. Finally, he said, "This was in Cincinnati?"

"*Outside* Cinci," I replied. "I'm not sure where exactly."

Milt jotted notes. "We can dig that up." He closed his pad. "Thanks for telling me this, Doc. We might have stumbled on it anyway, but thanks." He stood up and smiled. Not the crocodile smile, the friendly Polack smile. "Always good to get this kind of background on a serial. Ties up the ends as to motivation and pattern."

"Nothing will happen to Nancy, will it? I mean, no one is going to smear her name or anything? She was just trying to do what's right, by opening those sealed records, and I'd hate to think her parents would be hurt."

"Don't worry, Doc." He winked. I thought of Nolan and shivered.

Milt walked toward the door. Then he turned to me, concern on his face. "We're going to pull the surveillance off you and get to work finding Mr. Webster. His name's gonna be a household word throughout the cop universe." He paused. "You'll need to watch out for yourself. He's threatened you once, already. *Now*?" I didn't answer, so he continued. "Want me to post a cop outside nights?"

"Thanks Milt. I don't think that'll be necessary."

"You sure? Maybe just some drive bys?"

I shook my head. "I have my security system. And I have my…" I almost mentioned the pistol. "I'll be fine." I smiled. "Don't want to put the taxpayers to the expense."

But there was more to it than that. After being in police crosshairs for a week, I was looking forward to a little privacy again. And I had a feeling that maybe Nolan had left town. Got while the getting was good. Still, a small voice asked, if that's so, who showed up at the municipal building Friday? Who broke in Saturday night? Who was following you? "No one," I mumbled.

"How's that, Doc?"

"Nothing. Just cursing my own foolishness."

He shrugged and headed toward the door. "Let me know if you change your mind about the drive bys."

I said I would, but I knew I wouldn't.

~ * ~

I sat in Irv's office as he leaned back in his chair and looked at the ceiling.

"That's my plan. At least for now," I said.

"Seems like a lot of work, Randy." Irv chuckled. "For a county employee, anyway."

"Well, we're way behind on inspections, at least ten outstanding, a couple going back a week or more. So, I'll just have to nose it to the grindstone until we get replacements for Cash and Nolan."

Irv shook his head. "Jesus Petes. Cash gets killed, and now Nolan. Are the cops sure?"

"I don't know if they're ever *sure*, until they catch the guy at least. But that's their thinking, according to Garlicki."

"He would know. So, what now?"

"Now, I'll spend half the day doing inspections, starting with the oldest first, the other half paperwork."

"A one-man PCP, huh?"

I returned his grin. "I guess, for now. And don't forget, I have Jan."

"Right. You have Jan."

~ * ~

"Hey there, Randy-oh."

Jan hadn't been at her desk when I went down to see Irv, so this was my first time seeing her since Friday. I was surprised to say the least, shocked to say more. As I've mentioned, my admin always dressed on the slutty side, more with a naughty, goth flair than a brazen, flashy one. But today, she was in a zip-front tee shirt with the zipper all the way down, a push-up bra forcing her size B's into C+ fill for the gap. White booty shorts showed plenty of leg, while open-toe heels pushed her five-feet-two to five-five. But most surprising of all, she was now blond.

I guess my mouth hung open because she asked, "What do you think?"

At first, I couldn't answer, then I said, "This is new for you, isn't it?"

She laughed and spun around. "You like it?" I just continued to stare. "I was in a rut; thought I'd try a little change."

"Little?"

She planted a kiss on my cheek. "You're cute when you blush."

I managed to clear my throat. "I'm guessing the hot date from Friday prefers blonds."

Jan giggled. "Doesn't everyone?" She grabbed a sticky note from her desk. "That inspection scheduled for ten asked for one o'clock instead."

I stared at the note, waiting for the heat to leave my cheeks. I could feel Jan grinning at my embarrassment. "Okay. I, I guess I'll head south to that dog-poisoning complaint in Rutledge, then grab some lunch before the one o'clock."

"Yuck. Why would someone poison a dog?"

I grabbed my jacket from the rack. "Typically, they don't. People who hate their neighbors just think they do. But they all have to be checked out." I'd regained my composure and managed a fatherly smile. "Any recommendations for lunch?"

"Nolan tells me that Bozo's make's a good burger." Her grin changed to concern. "Where is he anyway? On vacation? Or do you think he split for good?"

I didn't tell her what I and now Irv knew; she'd soon learn it through jungle telegraph. "We shall see."

~ * ~

Spunky Cartwright had not been poisoned by the neighbor but by the chicken bones in the trash bag he'd ripped open. Still, I took a sample of the vomitus just to make sure; I'd ask the lab to check for rodenticide and organophosphates. A missing road sign made me late getting to Carlisle Way, where Mrs. Macklemore had another poisoning complaint, this one a pet rosebush rather than a golden retriever. I accepted a courtesy cup of bad coffee and listened to a forty-minute harangue on the evils of Yard-B-Beautiful Lawncare and Landscape, before investigating the aforementioned rosebush. Chemical damage was obvious, and I clipped a few branches for glyphosate residue. Each lab sample would set the county back five-hundred bucks, but the public must be served.

It was almost four when I got back to the office to do a couple of hours of paperwork. Jan had left, which was a relief. I'd grown accustomed to her outfits and sultry escapades through the years, but something about that blond hair and pushup bra really got to me.

"Too much of The Peeper, no doubt," I told the empty room. I silently thanked God Nolan wasn't around to see her.

The two hours became three. The sound of Deshawn's vacuum came and left the hall without ever entering my office. I emptied then rinsed the coffee urn in the breakroom. Then I stared out my window at my parking lot, watching the sinking sun turn my little maple tree to gold. No Kirby today. I jotted 'buy more cat chow" on a sticky note. I stuck the yellow square to the side of my keyboard, and I heard a noise in the hall. At least I thought I heard a noise in the hall, which was ridiculous as I was the only one in the building and the alarm was set (I'd checked). Still, I didn't fancy being here again after dark, so I redonned my sport jacket, locked my office, and left. On the way home, I treated myself to a little jazz and freewheeling.

~ * ~

It was after ten when I got home. Normally, I would have gone straight to bed, but I didn't feel tired. I felt energized, euphoric, edgy. I chalked it up to work; I hadn't worked that hard, that productively, since first starting at the PCP. It was like a drug, some amphetamine driving me on but leaving me unsatisfied. I knew I wouldn't be sleeping for a while, so I decided to grab a beer (no need to chance another bourbon hangover) and catch up on social media.

I skimmed the accumulated messages, which were various forms of junk: conspiracy videos, emojis, and cartoons. They vanished into the trash bin one by one, then twos and threes. I next scanned people I was following, enjoying some familiar faces (and bodies). A few posts made me chuckle, which was a glorious sound after days of stress. I skipped over political messages with various forms of 'Why do you think?' and 'Isn't it odd that?' epistles on the evils of government, big pharma, vaccines, or big oil. Things hadn't changed while I'd been offline, which was strangely reassuring. It was like following a soap opera; take a couple weeks off and you only had to watch one Friday to catch up.

I hearted Shannon T for her beaming smile and ample cleavage. A laughing emoji went to Marjee Brasnapper for her joke about the difference between a politician and a snake (hint: both are cold blooded, but only one has a heart). I saluted Karl K for his son's graduation from basic training at Pendleton. It was like old times.

Then I saw a post from Krazy Kat that made me both smile and drool (at least mentally). She was posed next to a cartoon pic of Betty Boop. They were both in matching red swimsuits, beads of water (or sweat) glistening on bare skin, cleavage featured in the foreground, a round bottom in the background. I considered a witty comeback, hesitated at the thought of going down that road again, then said what the hell. I was entitled. Things were looking up. It was therapeutic after my long ordeal. What could it hurt?

I pondered several witticisms, before settling on 'Boob Boob be dube!' This should appeal to old-school comics like me, and apparently like Krazy Kat. But I didn't want to duplicate the work of some other old-school wag (great minds, as Milt opined), so I first scanned the other responses to gauge the trends. As I'd hoped, these ran in the general direction of 'hubba hubba' and 'you are beautiful'. Only one even attempted wit, and this was on the gutter side.

'I'd love to lick you like a vanilla cone with cherries on top.'

I shook my head, noting that this reply had met with a scowly-faced emoji from Krazy Kat. I started to type, sure of getting a heart or maybe even a kissy face in reply, then noted something. The crude comment had apparently come from me. I blinked in amazement; fingers posed over the keys. This was not possible. Yet, there it was—my name and photo next to this gutter comment.

I stared at the comment, my name, my photo. I looked away, hoping it would disappear, but when I looked again, I was still the author. I remembered back in high school, when I'd thought I'd uncovered the big prize in a match-three scratch-off ticket. I looked at the card, looked away, then returned, always seeing three ten-thousand matches. It wasn't until the fourth or fifth glance that one of the zeros fell off, leaving me with two ten-thousands and a one-thousand. I hoped for that again, but the zero never dropped. Always, there were three: my name, my face, my crude comment. The answer finally hit me like a cold slap from an angry Krazy Kat.

"Nolan."

You're probably wondering why it took me so long to jump to the obvious conclusion. Nolan was still out there. Nolan was still messing with me.

The date stamp on the comment was Sunday evening. Roughly one day ago. But was that comment the only one he'd posted? I quickly scanned the feed, looking for salacious or risqué photos and cartoons. The first bikini shot had nothing but the usual hoots and whistles from the construction site. Likewise, a funny 'pardon this post' photo. But when I got to a lovely young thing named Trina Tease, resplendent in her American-flag halter, my name was there again, three comments down.

'My flagpole would definitely salute you.'

This sounded vaguely like me, but I had never written it. I had also not written the following line, nor would I ever.

'Then it'd fuck you!'

Trina's reply was predictable. 'Bye, asshole.'

My friend list had been reduced by one. More than one; many more. Since I'd been away, I was down a couple dozen names, no doubt offended ladies.

I checked the date stamp on the Trina comment—Wednesday about midnight. I'd been sleeping then. I shook my head and grabbed the mouse, intent on seeing if there was any more. But I stopped myself. What was the point? I could delete them, but not the impression they made. I couldn't even explain them. I tried to remind myself that these were only social media friends, strangers really, almost phantoms. But the damage to my reputation was real. And as bad as the damage was, I knew there'd be more. Nolan wasn't done with me yet. I could feel it in my gut, in my brain, in my soul. He would continue. Despite the police manhunt, he would continue. He wasn't done with me. So, I couldn't be done with him.

I left my computer and went down to pour myself a bourbon. Probably not the best idea, but at least it would help me sleep.

~ * ~

I woke to familiar sensations: a mild but unmistakable hangover and images of lidless eyes. The dream followed me again, more victims accusing me of dropping the ball. I needed to do something to end the nightmare. Then I remembered my last session on social media and knew I had another reason to stop Nolan as well. I took two Tylenol with a glass of juice and made a resolution. I would do something, something more than helping Garlicki.

Heading to the office, I had no clear idea of what that something was. But then a pathway presented itself.

Jan wasn't at her desk when I checked the complaint log. Two from last week weren't far from each other; one alleging lawn damage (no doubt under-watering mistaken for chemical burn) and an alleged poisoning of an old dog with neurologic signs (I thought of the vet-school gag about a twelve-year-old boxer named brain tumor). I should be able to finish handling these two complaints by lunch, a lunch I would spend at Bozo's, just four miles from the old-dog complaint.

The police were no doubt staking out Nolan's apartment. But he was spooked, unlikely to return there. I seemed to know this on an instinctual level, the same way I knew he wasn't done messing with me. I also knew something else, knew it on the same instinctual level. He wouldn't stop going to Bozo's any more than he would stop messing with me or stop killing. He'd gone there frequently when we were tailing him. Nancy had suggested it was a trigger for him, a way to psyche up as The Peeper. But I thought it was more. A trigger, yes, but also a relief valve. Something to calm the urges as well as feed them. A home away from home, human contact. Perhaps he needed that as much as he needed to kill. Perhaps he even used it to struggle against his inner Peeper, a form of misapplied self-medication. Yes, I was sure he'd be drawn to Bozo's. He might go there in disguise, but he would go. That was the key.

~ * ~

I didn't recognize the hostess, a short Asian gal with smooth skin and dark, almond eyes. But the waitress delivering my steak sandwich was Carly, the ebony lass who'd served Nolan and I last time I was there.

"Medium," she said with a trace of southern accent. "As I recall, that's how you like it."

I smiled. "You remember me?"

She dimpled one back. "Sure. You were here with Nolan a week or two ago."

"Good memory. Have you seen him lately? Nolan, that is?"

"No. Not in a few days." She frowned. "That's what I told the detective man who asked after him. Why do the cops want him, do you think?"

I shrugged. "Maybe unpaid parking tickets?"

Carly laughed and slapped my hand. "Silly."

"That's me. Dr. Silly. Maybe one of the other girls has seen him?"

She stared off in concentration, then smiled. "I can ask." She turned to a willowy redhead passing by with a pitcher of beer. "Hey, Rashon. You seen Nolan lately?"

"You mean the skinny guy with the ratty beard and roving hands?"

I caught Carly giving Rashon the high sign. "This is a *friend* of his. He's looking for him."

"Oh, sorry, sir. No. I haven't seen him in a week or more. Did you try one of the other restaurants?"

"Other restaurants?"

"Bozo's is a chain," Carly said. "Got stores in Middletown, Yellow Springs, Dayton, Columbus."

"I used to work at Yellow Springs," Rashon said. "Nolan showed up a couple of times."

"Probably when he was stalking Nancy," I mumbled.

"Pardon?"

"Oh, nothing. Thank you, Rashon."

Rashon smiled and left, showing me a backside that was definitely worthy of some roving.

"Will that be all," Carly asked, handing me my lunch tab.

"Yes," I said. "Thank you." She smiled and spun about—also handsworthy. I left a big tip.

~ * ~

I came back to the office and finished what paperwork I could. Jan evidently hadn't come in, leaving a voicemail that she had personal business to attend to. I never asked what 'personal business' it was, that wasn't my place as her boss. All of us had five PB days on our county calendar; one could use them as one wished, provided they did not interfere with essential operations. Given that no PCP operations were considered essential, this was never an issue.

At four-thirty I left to grab a beer and some dinner. You can probably guess my destination.

~ * ~

The navigator led me to a shopping mall in Yellow Springs. Bozo's wasn't hard to find—just follow the enormous clown pom poms. I took a quick drive around the half-full lot, but there was no beat-up, brown Honda. Nolan either wasn't here, or he'd traded in his wreck for a rent-a-wreck. To play it safe, I pulled on a ball cap and dark glasses, parked, and went inside.

The hostess was a bit leaner than the Midlothian girls, and my server, Marleen, was a bit beefier (farm stock, no doubt). As she went to fetch my beer, I scanned the bar. No Nolan. I leaned out of my booth for a better look but came up just as empty.

"Here you go, sir."

I accepted my draft and took a sip.

"Are you ready to order?"

"In a bit, I'm still deciding."

She smiled and turned away. I called her back.

"Perhaps you *can* help me though, Marleen. I'm looking for a friend. He's about thirty, thin, brown hair, scraggly beard." Her blank expression suggested no bells had been rung. "Usually wears old jeans?"

Marleen giggled. "That could be about anybody these days."

"Yes. But this guy might be a regular, or semi-regular. Comes in a lot. He, ah…" I tried to think of other Nolan characteristics. "Maybe calls you girls darlin. Calls the bartender skipper or boss? Winks a lot?"

Marleen shrugged and smiled. "I'm new, so I don't know the regulars yet."

"Sounds like Alonn," said a server passing by with a platter of dirty dishes. She was older, maybe early to mid-thirties. "Only without the beard."

"Alan? Ms…"

"Colleen. Sorry. I didn't mean to eavesdrop."

"That's quite alright, Colleen. His name is Alan?"

"Alonn. Like salon. That's how he pronounces it. He started coming in a couple weeks ago. Always chats up the girls." Her reference to 'girls' made her sound like a manager or supervisor, at least sometimes. "Wears dark glasses and the same old ball cap—PPC or something like that on the crown."

"PCP? Dark green?" A few years back, the county bought the inspectors green ball caps with PCP lettered in gold.

"Yeah, or brown. It's pretty dirty so hard to tell."

"Does he stay long when he comes in?"

She smiled. "Long enough to drink too much and become, well …"

"Less than respectful? Maybe handsy?"

Colleen tilted her head to the side and shrugged. "Occupational hazard."

"Have you seen him lately?"

She thought for a moment. "Yeah. Maybe couple of nights ago."

"Will he be here tonight, do you think?"

Colleen shrugged. "But you can probably catch him tomorrow. Everybody comes tomorrow."

I eyebrowed a question mark.

"Trivia night. Liv, our trivia gal, is kind of a favorite. I saw Alonn hitting on her last week."

"Let me guess," I said. "Blond? And um…" I cupped my hands amply over my chest.

Colleen tapped the tip of her nose.

"What time does trivia start?"

"Seven-forty-five on the dot," Colleen said. "Now, if you'll excuse me?" She turned away with her tray.

"Just one more question, if I may?"

Colleen turned back.

"Does he spell his name A-L-O-double-N?"

She shrugged. "Maybe. Maybe A-L-A-I-N. Maybe something else. Why?"

"Because A-L-O-N-N is an anagram of Nolan."

~ * ~

I was back at the office bright and early next morning. I was hoping to finish up my paperwork by noon and then tackle a couple more inspections, one just a few miles east of Clifton. I could have dinner in Yellow Springs and be at Bozo's in time for trivia night.

Part of me said I was on a wild-goose chase, just another failed stake out by inspector Clousea. Nolan wouldn't be there. This Alonn probably wasn't even Nolan. My description had been vague and there was no beard. As Marlene pointed out, skinny guys in beat-up jeans were as common as bird-crap on car hoods. Even ballcaps were a dime a dozen. But green caps with PCP on them? And beards could be shaved off. In fact, Nolan would know that the mind sees what it expects to see; if you're looking for a beard, you tend not to notice clean-shaven guys. Yes, it was a long shot, but deep down I knew it was a bet worth making.

Jan showed up about ten. I heard her talking in hushed tones to someone on the phone. When she hung up, I called over the partition.

"If your personal business was sex or female trouble, I don't need to know. Just hope you worked it out."

She popped her blond head into my office. It was still a shock seeing her new color, but it was more of a shock seeing her appearance. Instead of gothic makeup, bags hung beneath her eyes. Her hair was in disarray, and the jeans and sweatshirt she wore were in baggy contrast to her usual exotic attire.

"Somebody broke into my apartment. I woke up to him standing over my bed. Does that qualify as female trouble?"

"What? When?"

"Last night, just around one. I woke up with the feeling someone was watching me. At first, I figured it was Bryce, the guy I'm seeing."

"The one who likes blonds?"

"Not funny, Randy."

I dropped my smile fast.

"I opened my eyes, and there's this dark shape above me, just a big shadow between me and the window."

"What did you do?"

"What the fuck do you think I did? I screamed."

"What did *he* do?"

"He flinched, like he was the one who was surprised. Then he ducked into the hall and out the kitchen door."

"You must have scared him off."

"Yeah. Or Bryce did. I start screaming and Bryce shoots up in bed yelling, "What the fuck?" The perv starts running. I keep screaming. Bryce keeps saying "what the fuck?"." She shivered. "Almost gave me a heart attack."

"Must have been a burglar."

"Burglars don't watch you sleep, Randall. Pervs do that."

"What did you do then?"

"I turned on the light while Bryce put on his shorts and ran into the kitchen."

"And the guy was gone?"

"Yep. Bryce took a look around outside, but no sign of him."

"Did *you* get a good look at him?"

She shook her head. "I rent on a quiet country lane, Randy. Country quiet and country dark. All I saw was a darker shadow against the slightly lighter window."

"Did you call the cops?"

"I spent half the night with them and half of yesterday morning. Then Bryce stood guard while I *tried* to get some sleep." She yawned. "Maybe three-hours-worth."

"You okay? You wanna take the rest of the day off?"

She managed a wan smile. "I'm not going back to that empty house, even in daylight."

"No, I understand. But couldn't you stay with this Bryce guy?"

"I could, but he won't be home. He works elevator repair. Travels a lot."

"I hear that business has its…"

"Ups and downs. Right. Still not funny, Randy."

"Sorry. Can't you stay somewhere else? With a girlfriend or someone?"

"My friend Suzy is visiting her sister. And my other BFF was Rochelle." She paused for a moment, lips trembling, then simultaneously burst into tears and ran into my arms. She felt so small and helpless, more bones than flesh quivering inside the baggy shirt. "Oh, Randy. Do you think it was him? Was he standing over me?"

"Who? The Peeper?"

She pulled away, hands on my arms, frightened eyes staring into mine. "I dreamt last night he was standing over me, scissors snicking up and down." Her eyes flew wide. "If Bryce hadn't been there. If I was all alone on that quiet country lane?" Her face wedged back into my chest, tears and snot soaking my shirt. I let her cry, patting her back for support.

"There now. You're okay. Shhh."

"I can't go back there. I can't. I don't know if I can ever go back."

It felt good to hold her, to comfort her, to see that under that sarcastic façade was a real person, a frightened child in need of comfort and protection.

"Why don't you stay at my place?"

Her shudders slowed. Her sobbing seemed to ebb.

"No, I um, I couldn't. That wouldn't be right."

"Nonsense. I've got plenty of room. And it's a well-lit street with lots of nosy neighbors. I even have a burglar alarm. Nobody will bother you there."

"I don't know." She wasn't looking at me, but I could tell she liked the idea, just needed a little coaxing. "What would your nosy neighbors say?"

"Well, nothing to my face." She chuckled. "But from then on I'd be known as the neighborhood stud."

Jan chuckled again, then suddenly leaned up and kissed my cheek. "Thank you, sir."

I patted her back one more time. "You are welcome, madam."

She looked up, her red eyes saying thank you more than her words. "Just for a day or two. Until Bryce comes back."

I smiled and chucked her chin. "As long as you need."

Her eyes changed again, concern replacing gratitude. "Could I ask one more little favor?"

"You can even ask two."

"Would you drive back to my place with me so I can pick up some clothes and stuff?"

"I will if you want. But there's really no need. I've left Cheryl's things pretty much as they were. There are more soaps and creams than *you'll* ever need at your age. And her clothes may be a tad big on you, but I'm sure you can make something work."

"I don't know. Wear the clothes of a, well…"

"They're just clothes, Jan. That's all. Just clothes."

Her face took on the big-sister look she sometimes had when she talked to me, the look of the worldly wise lecturing the shrinking violet.

"You really didn't love her, did you?"

I didn't need to ask who *her* was, or even think much about it.

"Maybe in the beginning. Not for a long time."

She kissed my cheek again.

I know what you're thinking, but you're wrong. I admit that my willingness to help Nancy and have her stay over was tinged with an amorous ulterior motive, a motive that was ultimately crushed by first military muscle then Peeper perversion. But Jan was a different matter. It wasn't just the age difference between us or the generation gap that wasn't there with Nancy. I felt protective of Jan, which I know sounds odd given her jaded experience and my naivety. But I knew fundamentally that her sarcasm and world-weary swagger hid a tragic flaw, a flaw common to most of her generation. They were adult children who felt they knew everything, were open to everything, but failed to understand the real risk of anything. They'd been protected all their lives and couldn't seem to understand that there were sharks in the water. Oh, they feared the politically correct perils of date rape, climate change, pollution, and income inequality, but these were existential fears, more hypothetical than real. Helicopter parents instructed them to run from strangers, but that was a hard lesson to grasp when mommy or daddy was always there to keep the strangers away. When confronted by the concrete reality of a dark alley at two AM or a drunken boyfriend driving eighty the wrong way on the freeway, they were lost, unable to cope, defenseless. So, yes, I felt protective of Jan; thought of her almost like a daughter. That was no doubt part of my embarrassment when she recounted amorous sexcapades, the way a father might feel seeing his little girl in the pages of Playboy.

Even so, I might have foregone the offer of a place to stay had her problem been a vindictive ex-lover or an apartment full of roaches. But it wasn't these things, it was The Peeper. The Peeper was different. The Peeper was personal. Deep down, I felt responsibility for The Peeper, a need to bring him to justice. He'd taken Cheryl, a woman I no longer loved, as well as Nancy, one I was growing to. He'd stalked me, and women died because I fell asleep stalking him. Yes, The Peeper was personal. I knew this man but had failed to stop him or at least alert the police about him until it was too late. So, Nancy had died. So, she and all the others haunted my dreams. I was determined not to add Jan to the sea of lidless eyes following me to daylight.

"You can leave your car here and drive home with me."

Thinking of The Peeper made me think of Nolan, or should I say Alonn. I had a date with him tonight at quarter of eight. I could postpone it until next week, the cops might even nab him in the meantime. But I couldn't take the chance that the delay would add another lidless eye to my nightmare.

"We'll get you set up, then I'll have to go out for a few hours. Will you be alright?"

"Heavy date?"

I chuckled. "Not exactly. More like business. But I'm afraid to leave you alone." I thought of asking her to come with me, but that would be way too hard to explain. And I didn't want her there for what I needed to do. I didn't want anybody there but Nolan.

She squeezed my hand. "Don't worry about it. You have the alarm system, right?"

I nodded.

"Nobody but us chickens will know I'm at your place, right?"

"Well, maybe the nosy neighbors."

Now she laughed. "I'll risk it."

Chapter Twenty-eight

By seven, I was parked outside Bozo's, Yellow Springs. I'd left the freshly showered Jan chatting with her mother on the phone. Watching her there, curled up in one of Cheryl's robes brought on a strange mix of emotions: nostalgia, attraction, guilt. Perhaps if I'd done more to stop Nolan, the latter would be missing. I resolved to do something now. I'd considered leaving Jan the Bodyguard pistol, just in case. Instead, I tucked the revolver into the console of my Ford. I had a feeling I'd need it, in fact, I planned on needing it.

The Bozo's lot filled quickly; Colleen was right, trivia night was popular. I watched patrons going in—mostly guys. None looked familiar. None wore green ball caps with gold lettering.

Around seven-thirty, a van pulled up out front. From my spot on the far left of a middle parking lane, I watched a long shapely leg emerge from the passenger side, followed by an amply filled Bozo tee-shirt and blond hair surrounding a stunningly pretty face. She held a notepad and a hard-bound book with scraps of paper and yellow sticky notes marking pages. No doubt this was Liv. With her calling the tune, I could see why trivia night was so busy.

Liv leaned in to give the driver a kiss then waved him away amid a honking horn. A guy ran from the parking lot to her side. The guy grabbed her books (I thought of a schoolboy carrying his girl's things) and she laughed while wiping a strand of blond curl from her face. The two entered the bar.

I couldn't see much of her helper from my vantage point, he faced me only for a second, but I could tell he was thin, medium height, and clean shaven. I could also tell he wore faded jeans, dark glasses, and a green cap with gold letters. I couldn't see what the letters spelled, but in my mind, I saw PCP. I looked back at the car the guy had left; a navy-blue Tempo with the faded and chipped paintjob typical of a rent-a wreck.

~ * ~

Donned in my own sunglasses and cap, I skirted the perimeter of the bar. The trivia-night atmosphere was different than the lunchtime one. The shades were drawn, and the lights were low, forcing me to peek over my glasses to navigate. A small stage was set up to one side, a spotlight on Liv as she shuffled through her books. I didn't see Nolan but was careful to check each area thoroughly before edging into it. I didn't want to stumble on him unawares. Even if I was having trouble identifying him, he might not have difficulty identifying me, disguise or no.

As I stopped to scope out the bar, a waitress asked if I wanted anything. I ordered a bottle of beer and stayed by an outside window where some light filtered in. I could see most of the guys at the bar, none wore green ballcaps. My beer arrived and I gave her a five, getting a pretty smile when I told her to keep the buck change. I considered asking her if Alonn was around, but she might say his name or point, blowing my cover.

I'd just decided to move to a new spot in the room when Liv's voice came through the speakers. More correctly, it slid through the speakers, almost a husky purr not unlike the sound of silk drawn over beard stubble. Yes indeed, I could see why trivia night was popular.

Liv Roundtree introduced herself and explained the rules. Anyone could play, just ask a server for a contest form and pencil. Just then, a guy ran up to give her something; he'd been sitting at a front table with his back to me, but now I could see him. It was the guy from the parking lot, shades, green cap, and clean-shaven face. I still couldn't make out the ballcap lettering, but once again, I didn't think I needed to.

My server asked if I wanted another beer or a contest form before the trivia started, and I waved her off with a smile. I wasn't planning on staying for the contest. I had what I'd come for.

~ * ~

Night descended over the parking lot, although the kliegs made it almost as bright as day. Around nine, a guy and gal left, leaving a spot in the front with a better view of the blue Tempo. I considered moving, but stayed put; if I could see better, I could be seen better. From the edge of the lot, I was in a good position to follow the blue car when it left without having to navigate around other cars pulling out. I didn't want to confront Nolan in the lot, I wanted someplace more private.

Cool jazz from the speakers and warm breezes through the open window were lulling me to sleep. The second time I caught myself nodding off, I switched the radio to talk and drew the Bodyguard from the console, tucking the little black pistol into my waistband. The gun's hard edges weren't comfortable, but they were reassuring and would keep me awake.

"Not again," I whispered. "No sleeping tonight."

More people left around ten. Trivia must be over, the prizes awarded to the winners, maybe even a smile and a kiss from Liv. Nolan (Alonn) would no doubt be chatting her up, maybe offering a ride home. She'd politely refuse, all smiles, explaining about the guy in the van. Would that be enough to scare Nolan off, or would he follow her when she left? I thought the latter unlikely. He wouldn't want to run afoul of the van's owner, his perversion was reserved for helpless blonds on their own. Besides, he was Wonder Webmaster and could hack her home address anytime he wanted. I patted the gun at my waist.

"Not after tonight you can't, Mr. Peeper. It stops tonight."

Around eleven, the van pulled up in front of Bozo's and tooted its horn. A few moments later, Liv came out, looking a bit tired but just as lovely. Her legs seemed to take forever sliding into the shotgun seat, then the van pulled away. I watched the bar door, expecting Nolan to come out any minute. But nobody did. I made sure his blue Tempo was still there, then sat back to wait.

By eleven-fifteen, I'd been in the car for over three hours and had to pee; this had been the bane of my stake out efforts. I considered going into the bar to relieve myself but was afraid of running into Nolan or missing his departure whilst in the can. I considered pissing behind a tree but was afraid of getting caught inflagrante by the beams of curious headlights. I'd just decided to risk it anyway, when Alonn came out of the bar. I couldn't make out much but the cap and dark glasses, but I was sure it was him.

In the still night air, I heard the chirp of the door locks opening as he walked toward his car. When I saw his lights come on, I fired up the engine, put my Ford into drive, and hoped that my bladder wouldn't let me down.

~ * ~

The Tempo was easy to follow. While most of the other traffic headed for the highway, Nolan headed onto the less-travelled Dayton-Yellow-Springs Road. We quickly left the lights of the village, with only the moon, stars, and glowing headlights to cast eerie shadows on the surrounding farmland.

The local gentry no doubt went to bed with the sun and woke with the roosters, so there wasn't much traffic to hide my tail. Figuring that Nolan's spider senses would be heightened by running from the law, I dropped well back, trusting to the red glow of his taillights to keep me on trail. I sped up when the dots got smaller and slowed when they grew bigger. The road was straight, and the night was clear. All was well until the taillights suddenly vanished.

My foot instinctively hit the gas. Either Nolan had stopped, or he had turned. If it was stopped, I'd speed by him and pull over farther ahead to let him pass me.

"No, I won't," I said to the empty car. "I'll stop to see if he needs help. The good Samaritan bit. Then, before he can recognize me?"

I tapped the Bodyguard for reassurance. But instead, the feel of the cold lump of steel sent another cold lump into my gut. My heart raced, my breath increased to shallow sips of air, sweat drenched my face. Worst of all, my need to urinate tripled. It was the same when I had to speak in public, give a toast or make a speech.

"Liquid anxiety."

I chuckled at the old term, but nothing was funny. This was more than standing to address the chamber of commerce. This was life and death. I had trouble killing a mouse in a glue trap, now I was planning on killing a human being? I started to have serious doubts. Could I do it? Did I have the right to do it? Shouldn't I turn things over to the police? The latter question brought some comfort. I was hot on Nolan's trail. With luck, I could track him to his lair. Then, one anonymous call to the police and I'd have done my duty.

Would that be enough for the lidless eyes? I hoped it would, but whether it would or not, the new plan brought relief. I started to relax. The tightness in my chest eased. The hot sweat turned cold. I could breathe. I still needed to pee, but that would have to wait.

I searched the fields for some sign of the Tempo, a driveway, a light coming on in a farmhouse, anything. I looked so hard I sped through a stop sign. Slamming on the breaks, I screeched to a halt. My front wheels were well past the intersection of a three-way stop, with a road teeing off to the right. There was no sign marking the name of the road, and even if there had been, the streetlamp that was intended to illuminate the intersection was busted, probably target practice for some farm kid with a twenty-two.

Nolan must have turned down this nameless road. Unless I missed something, there was no other logical reason that the taillights disappeared. I backed up then turned right. I still had to pee, like a racehorse as they say, but that would wait until I ran Nolan to ground.

~ * ~

It had been dark on Dayton-Yellow-Springs Road, but at least I had the moon and stars. Even those were denied me on this narrower, nameless lane. Overhanging trees smothered off the sky. It was like being in a tunnel, or maybe a crypt. At least it was paved, allowing me to keep up my speed as I strained for signs of Nolan's car.

The road pitched down into a gentle valley, then crested the hill. Suddenly, there ahead of me, the glowing taillights reappeared. I had assumed that I was far behind, but now the taillights were dangerously close, less than one hundred yards. I punched the brakes, lengthening the distance. Once more we dipped into a valley. Once more the lights disappeared. Once more we crested a hill. But the lights were still gone.

I hit the brakes again and searched the darkness. Nothing. Creeping along at twenty MPH, I looked to the left but saw only trees. Then I looked right, and my headlights caught a mailbox leaning beside a dirt and gravel drive, dust motes swirling in the beams. The mailbox was old, with a once green paintjob now mostly rust red. I slowed further to read the numbers: '658'. There was no name.

I stopped and peered through the trees; nothing but night. I continued staring as I crept the car forward until a break in the foliage revealed a single light in the distance, its dingy yellow glow illuminating a dingy porch of a dingy farmhouse. A car was parked in front—a blue Tempo. Breathing a sigh of relief, I drove past the break in the trees and stopped, popping my Flex into park.

I sat for a moment, listening to the stillness, looking only at the cone of my headlights on the nameless track. Then I noticed my hands white knuckled at ten and two. It took some effort to loosen them; I actually had to will the fingers to let go of the wheel, peeling each back one by one. I pulled the palms to my chest, feeling their sweat soak through my sport shirt as my fingertips quivered like Saint Vitus dance. Finally, after a few moments that felt longer, the shakes ebbed. Fresh sweat soaked my palms as I wiped them across my glistening brow.

I had done it. I'd tracked Nolan to his lair, a nameless house on a nameless road. A perfect hideout for a serial killer. All I'd need to do was call the cops. I wouldn't even have to give my name. Just an anonymous tip that The Peeper was living at 658 on a nameless road just west of Yellow Springs and north of Dayton-YS Road. My whole body relaxed, which almost spelled disaster.

Once again, I found myself betrayed by a full bladder. Like that first night of surveillance, waiting for Nancy, I scrambled from the car. I ripped down my fly and pawed into my shorts. My stupid fingers refused to find their goal, making me certain that the dam would break while I frantically searched. Then, suddenly, I was free of the confines of my trousers, the night air cooling my fevered flesh, the smell of countryside replaced by the aroma of fresh pee.

I felt the night surround me, warm and humid, but mostly I felt relief. The stress of the chase seemed to flee with my urine stream. My strength seemed to flee as well, forcing me to lean against the car lest I drop to my knees. I closed my eyes as the stream continued, seeming to go on forever. I felt nothing but heavenly relief. I heard nothing but the steady splatter against the pavement. Then suddenly, the sweet contentment was replaced by terror.

"What you doin' there, *Boss*?"

The urine stream pinched off as quickly as it had started. My eyes flew wide, only to close tightly in the beam of a powerful flashlight. I instinctively turned away, my hands darting to stuff my manhood into my shorts.

"Not so fast, Boss. Face me, hands where I can see them."

The voice sounded serious, and I couldn't take a chance. I slowly turned, one raised hand shading my eyes from the glare of the flashlight.

"Why look at you. Dick out, pee-pee dribbling down your pants. Don't you know it's against the law to expose yourself in public?"

"I, um, do you mind if I cover up?"

"Yeah. I do. I like you better like this."

The beam moved from my face to my chest. I still couldn't make out my assailant, but I could see he held a long, dark tube in his other hand. I immediately thought of the shotguns you see in old movies; the two barreled variety farmers shoot at aliens and stagecoaches shoot at bandits. I kept my hands raised.

"What you following me for, Boss?"

"Um, I wasn't following you."

"Like hell. You been followin' me since I left the club. I watched your lights in the rear view, wondering. Then you turned down Snipe Road, and I *knew*. Nobody comes down Snipe this time of night. Nobody but me."

"No. I was just. I needed to, you know."

"What? Tap a kidney? So, you drive out here to the williwags to do it?"

"No. It's just that. I thought…"

"You thought what, Boss?"

The voice didn't sound familiar, except for the repeated use of the word 'boss.' Nolan had addressed me that way, not from respect but to point out that although I might be his boss, I had no real control over him. This voice was gruffer than I remembered, but that was no doubt an attempt to disguise his voice, just as the light in my eyes was supposed to hide his newly shaven face. Surely, he'd recognized me. Was it possible he wasn't sure what I was doing here? Or was he playing for time while he figured out how to dispose of me?

"You must be *Alonn*." I let a little sarcasm into my voice.

"How you know my name?"

"Listen, Alonn. Okay if I put down my hands and cover up here?"

He hesitated, then pointed the shotgun at me. "Yeah. Okay. Just no funny business."

The light was back in my eyes, blinding me as I stuffed into my pants.

"Okay. Now that you put the hoss back in the barn, you wanna answer my question?"

"You wanna get that light out of my eyes?'

The beam dropped to my chest, leaving residual yellow dots that still prevented me from seeing his face in the nighttime.

Alonn slouched a bit, shotgun pointed down, weight shifting to a back foot. I could sense him relaxing. And why not? I'd been subservient, non-threatening: I let him be in command. Maybe I could use that. I hadn't let on that I knew who he really was. Maybe I could use that too, surprise him with it.

"So, boss. Why were you following me from Bozo's?"

"You go there a lot, don't you, *boss*? Kind of a regular, huh?"

"What's it to you?"

"Got a real thing for that Liv, don't you?"

"So? She's pretty and funny and nice."

"And blond with big tits. Just your type, huh *Alonn*?"

"Sue me."

"Just like Shyreen."

"Who?"

"Had a thing for her too, didn't you?"

"I don't know no *Shy*-reen."

"Let's stop playing games, shall we, *Nolan*?"

"Who?"

Calling him by his real name had gained me a moment of surprise, but that would vanish just as quickly. I needed to act, and I needed to act now, before the shotgun came up with a boom.

My right hand flew to the grip of the Bodyguard, almost missing it. But I managed to hook the butt with my thumb, then bring the other fingers into play. The metal slid easily from my waistband, a feature of the snag-free design that Trey had praised, even while saying I wasn't supposed to carry it. The red eye of the laser stabbed the darkness as I leveled the pistol. The dot darted to the left of Nolan before I jerked it to his chest and watched it dance against his shirt. The shotgun barrel rose up, leveled at me. It was now or never; I either pull the trigger or end up as a plate of mashed Corlane. I fired.

I barely heard the shots, which were just muffled thumps, as if pounding a pillow with your fist. My other senses were not as addled. I winced at the flash repeatedly lighting the night. I smelled the musty aromas of woodland and fresh urine turn to an acrid stink of burnt powder.

The kick of the pistol was much as Trey had described it, substantial but tolerable. I don't remember how many shots I fired, but I ended up clicking empty over and over, so I guess it was five. I was pretty sure all hit him somewhere, because the red dot skittered but never left his silhouette.

As the red dot danced, so did Nolan, jerking as if Geppetto was tugging his strings. I remembered thinking that Pinocchio's nose grew when telling a lie, and wondering what part of Nolan would grow in hell? Odd what you recall during times of stress.

His flashlight flew one way, its broad beam arcing into the night, the shotgun flew the other. Both settled on either side of the crumpled body.

Slowly, shakily, I stumbled toward the prostrate form. The head was canted one way, the legs and arms splayed in all directions. Once again, I thought of a marionette losing the animation provided by its operator. Nolan Webster was no more. The Peeper's strings had been cut.

Looking down at the shadowy form that used to be a man (or maybe a monster), the world began to tilt. Lights flashed behind my eyes, much as the muzzle of the Bodyguard had flashed. I realized I wasn't breathing, probably hadn't taken a breath since before pulling the trigger. I stumbled toward the corpse (I knew he was dead by the lifeless way the body lay) then dropped my hands to my knees, taking in a ragged breath. I drew another breath; it was easier this time. The world swam back into focus. I stood erect, the dizziness passing with a wave of cold sweat, and walked more steadily.

I kicked the flashlight, its beam shifting to illuminate the prostrate body. The first thing I noticed was that the shotgun was not a shotgun; it was made of dark wood, with Rawlings burnt into the side. A cold, surreal feeling numbed my face. The world swam again as I dropped to my knees. The sour bitterness of bile filled my mouth, but only ended as a dry heave. I remember crawling toward my car, slinging the Bodyguard into the underbrush.

I must have made it in and driven off because I got home, somehow. I don't remember much about the trip, except for a warm breeze and the soothing sound of cool jazz. I don't remember going to bed, but I must have. I woke the next morning to the sound of my alarm clock tuned to WJZZ.

Chapter Twenty-nine

Dr. Horowitz shut off the digital recorder.

"That's quite a story, Dr. Corlane."

My frustration was growing. I'd gone to the police myself, told them about killing Nolan (or who I thought was Nolan). But still I'd spent days trying to explain to them. Now I was telling it all over again to their criminal psychologist. Who next? I half expected them to haul in one of those kindly old padres you see in prison movies; we'd play handball in the parking lot while I told him my life story. Even he wouldn't believe me. Even my attorney didn't seem to believe me. Meanwhile, The Peeper would keep killing, a thought that brought some succor; once he killed again, they'd know he wasn't me.

"But it's true. Every word. I had no idea he was carrying a baseball bat. With the light in my eyes and the darkness, it looked like a shotgun. I was just defending myself. Or at least I thought I was. Surely you can see that."

Horowitz smiled. It was, I thought, a patronizing smile. A smile reserved for small children asking juvenile questions. "Why again were you following this man?"

"I told you. I thought he was Nolan Webster. Who *is* wanted by the police for The Peeper slayings, you know?"

"But it wasn't Nolan Webster. It was one Alain Parker of 658 Snipe Road; the family place he'd occupied for his entire twenty-six years, the last three months by himself since his mother died."

"But I didn't know that!"

I was getting angry, which was probably a mistake that only made me look nuts. But I'm sure you can appreciate my frustration. I couldn't understand why this guy was being so dense.

"With all I've told you, can't you see that? I mean, the dark glasses, the ballcap with PCP on it, hanging out at Bozo's."

"Yes. I see. You thought all that was a disguise."

"Right. Anyone could have made the same mistake."

Horowitz looked at his notes.

"Possibly. But as I understand it, the dark glasses were to cover a lazy eye he had been self-conscious about since sixth grade." He flipped a page. "The ballcap lettering was not PCP but PTC, which stood for Premium Trucking Corporation; the place he worked." Now Horowitz looked at me, the patronizing smile back on his face. "And, although he flirted a good game, he'd started hanging out at Bozo's because he actually didn't have many dates."

"But I didn't know all that. I only saw him from a distance, and from a distance he looked like Nolan Webster in disguise."

Horowitz's face clouded in thought. "But couldn't you have asked about him? Gotten more information? Or even just walked up for a closer look?"

I sighed in frustration. How many times would I have to explain? I tried to keep my voice calm.

"I told you. I didn't want to spook him. He would have recognized me." I pointed an accusing finger. "Nolan had threatened me, you know. I was worried for my life."

"And that's why you bought the gun?"

"Yes."

Horowitz thought again. His eyes closed behind his wire-rimmed specks, his fat fingers folded over each other, strumming against the brown vest of his brown suit. I thought for the tenth time that he looked like a buddha statue, bald head and all.

"But why not turn the matter over to the police. Tell them you thought you knew where this Webster was and let them check it out?"

"Like I said, I was going to do that. Had *decided* to do that. But I had to pee. So, I pulled over and that's when this Alain jumped me."

"So, why carry the gun if you were going to leave it to the police?"

His smile was back. This time, it wasn't condescending or patronizing; it was accusatory. It made me feel guilty…and a bit ashamed. I looked at my hands.

"That was, ah, that was a mistake. When I started out that night, I was feeling, I don't know…"

"Feeling what?"

I shrugged. "Like I had to take matters into my own hands."

"An avenging angel?"

"Whatever you want to call it."

"Because this Nolan had been stalking you. Messing with your life? Threatening you?"

"Yes. I mean, no. It was more than that." I sighed again and looked him straight in the eye. "I thought he was The Peeper. He had to be stopped. All those women. Cheryl. Nancy. And then he went after Jan."

"Yes, we'll get to her in a minute." He flipped a few pages in his legal pad. "And that was the reason you felt this need for private justice? Protecting the weak? Righteous retribution?"

I was going to say yes, but it was too late to lie. It was on tape, the specifics jotted on his pad.

"Partially. Like I said. There were also the dreams."

His answering smile said, 'Ah hah'. "The lidless eyes."

I nodded. "The dead seemed to be calling out to me. Seeking justice, I guess. I couldn't sleep. I, I don't know, I felt like I had to give them justice or I'd never be able to rest."

The eyebrows below his shiny forehead raised into question marks. "Why do you think your mother was there? In your dreams, that is."

I shook a negative. "I don't know. Except that she raised me, taught me right from wrong. I guess, she was telling me to do the right thing."

He didn't seem to hear me, or if he had, didn't want to acknowledge what he'd heard. Either way, he jotted down another note.

"Let's get back to Ms. Sterling." Hands flat on the table, his eyes met mine. "You felt protective of her. Isn't that what you said? Like maybe a father feels for a daughter?"

"Yeah. I guess so."

"But you were also attracted to her. Especially her new blond hairdo."

"Well, it was more that she looked different. More exotic."

"And more attractive?"

"Well, sure. I guess. You know, blonds are more striking." I waved

224

another finger. "And I'd heard her amorous adventures long enough that, you know, I couldn't help but be a little…"

"Titillated?"

I shrugged.

"Did you masturbate while thinking of her?"

"What? No!" This was going too far, straying into areas that even head shrinker shouldn't tread.

He let it go and made a note.

"So, you invited Ms. Sterling over for protection. And because you felt a fatherly need to offer shelter. But that wasn't the case with officer Nagel?"

I'm sure I blushed. "No, at least not totally. Nancy was, well, I felt differently about her. I thought maybe we could have a relationship."

"Even though your wife had *just* died. Was just *murdered* in fact."

"Yes. No, I don't know." He was confusing me. "Look. I told you that Cheryl and I had been living separate lives for quite a while. Whatever love there was had basically gone. So, yes. I guess I was ready to move on."

"When did you find out Cheryl was cheating on you?"

"I didn't think she was. I'm still not sure."

"But the detective, this…" He looked at his pad. "This Garlicki. He asked around. Talked to her friends in this Ladies League. They confirmed she'd asked them to cover for her, if you ever called that is. Were they lying?"

I started to feel very uncomfortable. "I don't know."

"But you said that this Nancy Nagel had suggested that maybe your wife was cheating. Had laid the egg of the idea in your ear. Or should I say, on your computer screen." He smiled. "Isn't *that* right?"

"Yeah. I guess it made me suspicious."

"Did you know your wife was sleeping with Nolan Webster?"

I shook my head. I shook it violently. So violently I didn't know if I'd be able to stop. Finally, I did. "That's what the cops said, but I didn't believe it. Don't believe it."

"Maybe not consciously. But underneath?" I didn't answer. "Wouldn't that explain his, ah, DNA in her remains? Even if he wasn't The Peeper that is?"

"I don't know." I was angry. "What are you getting at?"

"Nothing. Except that maybe this underlying knowledge, this jealousy, this betrayal might have been a reason you were so fixated on him. Why you felt the need to stalk him, to punish him."

"I told you! I thought he was The Peeper. So did Nancy." I jabbed my finger in his face. "He was online friends with most of the victims. He knew about Weider-White. He was sleeping with Cheryl. I mean, he found Cheryl attractive, he'd said *that* much." I'm afraid I lost my cool. "She was blond with big breasts. They all were. That was his type. All of them."

"Just like Nancy."

"Yes."

"And your mother."

"My *mother*? Why do you keep bringing up my mother? What the fuck does this have to do with my mother?"

His patronizing smile was back. I was once again the little kid who'd asked about Santa Claus.

"Let's get back to that. Shall we?" He flipped pages in his pad. "I understand the police found certain items stashed behind a road map in the glove box of your car." He read from his notes. "A pair of surgical scissors. An autopsy knife. A box of surgical gloves, the same type found near Peeper victims. The scissors even had traces of blood on them." He looked at me quizzically. "How do you think they got there?"

I shrugged. "Like I told Garlicki, Nolan must have planted them. He's still on the loose, you know."

"Actually, they found him."

I'm sure my smile lit the room. "They *did*? Did he confess? Where was he hiding out? Some farmhouse or motel I'll bet."

"No, he was hiding in the freezer in your basement."

"What?"

"He's dead. Had been for a few days."

I was at a total loss. "How'd he get into *my* basement freezer?"

"The police are curious about that as well. I understand the body of the other pesticide inspector..." He checked his notes. "Carter McCall had been frozen also. They didn't catch it on preliminary work up but noted characteristic tissue changes at autopsy."

He looked at me clinically now. I was no longer the silly child asking silly questions. I was a bug under a microscope; some insect to be dissected and pinned to cork board.

"They say the freezing stopped decomposition and lengthened the estimated time of death by at least twelve hours."

I didn't know what to think, and I guess it showed on my face.

"Yes. I'm afraid that eliminates your alibi."

"I shouldn't need an alibi. I don't have to prove my innocence. Isn't that the law? Innocent until *proven* guilty."

He continued to look at me. There was still no smile, just that clinical detachment.

"I understand the police found other items when they searched your house." He didn't need to check his notes this time. "Most notably a jar of alcohol with bits of human tissue. Eyelids to be exact."

I tried to pull myself under control, but it was tough. It was as if the world was conspiring to place blame on me, an innocent man. I felt once again like someone from a Kafka novel, the prisoner on trial for a crime he hadn't committed. I summoned all my reserves of self-restraint.

"I can't explain that. Maybe Nolan planted those as well. Or if *he* wasn't The Peeper, then whoever the Peeper is must have done it. I understand they keep souvenirs, at least that's what they say in the movies. So yeah, The Peeper must have planted them to frame me. Maybe he planted Nolan too."

"And Mr. McCall as well?"

I threw up my hands. "How the hell do I know?"

I was the bug under the microscope again. "And why would this Peeper want to frame *you*?"

"How should I know? Deflect blame? Maybe he knew I was already under suspicion by the police. Maybe he's *with* the police. Did you ever think of that? Maybe it's a cop. Maybe somebody else who knows how to break into my place and plant evidence. How should I know? I just know *I'm* not some lunatic killer." I waved at him and swept my hands around the room. "No matter what the police think with this psychological inquisition they set up."

His smile said I was the silly child again. "Let's be clear, Dr. Corlane. I don't work for the police; I work for you. Specifically, for your lawyer, Mr.

Bradshaw."

"Bradshaw?"

"He set this up. Oh, no doubt the state will want to bring in their own expert as well. In the meantime, I've done some checking into your background and the police have provided me with materials they have access to. Perhaps we can elucidate some matters that might make state psychiatric evaluation unnecessary."

This was strange news indeed. "But Bradshaw is my lawyer. He's supposed to be on *my* side."

"He is. As am I. Shall we move on?" He removed his glasses and leaned back, looking at the ceiling. "Let's talk about Ms. Sterling again. When did you start feeling attraction for her?"

"What does that have to do with anything?"

"Humor me. When?"

"I don't know what you mean."

"Well, were you always attracted to her?"

I shrugged. "I just thought of her as a cute kid. One of the sexplorables so common to today's youth. She was, well, she was just Jan."

"But then you said you started to feel attraction for her." He grabbed his pad and flipped several pages. "An attraction like a father might feel for his daughter but be embarrassed by." He smiled. "Would you call that forbidden love? Taboo love? What?"

"I don't know."

"When did this feeling start?"

"What do you mean, *when*?"

"Well, you said yourself that you used to think of her as just this promiscuous kid, but then that you started to feel a taboo attraction. When did that start? Was it recent?"

"I guess so." I tried to think. He was right, there had been a change. At first, Jan was just Jan, a competent if sarcastic and sexually explicit admin. Then? "I'm not sure?"

"Was it the recent change in her? The new clothing? The dyed hair?"

I didn't have to think about that. "Well, yeah. I guess. Like I said, she looked more… *exotic*."

"Did she remind you of anyone?"

"Who?"

He shrugged. "She was blond now. Your wife was blond, wasn't she?" I nodded. "And officer Nagel was blond. And this Weider-White woman you found attractive, the one you sent the risqué comment to?"

I stabbed a finger at him. "I didn't send that comment."

"Okay. But she was blond, no?"

"What are you getting at?"

"Just that you prefer blonds or seem to." I started to respond but he cut me off. "What color was your mother's hair?"

"My mother? Again, with my mother. Why are you so interested in her?"

"She was a blond, wasn't she?"

"Yeah. So?"

"When was your first sexual experience?"

"What?"

"Your first time? The average age for males is seventeen. Was your first time before then?"

"Listen, *Doctor*. You're getting damned personal, and I don't appreciate it."

That smile again. I wanted to slap it off his condescending buddha face.

"Humor me. You know us Freudians. When was it?"

I was feeling damned uncomfortable again. "What do you mean, um, like sex with a girl?"

He raised his brows. "Unless yours was a homosexual experience. Was it?"

I shook my head violently. "No. Of course not."

"Then when?"

I let out a long exhalation and tried to hold onto my temper. "If you must know, it was after."

"In college?"

"Yes."

"Freshman year? Junior? When?"

"Why is this important?"

"Professional curiosity." That smile again. "When?"

"If you must know, it was graduate school."

"I see. Are we talking about the late Mrs. Corlane?"

I put on my best condescending smile and nodded. Let's see how he liked it.

Horowitz jotted a note. "Why do you think you waited so long? Was it an issue of shyness?"

"Well…"

"Was there a strict religious prohibition?"

I laughed. "Yeah, I guess you could say that."

"Your mother was a religious woman?"

I tapped my nose like in charades, the condescending smirk on my face the whole time. "You have a knack for understatement."

"What denomination? Lutheran? Baptist? Catholic?"

"Bible. Old Testament, New Testament, chapter, verse."

He smiled. "My father was a rabbi. I know the feeling. I learned many Torah chapters by rote. You?"

"And a man who injures a countryman-as he has done, so it shall be done to him…fracture for fracture, eye for eye, tooth for tooth."

"Leviticus."

"24:19-21."

"So, you remained a virgin until marriage?"

I didn't answer. The whole discussion was making me ill at ease. My silence didn't seem to bother Horowitz. He just scribbled on his pad.

"I assume masturbation was also proscribed?"

I still refused to answer, but that didn't stop his questions.

"Did you do it anyway?"

I remained silent.

Horowitz put down his pen. "I'd like to try a little experiment. Please close your eyes."

"Why?"

"Just close your eyes and relax."

I complied, mostly to get this over with.

"Now relax and listen only to the sound of my voice."

~ * ~

"You will remain in a deep sleep but be able to hear the sound of my voice. Do you understand?"

"Yes."

I was tired, very tired. It was as if the strength had drained out of me; the very life drained out of me. Discomfort departed, leaving behind a disconnection from reality. It was like a dream, things swirling in the netherworld between waking and sleep, reality and fantasy.

I seemed to be watching myself from far above, floating numbly somewhere in the interrogation room. My will likewise floated above me, ready to depart; Horowitz's questions cutting it free like the string of a balloon. I heard myself speaking, but it was sloppy and disjointed. Yet, the words continued to escape my mouth, rising to the surface like the bubbles from a drowning man.

"I want you to think back to your teenage years. You lived at home with your mother who had proscribed masturbation. Did you do it anyway?"

"No."

"You had no sexual outlet of any kind prior to your marriage in graduate school? That would be quite unusual."

"We were an unusual family."

"What were your mother's thoughts on the topic?"

"Sex or jacking off?"

"The former."

"She had her own ideas on that; partly taken from the bible. 'The spirit is willing, but the flesh is weak'."

"That's New Testament, isn't it?"

"Matthew. 26:41."

"What did it mean, from *her* perspective?"

My eyes remained closed. A sense of calm filled me, the surreal feeling deepened. The world about me fled. The years likewise fled, flipping back like the pages on a calendar. I couldn't seem to resist it—a form of compulsion. Like being in thrall to a snake charmer. I kept speaking, unable to dam back the words.

"That men and women were inherently wicked. That there was nothing you could do about it."

"Original sin?"

"Adam knew it. Eve knew it. Giving in was inevitable. But…"

"But?"

"There were ways to limit the sin. Ways to…"

"Go on, Doctor Corlane. Let go of the long-hidden secrets. Confession is good for the soul."

"Numbers, 5:6-7," I was barely mumbling now.

"Quite right. How did one limit the sin?"

"By keeping…"

"Go on."

"By keeping it private. Out of public view. Within the family."

"I see. Within the family."

I could still hear him, but his words were faint.

"This private sinning kept within the family. Did it ever send you to your mother in the reaches of the night?"

I didn't answer.

"Did she come to you? Do you remember?"

Images swam into my head. I didn't consciously dredge them up, they just floated to the surface. I spoke what I saw, unsure if Horowitz was hearing it or if I was reciting in a dream.

"Midnight—12:00 on the bedside clock. I'd wake, although there was no alarm, just a sliver of light from the open door. My mother would call my name softly, but I could hear it. Then she'd walk toward me. I could see the outline of her against the light as she pulled off her nightgown—the roundness, the soft curves, the blond hair brushed straight for bed. I'd raise the covers as she lay down. Then she spoke, always the same words."

"What words?"

"This is our secret, our redemption. This is all we need."

Chapter Thirty

"Corlane analysis: Session two."

Dr. Horowitz spoke for the sake of the digital recorder, its red eye staring accusingly at me. Today, he was dressed in a grey suit, but otherwise looked the same.

I didn't remember much from the last session. He told me that I had passed out, and indeed I came to in my private cell here in county lockup. Came to twelve hours later, feeling remarkably refreshed. I hadn't realized how troubled my sleep had been or the benefits of a good night's worth.

Horowitz smiled. It wasn't his condescending smile or his perfunctory clinical smile. This was a new one I'll call his 'friend to man' smile.

"Feeling better, Dr. Corlane?"

I tried to match his smile. "Fine."

"Well rested? Spirit lighter?"

"Yes, fine."

"Splendid."

I had a sudden thought. "Doctor, the police don't, I mean, I don't have much knowledge of what's going on outside."

"You have a question about the outside?"

'Well, yes, I guess. Have the police, has anyone mentioned an orange tabby cat?"

He raised his brows. "A cat?"

"Yes. In the municipal parking lot, over by the big maple."

He looked at me calmly. "Not to my knowledge. Why?"

I shrugged. "I've been taking care of it, feeding it. Reminded me of a cat my mom had growing up. I don't know why I thought about it now; I guess I just wanted to know if it was okay."

He smiled. "Shall we continue talking about your mother?"

I didn't answer. Horowitz ignored the silence.

233

"When did she die?"

"My senior year of undergrad."

"How did she die?"

"I, um, I don't remember." The good feeling I had started the day with evaporated, leaving behind a familiar sense of discomfort. I tried to recall what we had already discussed but couldn't. It made me angry, and I didn't know why, which made me angrier still.

"That would be quite unusual."

"Why? Why the fuck would that be so unusual, *doctor*?"

He ignored my outburst. "Because for most people, the death of a parent is a strong memory not easily forgotten, even after more than twenty years."

"OK. I'm unusual."

"Indeed. But please think back. I'm sure it will come to you."

"Why the fuck are you so interested in my mother's death?"

"Why are you so angry?"

"Answering a question with a question? Is that an old psychologist's trick?"

He just smiled.

"Fine. If you must know, I think she was killed."

"Murdered? How?"

"I don't know. The police didn't give me many details. And I didn't ask."

"That is also unusual. Most people would be curious."

"As we already concluded, I'm unusual."

"Indeed. Would you like to find out?" He reached into his briefcase and withdrew a manilla folder. It was old and dog-eared.

"What's that?"

"A report from the Ridgeville Ohio police department. I believe that was your hometown, no?" He waved the report. "Would you like to read it?"

"You're the one interested. You read it."

My flip remark couldn't cover my sudden distress. My face flushed crimson. My heart changed from a steady thump to a birdlike flutter. I had trouble breathing.

"Fine. I'll read it to you." He removed his glasses and squinted down at the contents of the folder. "Victim is a nude white female approximately forty years of age, five feet seven inches tall, blond hair, blue eyes, a small mole above left lip. She has been stabbed multiple times. The left breast has been removed and the abdomen opened; the uterus exteriorized. There are no signs of defensive wounds, with the body being otherwise unmarked. The corpse's eyes were wide open, looking straight up as if in terror or disbelief."

He looked up from the page. "Ring any bells?"

I didn't answer. I couldn't answer; stout cables constricted my breath to ineffectual sips of air.

Horowitz tapped the folder. "It says further on that you were investigated for the crime, but that you had a solid alibi. Evidently you had been in the company of a young lady when the crime was perpetrated; had spent the night in fact."

I still couldn't answer.

"Was that indeed the case? Were you sleeping with this young lady the night of your mother's murder?"

I remained silent, hoping he would go away so that I could breathe.

"We touched on this yesterday. Do you remember?"

I thought about it before managing a strangled, "No." It seemed odd that I should have forgotten something we discussed only yesterday.

He paused before continuing. "You told me that your first sexual experience was your marriage, years *after* your mother's death. Do you remember?"

I didn't answer. I couldn't answer.

"Maybe I can help," said Horowitz. He snapped his fingers.

Images flashed through my head in rapid succession; a literal flashbang of images popping in one after the next. All we had discussed filled the memory gap; I couldn't stop it. The phrase 'drinking from a firehouse' came to me amid the jumble of images and memories. I should have been shocked by the sudden assault, unable to process it. The memories, some from decades past, should have shocked me as well. Instead, a calm descended over me, almost Horowitz's clinical detachment. I found I was able to sort out the information and I had no qualms about discussing it.

"You *weren't* sleeping with this young lady, were you?"

"No." I felt no hesitation answering. "I had gone over there to study, but no."

"Why did she cover for you?"

"She had a crush on me, but she was short, chubby, with curly brown hair."

"Not exactly your type." His smile was back, this time tinged with compassion.

"No. But she was willing to swear to what I asked her in hopes that we could have more than friendship."

"When had you left her?"

"About ten."

He tapped the report again. "This says that a second person was killed that night. A white male. His body was found beside your mother's."

"Her boyfriend, George."

"Her lover?"

"Yes."

"But you told me yesterday that your mother had no lovers. That she observed biblical proscriptions from such activity—outside the family that is."

I continued to speak, but it was as if I was listening to someone else. My brain didn't know what was going to be said until my lips said it. It was a disturbing sensation, but strangely compelling as well.

"He was a minister. A *Baptist*." I marveled at the disdain in my voice. "She met him at a bible-study. Then brought him home for dinner a couple of times."

"Did you like him?"

"No."

"Did you hate him?"

"No."

"How did you feel?"

"Threatened."

"You saw him as a rival?"

"Yes."

"The night you left the young lady, the one that had a crush on you."

"Marjory Dorn."

"When you left Ms. Dorn. Where did you go?"

"Home."

"Why are you smiling?"

"I can still remember my old Camaro, the smell of pine air freshener changing to cut grass and flowers as I opened the window and turned on the jazz station."

"Was Reverend George there when you came home?"

"Yes."

"He was with your mother?"

"Yes."

"What were they doing?"

Suddenly I couldn't answer. The coils were back around my chest. My heart had risen to my Adam's apple.

"Were they in bed together?"

Still, I remained silent, my mind awash in new images, new sensations, snippets of old memories made fresh. Entering the house, the kitchen looking large in its emptiness. Sensing something was wrong but not knowing what. The feel of the knife handle, its carving blade gleaming in the fluorescent glow. My footfalls as I ran down the hall, my own voice echoing from the walls of the narrow passage. The homey aroma of spices changing to the acrid smell of sweat and musk, then morphing again into the stink of copper, its taste in my mouth like old pennies. Rumpled linen soaked with red that looked almost black in the half-light. Eyes staring widely, almost lidlessly in surprise. A surge of anger, betrayal. Then. Then.

"What did you do, Randy?"

I was no longer middle-aged Dr. Randall Corlane, widower, chief of the Midlothian Pesticide Control Program. I was twenty-year-old Randy; biology major, son of Dolores Corlane. But I was more. I was a wild dog fighting for his alpha status. I was every Dear John who had ever been jilted. I was every religious zealot who'd ever slain an infidel. I was an angry God, my wrath descending to rip the commandments asunder with a fiery stroke of my stout right hand.

"I am death," I shouted, leaping to my feet, chair tumbling behind me. "The mighty god of vengeance." I heard the snap of fingers. Then I heard nothing.

Chapter Thirty-one

That is the entire story, to the best of my memory. The rest is not worth telling.

There was no trial, nor was there a need for a prosecution head shrinker; Dr. Horowitz spared me that at least. He smiled as he told me that my therapy would be long and hard. I recognized his clinical smile, the one that put me under that microscope; his special project that would no doubt fill the pages of many a journal article—perhaps a book. He didn't say it, but I knew I would never be free again. From now on, my days would be filled with therapy, soap operas, robes and slippers, sterile white walls, soft foods that required no sharp utensils, the harsh glow of fluorescent lights. Perhaps, occasionally, visiting psychiatrists would smile and ask their questions. This was my new existence, the new normal. A normal that was not particularly appealing to me.

I've filled a total of nine legal pads with this telling. Under suicide watch, I have been relegated to felt-tip markers. Dr. Horowitz was kind enough to bring me the fine-liner I used at the office, along with the four-pack of refills I kept in my desk drawer. I've gone through three ink cartridges so far and will be using the last one shortly; this last being a very special cartridge filled not with ink but with aldicarb, the only acutely toxic insecticide still legally available. I filled this cartridge months ago, not really knowing why. No doubt my subconscious mind was wiser than my conscious one. At a lethal dose of one thousandth of a gram per kilogram body weight, the three grams of aldicarb in the cartridge should be more than enough to get the job done.

The dreams have not stopped, but I fear them less; Horowitz also gave me that. The lidless eyes no longer rebuke me, no longer cry for justice. They only stare. Nancy. Cheryl. Suzanne Weider-White. My mother. Jan. I'm curious as to why Jan has joined the party, her bleached-blond hair swirling around her staring orbs. I've asked Horowitz about this, but he declines to answer. Nor will he let me read the papers or watch the news. As you can imagine, social media is out as well.

I still worry about Kirby. Is he okay? Was he ever really there?

Tonight's dessert is banana pudding. It's not as good as my mother used to make, but it is nostalgic. The aldicarb gives it a slightly bitter taste. I wonder if there will be dreams.

About the Author

Award winning author John Bukowski is a former veterinary practitioner, health researcher, and medical writer who now writes short fiction and fast-paced novels, including *Project Suicide* and *Checkout Time*. Project Suicide won third place at the 2024 BookFest Awards. *Checkout Time* won second place at BookFest and was a 2024 finalist for both the Silver Falchion and Imadjinn awards. Bukowski has also authored nineteen published short stories and a variety of consumer materials, including handbooks, website content, and radio scripts. He's a Detroit native who currently resides in Eastern Tennessee. Further examples of his writing can be found on www.thrillerjohnb.net.

www.ingramcontent.com/pod-product-compliance
Lightning Source LLC
Chambersburg PA
CBHW051429170626
46809CB00006B/2378